SHERLOCK HOLMES

The Secret Notebooks

JUNE THOMSON

JAICO PUBLISHING HOUSE

Ahmedabad Bangalore Bhopal Chennai
Delhi Hyderabad Kolkata Lucknow Mumbai

Published by Jaico Publishing House
A-2 Jash Chambers, 7-A Sir Phirozshah Mehta Road
Fort, Mumbai - 400 001
jaicopub@jaicobooks.com
www.jaicobooks.com

Published in arrangement with
Allison & Busby Limited
12 Fitzroy Mews
London W1T 6DW

To be sold only in India, Bangladesh, Bhutan,
Pakistan, Nepal, Sri Lanka and the Maldives.

SHERLOCK HOLMES
THE SECRET NOTEBOOKS
ISBN 978-81-8495-578-1

First Jaico Impression: 2014

Printed by
Repro India Limited, Mumbai

JUNE THOMSON, a former teacher, has published over thirty novels, twenty of which feature her series detective Inspector Jack Finch and his sergeant, Tom Boyce. She has also written six pastiche collections of Sherlock Holmes short stories. Her books have been translated into many languages. June Thomson lives in St Albans, Hertfordshire.

By June Thomson

THE SHERLOCK HOLMES COLLECTION

The Secret Journals of Sherlock Holmes
Holmes and Watson
The Secret Documents of Sherlock Holmes
The Secret Notebooks of Sherlock Holmes
The Secret Archives of Sherlock Holmes

THE JACK FINCH MYSTERIES

Going Home

CONTENTS

Foreword p. 7

The Case of the Upwood Scandal p. 11

The Case of the Aluminium Crutch p. 43

The Case of the Manor House Mystery p. 69

The Case of the Cardinal's Corpse p. 105

The Case of the Arnsworth Affair p. 139

The Case of the Vanishing Barque p. 165

The Case of the Gustaffson Stone p. 201

FOREWORD

by

Aubrey B. Watson LDS, FDS, D.Orth.

Those of you who are already familiar with the four earlier collections[1] of hitherto unpublished accounts of cases which Sherlock Holmes and Dr John H. Watson investigated will not need reminding of the curious circumstances under which they came into my possession.

However, for the benefit of new readers, I give this brief summary of how I acquired them through the Will of my late uncle Dr John F. Watson, a Doctor of Philosophy at All Saints College, Oxford.

Despite the similarity of the names, my late uncle

[1] These are: *The Secret Files of Sherlock Holmes* (1990); *The Secret Chronicles of Sherlock Holmes* (1992); *The Secret Journals of Sherlock Holmes* (1993); *The Secret Documents of Sherlock Holmes* (1997); and *The Secret Archives of Sherlock Holmes* (2012). Aubrey B. Watson.

was not in any way connected with Dr John H. Watson, Sherlock Holmes' friend and chronicler, although it was because of this resemblance that he had made a study of his namesake's life and background and had become, in consequence, something of an authority on the subject. For these reasons, a certain Miss Adelina McWhirter approached my late uncle in September 1939, just before the outbreak of the Second World War, with a proposition which she thought might interest him.

An elderly and apparently respectable spinster, she claimed to be related to Mr Holmes' Dr Watson on the maternal side of the family and had inherited a battered tin despatch box with the words 'John H. Watson, M.D., Late Indian Army' painted on its lid. It was this box, she said, which had belonged to Mr Holmes' Dr Watson and contained the papers relating to those cases which had not been published and which Dr Watson had placed for safe-keeping in the vaults of his bank Cox and Co. at Charing Cross.[2]

Finding herself in straitened circumstances, Miss McWhirter wished to sell both the box and its contents and approached my late uncle, who agreed to buy them.

---

[2] In 'The Problem of Thor Bridge', Dr Watson writes: 'Somewhere in the vaults of the bank Cox and Co., at Charing Cross, there is a travel-worn and battered tin despatch box with my name, John H. Watson, M.D., Late Indian Army, painted upon the lid.' Strictly speaking, Dr Watson never served in the Indian Army but in the British Army serving in India. The despatch box was presumably army issue. Aubrey B.Watson.

However, soon after his purchase of the Watson archive, war was declared and my late uncle, fearful for their safety during the coming conflict, copied out the papers and, taking a leaf out of Dr John H. Watson's book, deposited the original manuscripts, still in the despatch box, in the main branch of his bank in London. Unfortunately, the bank suffered a direct hit during the bombing of 1942 and although the despatch box was recovered from the rubble, it was so badly damaged as to be unrecognisable while its contents had been reduced to a mass of burnt paper.

My uncle was placed in a quandary. While he still had his own copies of the Watson manuscripts, he had nothing to prove the existence of the originals except for the damaged box and its charred contents, which hardly amounted to proof. Nor could he trace Miss Adelina McWhirter. She had, it seemed, moved out of the residential hotel in South Kensington where she had been living without leaving a forwarding address.

Therefore, having no means of proving the authenticity of the Watson archives, and fearful of his reputation as a scholar, my late uncle decided not to publish and, on his death at the age of ninety-eight on 2nd June 1982, his copies of the originals were left to me, his only living relative, in his Will. As for the despatch box and its contents, no trace of them remained and I can only assume that, when he passed away at the Eventide Nursing Home in Carshalton, Surrey, the staff threw them out as so much rubbish.

I, too, have hesitated for a long time over the question of whether or not to publish these accounts but, having no one to whom I can bequeath them and having no academic reputation to protect, being an orthodontist by profession, I have decided to risk rousing the obloquy of serious Sherlockians by placing these accounts before the public, together with the footnotes which my late uncle added to his original manuscript copies.

However, I must point out that I accept no responsibility for their authenticity.

THE CASE OF THE UPWOOD SCANDAL

It was a bitterly cold November morning, not long after my old friend Sherlock Holmes and I had returned to London from Devonshire following the tragic conclusion of the long and complex Baskerville case,[1] when a visitor, a Mr Godfrey Sinclair, called at our Baker Street lodgings. His arrival was not unexpected, for Holmes had received a telegram from him the previous day requesting an interview, but the reason for his visit was quite unknown, Mr Sinclair having failed to mention the nature of his business. It was therefore with some curiosity that we waited for Billy, the

[1] The date when Sherlock Holmes undertook the investigation entitled 'The Hound of the Baskervilles' is disputed, but internal evidence suggests the late 1880s. The great Sherlockian expert William S. Baring-Gould has opted for the autumn of 1888. The account of the inquiry was first published in serial form between August 1901 and April 1902. Dr John F. Watson.

boy in buttons,[2] to show this new client upstairs.

'At least we know one fact about him. He is a man with a proper sense of the value of time. A businessman, would you say, Watson? Certainly not a dilettante,' Holmes remarked when, on the stroke of eleven o'clock, the hour fixed for his appointment, there was a peal on the front-door bell.

However, I noticed when Mr Sinclair was shown into the room, that his appearance was not quite that of a conventional businessman. His clothes were just a little too well-cut and the gold watch-chain looped across the front of his formal waistcoat a touch too decorative for a banker or a lawyer, and I marked him down as having a connection with the theatre, perhaps, or some other occupation in which the fashion of one's coat was of great importance.

He also had the bearing of someone used to the public gaze, an impression borne out by an air of social ease and almost professional *bonhomie*. And yet, beneath this social gloss, I fancied I detected a certain caution, as if he preferred to be the observer rather than the observed. Although only in his thirties, he gave in addition the

---

[2] The first reference to Billy, the pageboy or 'the boy in buttons', surname unknown, is in 'The Adventure of the Yellow Face', ascribed by some commentators to 1882. There are several references to him in the canon. His duties included running errands and showing clients upstairs to the sitting-room. His wages were presumably paid by Sherlock Holmes. He should not be confused with another pageboy, also named Billy, who features in the later adventures at the turn of the century, such as 'The Adventure of the Mazarin Stone' and 'The Problem of Thor Bridge'. Dr John F. Watson.

impression of a much older man, experienced in the ways of the world and consequently wary of its practices.

Holmes was also conscious of his client's reserve, for I noticed his own features assumed a bland, non-committal expression as he invited Sinclair to take a seat by the fire.

In accordance with his punctual arrival, Sinclair came straight to the point in a pleasant but competent manner.

'I know you are a busy man, Mr Holmes,' he began, 'and I shall not waste your time with a long explanation of my affairs. To put the matter briefly, I am the owner of the Nonpareil Club in Kensington, a private gambling establishment which is, of course, by its very nature against the law.[3] Two of its members are a Colonel James Upwood and a friend of his, a Mr Eustace Gaunt, who joined the club only recently and about whom I am less familiar. Although several card games are played at the Nonpareil, including baccarat[4] and poker, Colonel

---

[3] Until the Betting Act of 1960 was passed, all betting in public places was illegal, but gaming clubs such as Crockford's were well established, although they ran the risk of being raided by the police and shut down. Dr John F. Watson.

[4] It was because of a game of baccarat that Edward, Prince of Wales, became involved in the Tranby Croft scandal. He and some fellow guests were staying at a country house called Tranby Croft, the home of a rich shipowner, Arthur Wilson, in 1890 when a fellow guest, Sir William Gordon-Cumming, was accused of cheating at the game. He was made to sign a paper promising never to play cards again, which the fellow guests, including the Prince of Wales, also signed. But the scandal leaked out and Gordon-Cummings brought a libel action. The Prince was subpoenaed as a witness. The case was lost but the publicity damaged Edward's reputation. Dr John F. Watson.

Upwood and Mr Gaunt prefer whist. Both appear to be accomplished at the game and visit the club regularly on a Friday evening at about eleven o'clock for a rubber or two.

'Generally speaking, the stakes are moderate and there is nothing in their play to arouse suspicion. Their gains and losses are more or less balanced. However, on two occasions in the past six months, they have won considerable sums, in one case of over £500, in another of £800. I noticed on these two evenings they were particularly careful in choosing their opponents, although it was subtly done and I doubt if anyone else observed this, certainly not the gentlemen they played against.'

'Who were?' Holmes interjected.

'I would prefer not to name them, if you have no objections, Mr Holmes. Suffice it to say that all four of them were wealthy young men, scions of well-known aristocratic families and inclined to recklessness, who had on the evenings in question indulged a little too freely in the club's champagne.

'Their losses probably meant less to them than they would to some other members, but that is not an excuse for cheating at cards, if that is what Colonel Upwood and Mr Gaunt were doing, as I strongly suspect they were. However, I have no proof. That is why I have come to you, Mr Holmes. I would like to know one way or the other for my own peace of mind and for the good name of the Nonpareil. If they are cheats, then my response is quite clear. I shall speak to the gentlemen in question, cancel their membership and warn the other clubs to which they belong of their activities. Are you prepared to take on the case, Mr Holmes?'

Holmes replied with alacrity.

'Certainly, Mr Sinclair! Your card-players are a refreshing change from the usual run-of-the-mill criminals. But I cannot promise immediate results. If the two gentlemen in question are indeed cheating, then they will clearly not indulge themselves every week. You said they play regularly on a Friday evening. Then I suggest my colleague, Dr Watson, and I call at the Nonpareil next Friday at half past ten and the subsequent six Friday evenings at the same time. If nothing suspicious occurs on any of these occasions, then we shall have to review our strategy. By the way, I think it prudent if we assume false identities during the investigation in case our names are familiar to any of your members. Dr Watson will therefore be Mr Carew and I shall be Mr Robinson.'

'Of course. I quite understand,' Sinclair replied, getting up and shaking hands with both of us before giving Holmes his card. 'Here is my address. I shall expect to see you both next Friday at the time agreed.'

'Well, well!' Holmes declared after Mr Sinclair had left the room and we heard the street door close behind him. 'What do you think of the affair, Watson? Gambling, indeed! A case after your own heart, would you not say, my dear fellow, although, in your case, it should be horses or billiards, not cards?[5] How is your whist-playing, by the way?'

'I play a little,' I replied a little stiffly, for I was somewhat piqued by Holmes' teasing manner.

'Enough to win £400 at a sitting?'

'Hardly, Holmes.'

'Then we must not plunge ourselves too deeply in the game on Friday evening,' Holmes rejoined. 'A rubber or two should suffice, combined with a little stroll about the gaming-room to establish the lie of the land and to acquaint ourselves, if only at a distance, with Messrs Upwood and Gaunt. You know, Watson, or rather Carew, to accustom you to your new *nom de guerre,* I am quite looking forward to the assignment,' Holmes continued, chuckling and rubbing his hands together. 'It is not often one is paid a fee for indulging oneself at one of London's better-known gambling clubs.'

The Nonpareil, as we discovered when we alighted from our hansom on the following Friday evening a little before ten o'clock, was not quite what I had been expecting. I had envisaged a more flamboyant establishment, its windows ablaze with a myriad of gas lamps and with a uniformed flunkey in knee breeches and a satin waistcoat to escort us inside.

[5] Dr Watson enjoyed betting on horses and confessed that half his army pension was spent at the races. *Vide*: 'The Adventure of Shoscombe Old Place'. There is no evidence that he bet at billiards. Dr John F. Watson.

Instead, we found ourselves mounting the steps of one of the tall, elegant houses which lined a quiet side street in South Kensington. The only decoration on its plain façade of brick and stucco was the rather severe iron railings to the first-floor balcony and the basement area. As for the blaze of gas lamps, only a subdued glow escaped round the edges of the tiers of heavily-curtained sash windows, lending the building a soft, shrouded air, like the proscenium in a theatre before the curtain goes up to reveal the stage.

There was no satin-coated footman to welcome us either, only a tall, pale-faced butler, dressed in black, who had the sombre gravity of an undertaker's mute.

As he took our cloaks and silk hats, I had an opportunity to glance about me and was, despite the initial disappointment, impressed by what I saw, although the interior of the Nonpareil no more corresponded to my image of a gaming-house than its exterior.

The foyer was square and plain, floored with black and white marble tiles and, like the façade of the house, unadorned apart from two enormous gilt-framed looking-glasses, each accompanied by matching marble-topped console tables, which faced one another and created a bewildering profusion of reflections of Holmes and myself standing within a diminishing arcade of other gilt-framed mirrors, glittering under the lights.

When I had recovered from this momentary visual

confusion, I saw that a pair of double glass doors led into a drawing-room furnished, like a gentlemen's club, with leather armchairs, ceiling-high bookcases and low tables on which were displayed newspapers and periodicals, meticulously folded. A bar, sparkling with crystal glasses and ranks of bottles, occupied one wall.

Another pair of double doors in the far wall allowed a glimpse of a supper-room beyond, where there was a long buffet table loaded with tureens of soup and huge platters of food, together with piles of plates and silver cutlery. Small round tables, covered with starched white linen, were scattered about at which several gentleman were already seated, making use of the club's hospitality. More were occupying the leather chairs in the drawing-room with brandy or whisky glasses in their hands, while soft-footed waiters padded about carrying silver salvers containing more glasses of wine, champagne or spirits.

The atmosphere was hushed. There were no loud voices, only a subdued murmur of conversations and the tinkling of glass, while the air was fragrant with the warm scent of cigars and wood smoke from the blazing fires, the aroma of leather, rich food and the fresh flowers which decorated both rooms as well as the entrance foyer.

Mr Sinclair must have been watching for our arrival for, hardly had we divested ourselves of our outer garments, than he came forward to greet us.

'Mr Carew! Mr Robinson! I am delighted to welcome you as new members!' he cried, holding out his hand to each of us in turn before escorting us up the staircase to a broad upper landing and from there into a large double salon running the width of the house. This, I assumed, was the gaming-room, the heart of the Nonpareil Club.

Unlike the discreet apartments on the lower floor, this huge chamber was sumptuously furnished and brilliantly lit. Four large chandeliers hung from the coffered ceiling, their radiance enriching the already flamboyant splendour of the gilded leather chairs, the ormulu and silver mounts on the furniture and the towering swags of scarlet and gold brocade which hung at the windows. The walls were painted with scenes from an Olympian banquet at which gods and goddesses, draped in diaphanous robes and crowned with gilded laurel leaves, dined to the music of lyres and flutes.

It was all much too extravagant and elaborate – a deliberate effect, I suspected, designed to create an atmosphere of excitement and hedonistic pleasure in order to encourage the players seated at the baize-covered tables placed about the room to indulge themselves more freely than they might have done in a more decorous setting. Although there were no overt signs of excitation, no raised voices or boisterous behaviour, the atmosphere was vibrant with an almost inaudible ebullience, like the faint humming from a hive of bees or the trembling left in the air after a violin has played its last note.

Mr Sinclair paused with us in the doorway, as if to let us, as new members, grow accustomed to our surroundings, murmuring as he did so, 'Look to your left, gentlemen, at the table nearest the far wall.'

We moved on, Sinclair stopping now and again to introduce us to those members who were not engaged in play, and both Holmes and I took the opportunity to glance covertly towards the table he had indicated.

Colonel Upwood was immediately identifiable by his military bearing. A bulky man, he sat stiff and upright in his chair, his tanned, weather-beaten features suggesting he had served in the East. During my own service in Afghanistan,[6] I had seen many faces similar to his. The flesh becomes dry and lined, like old leather, particularly about the eyes, where the effort of continuously squinting into the bright tropical light forms a myriad of tiny wrinkles in the skin, the inner crevices of which remain pale where they have not been exposed to the sun. These tiny lines created the impression of a jovial man, much given to laughter, but the eyes themselves were cold and watchful, while

---

[6] After training at St Bartholomew's Hospital in London and the Army Medical School at Netley, Hampshire, he was posted to India where he joined the 66th Berkshire Regiment on foot as an army surgeon in Afghanistan. He was wounded at the Battle of Maiwand in 1880 and was invalided out of the army with a pension of 11/6 a day, approximately 57 pence. *Vide: A Study in Scarlet.* Dr John F. Watson.

the mouth, under the clipped white moustache, had a grim, humourless twist to it.

His companion, Eustace Gaunt, who faced him across the table, was, by contrast, a thin, weak-chinned man, with reddish-brown hair and moustache. Although generally of a very undistinguished appearance, his most striking feature was his brilliant, dark-brown eyes, which were never still but were constantly darting to and fro. His hands were delicate, like a woman's, and had the same restless quality as the eyes, fluttering over the cards laid out upon the table or moving up to finger his cravat or the white rose in his buttonhole. The rest of him remained curiously immobile, like a dummy on display at a fashionable tailor's.

They made a strange, ill-assorted couple and, as Mr Sinclair drew our attention to them, I saw Holmes give a small start of surprise, followed by a stifled chuckle of amusement.

'Most interesting, Watson!' he murmured in my ear – a reference, I assumed, to their incongruous partnership. But there was no opportunity to follow up his remark, as Sinclair was arranging for partners to join us in a rubber or two of whist.

It was an uneventful evening. Holmes and I won a little and lost a little, our gains almost cancelling out our losses to our final disadvantage of three guineas. However, after the initial excitement of the novelty and sumptuousness of our surroundings had worn off, the occasion became rather prosaic. Because of his phenomenal gift of storing information which he can later recall at will,[7] Holmes was potentially an excellent card-player, for he could remember exactly which cards had been played and which remained in our opponents' hands. But the mental challenge was too trivial to keep him occupied for long and his attention soon strayed from the game, his gaze wandering from time to time in the direction of Colonel Upwood and Mr Gaunt. Neither man, however, seemed aware of his interest.

I, too, am not a dedicated card-player. After the excitement of the race-course, where the physical prowess of both horse and jockey can send the blood tingling through the veins, I found whist too static for my taste. I missed the roar of the crowd and the thunder of hooves on the turf. Even billiards had more allure, for in that sport the players at least have the opportunity to move about the table, while the co-ordination of hand and eye calls for real skill. In comparison, card games seemed quite tame.

It was two o'clock in the morning before Colonel Upwood and Eustace Gaunt left the club, having won, according to Holmes' calculation – for he had been surreptitiously assessing their play – the modest sum of about twelve guineas, not enough to warrant a charge of cheating.

---

[7] Sherlock Holmes once stated: 'I hold a vast store of out-of-the-way knowledge, without scientific system, but very available for the needs of my work.' *Vide*: 'The Adventure of the Lion's Mane'. Dr John F. Watson.

We waited for half an hour before taking our own leave, so that our departure should not coincide too closely with theirs and perhaps arouse suspicions.

'I suppose,' I remarked when we were inside a hansom, rattling our way through deserted streets towards Baker Street, 'that the whole wretched experience will have to be repeated next Friday.'

'I am afraid so, my dear fellow,' Holmes agreed.

'What a waste of an evening!'

'Not entirely,' he corrected me. 'We have gained some very useful information about Gaunt and Colonel Upwood, including their methods.'

'Have we, Holmes? I saw nothing out of the ordinary about their play. They were apparently not cheating or they would have won more than they did.'

'So it would seem,' Holmes conceded. 'But we must wait upon events, Watson, rather than anticipate them. Like all greedy men, sooner or later they will succumb to the temptation of easy money. Meanwhile, I suggest we bear our souls in patience.'

He said nothing more about the case until the next Friday evening, when we again presented ourselves at the Nonpareil. As we mounted the steps to the front door, he remarked to me casually over his shoulder as he rang the bell, 'Perhaps tonight the game really will be afoot!'

But events were to prove otherwise.

As before, Godfrey Sinclair again introduced us to a pair of partners in the gaming-room and the four of us sat down together at one of the small baize-covered tables to play. On this evening, however, the *ennui* was broken a little by Holmes' insistence that we rose from the table from time to time to stretch our legs by sauntering about the room as other gentlemen were doing, pausing on occasion at other tables to observe the play.

We halted for less than a minute at our suspects' table, no longer than at any of the others, and no one in the room, I am convinced, saw anything suspicious in either our expressions or our bearing. Holmes' face, I observed when I took a sideways glance at him, registered nothing but polite interest. Only someone who knew him as well as I would have been aware of his inner tension. Like a fine watch spring wound up almost to breaking point, he was vibrant with suppressed energy, every nerve alert, every sense concentrated on the two men who sat before us.

As far as I could see, there was nothing unusual about their behaviour. Colonel Upwood sat four-square upon his chair, hardly moving or speaking apart from an occasional jovial comment to the other players about the fall of the cards.

'My monarch has been defeated in battle, I see,' he remarked as his King of Clubs was trumped. Or, 'Never trust a woman!' when his partner's Jack of Hearts was taken by an opponent's Queen.

As for Eustace Gaunt, I noticed his nervous habit of touching his cravat or his buttonhole, a red carnation on this occasion, was still in evidence. So was the restless movement of his eyes.

The play was not very inspiring and we soon moved on to halt briefly at other tables. As we did so, I noticed that, as soon as we were no longer in the suspects' vicinity, Holmes' nervous tension subsided and he became merely bored, his eyes hooded with lassitude while his lean profile bore the pinched expression of insufferable weariness.

The next two Friday evenings followed much the same pattern. Upwood and his partner neither lost nor won any large sums of money and even they seemed to be growing fatigued with the play, for they left early at half past midnight, to my inexpressible relief.

I half expected the next occasion would be the same and I had to brace myself for the extended tedium of an evening of whist.

Holmes, too, seemed in low spirits, sitting in silence as we rattled in our hansom towards the Nonpareil Club. I felt that, like me, he had begun to despair of ever reaching an end to the inquiry and that it would continue indefinitely as a weekly torment, much like that suffered by the man in the Greek legend who was forced to keep pushing a large stone up a hill, only to have it roll down again.[8]

But as soon as we entered the gaming-salon, I detected

---

[8] According to Greek mythology, Sisyphus, king of Corinth, captured and chained up Death, who had to be rescued by the god Ares. As a punishment, he was forced to push a large stone repeatedly up a hill, only to have it roll down again. Dr John F. Watson.

an immediate and dramatic change in his demeanour. His head went up, his shoulders went back and he gave a low, triumphant chuckle.

'I think we are about to witness the dénouement of our little investigation, my dear fellow,' he murmured to me under his breath.

I followed his gaze to the table where Eustace Gaunt and Colonel Upwood were already seated in the company of a pair of young men who, judging by their heightened colour and over-loud voices, had indulged themselves too liberally in the bar downstairs.

'The sacrificial lambs are on the altar,' Holmes continued in the same low tone as Colonel Upwood dealt the cards. 'The ritual fleecing of them will begin any moment now.'

We retired to another table and played a rubber of whist with two gentlemen who often acted as our opponents, but neither of us were at our best. Both of us were distracted by the game going on across the room, where soon a small, interested group of fellow members had started to gather. Even our opponents' interest began to shift to this new centre of attention until eventually all four of us by mutual consent laid down our cards and, getting to our feet, strolled across the room to join the company, which now numbered about fifteen.

It was clear from the bank notes and sovereigns lying on the table that Colonel Upwood and his partner had already won a considerable sum of money and were likely to win more, for their opponents, the two young gentlemen, although showing signs of unease, seemed determined not to admit defeat but to continue the game.

They were encouraged in this frame of mind by Gaunt and Upwood, whose tactics were subtle. Like two experienced anglers fishing for trout, they kept their victims in play, using the bait of letting them win two or three games in a row, thereby lulling them with a false promise of imminent success. The following game, of course, they lost.

From Holmes' earlier remark about sacrificial lambs, I assumed Gaunt and Upwood were cheating. However, although I watched them with the closest attention, I could not for the life of me see anything in either their manner or their behaviour which could warrant such a charge. There appeared to be no sign of *légerdemain* in the way they dealt the cards. Their hands always remained in full view on top of the green baize and, unless they were accomplished magicians, which I doubted, they were not substituting one card for another.

In all respects, they acted exactly as we had seen them behave on those other Friday evenings when we had watched their play. As before, Gaunt's nervous mannerisms were in evidence, but no more than usual. Upwood also made the occasional facetious remark, referring to the Queen of Spades as 'the Black Beauty' and to the Diamonds as 'sparklers', an exasperating habit but one which appeared to be quite innocent of deception.

After a few minutes only, Holmes touched me briefly on the arm and murmured, 'I have seen enough, my dear fellow. We may leave.'

'But what have we seen, Holmes?' I demanded as I followed him to the door.

'Proof of their cheating, of course!' Holmes replied dismissively, as if that fact were self-evident.

'But, Holmes . . . !' I began.

There was no opportunity to add any further protest for, just outside the salon door, we met Godfrey Sinclair hurrying across the upper landing, summoned no doubt to the gaming-room by one of his subordinates, his normally urbane manner considerably ruffled.

'Mr Holmes . . . !' he began anxiously, but fared no better than I had.

'Yes, Mr Sinclair, they are indeed cheating,' Holmes informed him in the same brisk manner he had used to me. 'I advise you, however, to do nothing about it at this moment. I have the matter in hand. Call on me on Monday morning at eleven o'clock and I will explain to you exactly how the situation may be resolved.'

And with that he swept off down the stairs at a rapid pace, leaving his client standing at the top, open-mouthed at the decisiveness of Holmes' conclusion.

Knowing Holmes in this assertive mood, I did not mention the matter again and it was not until the following evening that he himself made any reference to it, although in such an oblique manner that at the time I was not aware of its significance.

'Would you care to spend the evening at a music-hall, Watson?' he asked in a negligent manner.

I glanced up from the *Evening Standard*, which I had been reading by the fire.

'A music-hall, Holmes?' I repeated, puzzled by Holmes' sudden interest in this form of entertainment, which I had never known him to favour in the past. An opera, yes; or a concert. But a *music-hall*?

'Well, it would make a pleasant evening out, I suppose,' I replied. 'Which one were you thinking of?'

'I understand the Cambridge[9] has several excellent performers on its programme. Come then, Watson. We shall leave at once.'

Seizing up his coat, hat and stick, he set off down the stairs, leaving me to hasten after him.

We arrived in time for the second half of the evening's entertainment, which consisted of several acts, none of which I could see might be of particular interest to Holmes. There was an Irish tenor who sang a sentimental song about a young lady called Kathleen, a lady wearing a huge crinoline which opened like a pair of curtains to release a dozen small dogs which then proceeded to

---

[9] I have been unable to trace a Cambridge Music-Hall, except for a small establishment in the East End of London, and I suggest it is a pseudonym for the Oxford Music-Hall in Oxford Street in London, where many famous performers appeared. Dr John F. Watson.

jump through hoops and dance on their hind legs; and a lugubrious comic with a huge nose and a check suit who told sad jokes about his wife which the audience seemed to find extremely funny.

The comic was followed by a certain Count Rakoczi, a Transylvanian of Gypsy origin, whom the Chairman[10] announced with a thump of his gavel as 'A Maestro of Mind-Reading and Mental Manipulation!'

I felt Holmes stiffen in his seat beside me and, guessing that it was this particular act which he had come to see, I myself sat up and concentrated on the stage as the curtains parted to reveal a man who, although short of stature, was of striking appearance.

His face and hands were of an unnatural pallor, enhanced by artificial means, I suspected, which contrasted dramatically with his black hair, dashing black mustachios and small pointed beard which gave him a Mephistophelian air. This black and white colour scheme was repeated in his apparel, in his gleaming silk hat and long black cloak which he removed with a flourish to reveal its white satin lining, as well as his black evening clothes and his shirt front, as blanched and as glistening as a bank of snow.

He passed his hat and cloak to his lady assistant who, in contrast to Count Rakoczi, was more exotically attired in a long robe which appeared to be made entirely out

[10] The Chairman introduced the acts, usually in a comically extravagant manner, and presided generally over the performance. Dr John F. Watson.

of silk scarves of every colour of the rainbow and which floated about her with each movement she made. Her headdress was fashioned from the same multicoloured silk into an elaborate turban and was sewn all over with large gold sequins which flashed like fiery stars under the gas lights.

As the applause died down, Rakoczi stepped towards the footlights to announce in a strong accent – Transylvanian, I assumed, should there be such a language – that he would identify by telepathic communication alone any object supplied by members of the audience, which his assistant would hold up. He himself would be blindfolded with a mask which he invited the Chairman to inspect.

The mask of black velvet was duly passed to the Chairman, who made a great show of holding it up for the audience to see before fully examining it with meticulous care. Having assured us that it would be impossible for Rakoczi to see anything through it, he then handed it back to the Count who, to a dramatic roll on the drums, pulled it down over his eyes. He then took up his position centre stage where he stood very erect, his arms folded across his chest and his blindfolded face raised towards the upper gallery. While this was happening, his assistant, gallantly aided by the Chairman, who rose to offer her his arm, descended the steps from the stage into the auditorium to a rustle of anticipation from the audience.

She moved up the aisle, stopping here and there to

collect an item from individual members of the public which she held up for the rest of the audience to observe, addressing Rakoczi as she did so with various casual remarks in a strong contralto voice which also had a foreign accent, in her case more French than Transylvanian.

'What do I have here, Maestro?' she demanded, holding up a gentleman's gold pocket watch and letting it spin gently at the end of its chain. 'Oh, come!' she protested when he hesitated. 'It is a simple question. We are all waiting for the answer.'

Rakoczi lifted his hands to his face, pressing his fingers theatrically against his temples as if trying to concentrate his thoughts.

'I zee somezing gold,' he said at last. 'Round and shining. It iz hanging from a chain. Iz it a gentleman's vatch?'

'Can you tell me anything more about it?' his assistant persisted as the audience began to murmur its amazement.

'There are initials engraved on it,' Rakoczi continued. 'What initials are they? Let me have your answer!'

Again the fingers were pressed against the temples.

'I zee a *J* and an *F*.'

'Is he correct?' the lady assistant enquired, turning to the owner of the watch, who rose to his feet greatly astonished.

'Indeed he is,' the gentleman announced. 'My name is John Franklin. Those are my initials.'

There was an outburst of applause, which Rakoczi

acknowledged with a bow as his assistant moved to another member of the audience.

Altogether, Rakoczi correctly identified five more objects – a signet ring, a black silk scarf, a pair of spectacles, a silver bracelet and, as the *pièce de résistance*, a lady's silk purse embroidered with roses, which he not only described in detail but named the number and the type of coins it contained.

During this mind-reading demonstration, I found my attention being drawn more and more to the Count rather than to his assistant, despite her more obvious charms, although Rakoczi, standing there centre stage in his black and white apparel, was himself a compelling figure. There was, however, something else about him which fascinated me. I felt I had met him somewhere before, quite where or when I could not remember. All the same, there was a disturbingly familiar quality about some of his movements rather than his features or his bearing.

I was still puzzling over this when the performance finished and the lady assistant returned to the stage, where Rakoczi, divested of his velvet mask, took her by the hand and, leading her towards the footlights, bowed with her to thunderous applause from the audience.

Hardly had the heavy curtains been drawn across the stage than Holmes got to his feet.

'Come along, Watson,' he whispered urgently. 'It is time we left.'

Giving me no opportunity to protest that there

were two turns still to be performed before the end of the programme, a unicyclist and a famous soubrette well-known for her comic Cockney songs, who was top of the bill,[11] he hurried towards the exit, leaving me with no other option but to stumble after him.

'Where are we going now, Holmes?' I asked as I caught up with him outside the theatre, for it was clear from the purposeful manner in which he strode up the street that he had a specific destination in mind.

'To the stage-door,' he replied briskly.

'But why there?' I asked, much mystified by his answer.

'To interview Count Rakoczi, of course,' he retorted, as if the explanation were obvious.

The stage-door, a dingy entrance poorly lit by a single gas flare, was situated in an alleyway which ran alongside the theatre. Once inside, we found ourselves facing a small, booth-like office with an open hatchway, behind which the doorkeeper, an elderly, bad-tempered looking man smelling strongly of ale, kept guard, who, from his glowering expression, seemed determined to refuse any request we might make. However, a florin soon weakened his resolve and he agreed to deliver one of Holmes' cards, on which he had scribbled a short note, to Count Rakoczi's dressing-room.

---

[11] This is probably a reference to Marie Lloyd, a very popular music-hall artiste who sang comic Cockney songs and performed sketches. Her real name was Matilda Alice Victoria Wood (1870–1922). She first appeared at the Eagle Music-Hall under the stage-name Belle Delmare. Dr John F. Watson.

Shortly afterwards he returned to conduct us to this room, where we found Rakoczi standing facing the door as we entered, a look of acute anxiety on his face.

He had stripped off his stage persona, not just the evening clothes, which he had substituted for a shabby red dressing-gown, but also the appurtenances of his physical appearance, including the pallid complexion, the curly black mustachios and pointed beard together with the jet-black hair. He stood before us totally transformed from the dashing figure he had presented on the stage to a very ordinary man with reddish hair and a slightly undershot chin.

'Mr Gaunt!' I exclaimed out loud.

Those restless eyes which I had noticed at the Nonpareil Club darted from Holmes to me and then back again to Holmes, while one hand went up in a characteristic gesture to pull nervously at the lapel of his dressing-gown.

'You received my card and read the note, I assume?' Holmes remarked in a pleasant voice which nevertheless held a touch of menace. When Gaunt failed to reply, Holmes continued. 'I have several courses of action open to me, Mr Gaunt. I could go straight to the police or alternatively I could inform Mr Sinclair or the manager of this theatre of your criminal activities. Any of these choices could lead to your arrest and imprisonment. Alternatively, I could leave you to remedy the situation yourself without my interference.'

Holmes paused and raised his eyebrows but Gaunt still failed to speak, although a slight inclination of his head indicated agreement with my old friend's last suggestion.

'Very well,' Holmes continued in a brisk, business-like manner, 'then this is what you must do. You must go immediately to Colonel Upwood and explain the situation to him. The two of you will then arrange to send to Mr Sinclair at the Nonpareil Club your resignations together with a full list of all the club members whom you have cheated and a precise record of the amounts. With that letter, you will send the money owed, so that Mr Sinclair can return it to your victims.

'Furthermore, you and Colonel Upwood will send me a written guarantee, making sure it is signed with your real name, that neither of you will ever play cards again for money. If either of you break that undertaking, I shall make sure that every gentlemen's club is told of your past misdemeanours, as well as every music-hall manager and Colonel Upwood's commanding officer. As a result, your reputations will be ruined. Do I make myself clear?'

'Yes, yes, indeed you do, Mr Holmes!' cried Gaunt, beating his hands together in so frenzied a manner that I feared he might burst into tears. To my great relief, Holmes nodded in my direction and we left the room before the man succumbed to this final humiliation.

'It was sheer good luck that I realised Gaunt was none other than Count Rakoczi, the self-styled telepathist,' Holmes remarked as we left by the stage-door and stepped out into the narrow alley. 'I saw a poster of him several weeks ago outside the Cambridge Music-Hall and recognised Gaunt as the same man the moment we entered the gaming-room at the Nonpareil. Of course, you realise how he and Upwood arranged the fraud?'

'I think so, Holmes. They used a form of code, did they not, to communicate secretly between themselves?'

'Exactly so, Watson. In the case of the music-hall act, it was certain words or phrases used by Rakoczi's assistant which told him what she was holding – a watch, say, or a purse. Other words indicated colour, number, initials and so on. No telepathy was involved; only a good memory and a convincing stage presence. Of course, the assistant also had to make sure that she chose only those items for which their system already supplied a code word.

'I am convinced that Colonel Upwood saw their performance and realised it could be adapted for cheating at whist, using not just words and phrases but also certain gestures to indicate which cards each of them held in his hand, thereby controlling the play. Gaunt already had several nervous mannerisms which he made a point of using habitually so that no one would think it suspicious when he fingered his collar, for example, or stroked his chin at the card table.

'It was a deception which they could not use too often, otherwise Sinclair and the club members would have suspected them of cheating. So they took pains to choose their victims with care, not experienced card-players but rash young men with plenty of money who might be expected to plunge in too deeply.'

'And always on a Friday,' I pointed out. 'Why was that, Holmes?'

My old friend shrugged.

'Possibly because it was the only evening in the week when Gaunt could persuade the manager of the Cambridge to change his placing on the bill, allowing him to leave a little earlier than usual so that he had time to remove his stage costume and make-up and take a cab to the Nonpareil.'

As he was speaking, he drew me quickly into a doorway, from the shelter of which we could watch unobserved the main entrance as well as the stage-door of the theatre. A few seconds later, we saw Eustace Gaunt, alias Rakoczi, emerge from this side entrance, dressed in street clothes, and walk hurriedly along to the main thoroughfare, where he hailed a hansom.

As it drew away, Holmes remarked with a chuckle, 'I think we may guess Gaunt's destination, my dear fellow. If I were, like you, a gambling man, I would wager half a sovereign that he is on his way to Colonel Upwood's to lay my ultimatum before him.'

Holmes was, of course, correct, as usual.

The following day, he received two letters, one from Colonel Upwood, the other from Eustace Gaunt who signed himself as Alfred Tonks, presumably his real name. Both men unreservedly accepted the terms which Holmes had laid down.

That same morning, Godfrey Sinclair arrived to thank Holmes for his successful handling of the case and for avoiding the scandal which would have ensued had the affair been made public.

The two men had resigned their membership of the Nonpareil, and Upwood, who presumably was in charge of their finances, had enclosed a list of names of all those they had cheated together with enough bank notes to repay the money their victims had lost.

'A most satisfactory ending, my dear fellow,' Holmes remarked, rubbing his hands together gleefully after Sinclair had left. 'I suppose your faithful readers can expect a written account of the inquiry, suitably embellished in your own inimitable style. What will you call it? "The Adventure of the Colonel's Cardsharping" or "Scandal at the Nonpareil Club"?'

In fact, I decided to call it neither, nor shall I publish an account of the case.

A few days after this exchange, I received an answer to a letter I had written to my old army friend, Colonel Hayter,[12] asking if he knew anything about a Colonel Upwood, as he had maintained closer contact than I with our former regiments[13] and was better acquainted with army gossip.

---

[12] Dr Watson first met Colonel Hayter in Afghanistan, where he gave him medical treatment. The two men kept in touch and, on Colonel Hayter's retirement to Reigate, he invited Dr Watson and Sherlock Holmes to stay with him. Dr John F. Watson.

[13] Dr Watson's regiment was the 66th Berkshires. It is not known which regiment was Colonel Hayter's but he may also have served in the Berkshires. *Vide*: 'The Adventure of the Reigate Squire'. Dr John F. Watson.

He wrote back to tell me that, although he had never met Upwood, he knew a little about his background and his service record, in particular one episode which my old friend thought would interest me, knowing of my own army experiences.

Colonel Upwood had taken part in the relief of Kandahar,[14] the garrison town in Afghanistan to which the British forces, including myself, had retreated after our tragic defeat at the battle of Maiwand on 27th July 1880. The town was besieged by a vastly superior Afghan force led by Ayub Khan, and was relieved twenty-four days later by the heroic action of a British force of 10,000 men, led by Major General Frederick 'Bobs' Robert, which, after a forced march from Kabul to Kandahar of 320 miles across the mountains in the scorching summer heat, attacked Ayub Khan's camp, killing thousands of his men and putting the rest to flight. Compared to these losses, our own, thank God, were mercifully light, amounting to only 58 men killed and 192 wounded.

Without the intervention of that gallant force, those of us at Kandahar might have been starved into surrender with consequences which do not bear contemplating.

Among that relieving force was Upwood, then a

[14] Kandahar was a strategically important Afghan town situated 155 miles inside the frontier with India, which was captured and garrisoned by a force of 2,500 soldiers, both British and Indian. The siege was raised on 31st August after twenty-four days. Dr John F. Watson.

Major, who was wounded in the left arm during the attack and was consequently, like myself, invalided out of the army with a pension.[15]

One might therefore claim that my life was saved as much by the action of Upwood and his brave comrades as by that of Murray, my orderly, who, after I myself was wounded, threw me across the back of a pack horse and joined the general retreat to Kandahar.

In view of this, I feel it would be disloyal of me to publish this account of Colonel Upwood's subsequent fall from grace at the Nonpareil Club and therefore it will be consigned to my old army despatch box along with other unpublished papers, a fitting resting place, I feel, for this particular manuscript.[16]

---

[15] See footnote to p. 20.

[16] See footnote to Foreword, p. 8.

THE CASE OF THE ALUMINIUM CRUTCH

On several occasions in the past, Sherlock Holmes had referred briefly to a former inquiry which he had undertaken before my advent as his chronicler but he had found neither the opportunity nor the inclination to give me a full account of it, although I had pressed him to do so numerous times.

'Oh, that old case!' he would say dismissively. 'A singular investigation indeed, my dear fellow. I must tell you about it one of these days. I think you will find it quite interesting.'

In the event, it was a casual remark made by Inspector Lestrade which at last prompted Holmes to make good his pledge.

Lestrade had called on him one evening in order to ask his advice on an urgent case with which he was having difficulties, that of the missing heir to the Blackstock estate.

As he rose to take his leave, he added, 'By the way, Mr Holmes, do you remember Whitey Johnson, the jewel thief?'

'Whitey Johnson!' Holmes exclaimed. From the kindling expression in his eye, I could tell his interest was immediately aroused. 'Indeed I do remember him! But I thought he was still in prison. He is surely not up to his old tricks in there?'

Lestrade chuckled, his sharp, foxy features crinkled up with amusement.

'Not any longer. He died in Pentonville last week; lost his balance going down some stairs and broke his neck, or so the Governor informed me. That aluminium crutch of his was to blame. It slipped out from under him. So you might say it was his downfall in more ways than one.'

The remark was evidently intended to be humorous, for Lestrade rubbed his hands together with glee as Holmes escorted him to the door.

On resuming his seat by the fire, my old friend looked across at me with a rueful expression.

'Whitey Johnson dead! I am sorry indeed to hear that. His was one of the first cases that Lestrade asked for my assistance in solving. For a villain, he was, I recall, a very mild-mannered little man.'

'Was he?' I asked with a touch of asperity. 'Although you have referred to the case several times over the years and promised me a full account of it, I have not yet had that pleasure.'

'Then you shall have it this very minute, my dear fellow,' Holmes replied. Pausing only to fill his pipe with tobacco from the Turkish slipper,[1] he lit it and leant back in his chair, his lean features taking on a pensive expression as the wreaths of smoke rose to encircle his head.

'It must have been in the late 1870s when I was still living in Montague Street,'[2] he began. 'By that time, my reputation as a private consulting agent was becoming better known and my clientele was spreading beyond the immediate circle of my former Varsity acquaintances and their friends. News of it had even reached as far as Scotland Yard. So it was that one morning Inspector Lestrade[3] called on me to ask for my help with a case which, up to that moment, had defeated the official police. As a force, they were shockingly lacking in imagination, a quality of mind which, allied to the power of deduction, is essential if any successful detective is to make a success of his career.

'The particular investigation for which Lestrade needed my assistance involved a pair of jewel thieves,

---

[1] Sherlock Holmes was in the habit of keeping his tobacco in the toe of a Persian slipper which hung on a hook near the fireplace. *Vide*: 'The Adventure of the Speckled Band'. Dr John F. Watson.

[2] On first coming down from university, Sherlock Holmes rented lodgings in Montague Street, a turning which runs alongside the British Museum. Dr John F. Watson.

[3] The first case for which Inspector Lestrade asked Sherlock Holmes for his help was a case of forgery. *Vide*: *A Study in Scarlet*. Dr John F. Watson.

a man and a woman, both well spoken and respectably dressed, whose *modus operandi* never varied. Together they would go into a jeweller's shop, one of the smaller, less fashionable premises in a busy shopping neighbourhood, where there was only one assistant serving behind the counter, usually the owner himself. They would also take care to choose a time when the shop was likely to be empty and made sure there was nothing about their manner or their appearance to draw attention to themselves. In fact, the woman always wore a hat with the veil drawn down over her face, while her male companion was variously described as having a moustache, a beard, eye-glasses, and hair that was fair, dark or red, so one could safely assume that he wore different disguises.

'They gave the impression of being a married couple who were well-to-do and who were about to celebrate some special occasion, their wedding anniversary perhaps, or the lady's birthday, in consequence of which the husband had decided to buy his wife a ring. The shopkeeper was delighted to serve them and laid out for their inspection a selection of his very finest rings for the lady to try on.

'It was while the lady was making her choice that the theft took place. Without any warning, the man would suddenly snatch up a handful of the rings and run out into the street while at the same moment the lady would faint, collapsing across the counter in a swoon.

'You may imagine the shopkeeper's shock and

bewilderment. In the confusion of the moment, he was not sure what to do. Should he go to the assistance of the lady? Or should he pursue the thief who had made off with his property? In all four cases which Lestrade had investigated, the sense of ownership overrode any notions of chivalry and the victim set off in pursuit of the robber. But those few seconds' hesitation were vital. By the time he had run out into the road, the thief had disappeared amongst the passersby. It was only then that it occurred to him that the woman was the man's accomplice and that he had moreover left her alone in his shop surrounded by cabinets full of jewellery. It was small consolation that the cases were locked; the glass could easily be smashed. He could only comfort himself with the thought that the more valuable pieces were locked away in the safe. Immediately, he ran back to his shop but, of course, the lady had vanished.'

Holmes broke off at this point to look across at me quizzically.

'I can tell by your expression, Watson, that some aspect of my account is troubling you. Which is it, my dear fellow?'

Although I had known Holmes for several years, he still had the capacity to astonish me by his perspicacity and the acuteness of his observation.

'I do not understand the part Whitey Johnson played in the robberies, Holmes,' I confessed. 'You said nothing about the male thief being a cripple. Surely a man with a crutch would be easily identifiable, no matter how many forms of disguise he may have used to alter his appearance. Or was he perfectly able-bodied and the crutch was merely another ploy to throw his pursuers off the scent?'

'Excellent, Watson!' Holmes exclaimed. 'Your powers of deduction improve by the hour! I can see I shall soon have to look to my own laurels. For you are quite right, my dear fellow. Whitey Johnson, who was incidentally a genuine cripple, took no part in the actual robbery. His role was more of a diversionary nature, as I discovered when I interviewed the victims. In other words, to use the language of the criminal underworld, he acted as the "stall". Two out of the four shopkeepers had been impeded in their pursuit of the thief by a man with a crutch who had stepped out in front of them at a crucial stage of the chase, allowing the robber to get clean away, although neither of them thought these incidents were deliberate and had failed to mention them to Lestrade. It was only when I pressed them for further details, however trivial, that either of them mentioned it. But, in fact, the man with the crutch played an even more significant role in the robberies than that of a mere "stall". I wonder, my dear Watson, if you, with your enhanced powers of deduction, can suggest what that role might have been? You look puzzled. Then consider the facts. Firstly, what items of jewellery were the thieves interested in stealing?'

'They were rings, were they not, Holmes?'

'Quite so. They never asked to look at bracelets or necklaces or even brooches. Always rings. Now consider one other factor – the crutch which the third member of the gang carried. What was it made of?'

'Wood?' I suggested, considerably mystified by this aspect of the case. What possible significance could the material of which the crutch was constructed have on the bearing of the matter?

'No, no, Watson!' Holmes corrected me with a touch of impatience. 'Remember what I said to you earlier. It was an aluminium crutch. *Aluminium!* That is of great, if not crucial importance, to the whole affair. Now do you make the connection?'

'I am afraid not, Holmes,' I replied, feeling abashed.

'Pray do not trouble yourself, my dear fellow. The solution may come to you later. For the moment, allow me to continue with my account. I now knew that I was dealing with a gang of professional thieves, three in number, which consisted of a woman and two men, one of whom was possibly a cripple, although at that stage in the inquiry, I could not be positive about this particular fact.

'Now at that time, I had already recruited my own little gang of street urchins, whom you are already acquainted with, Watson.'

'The Baker Street Irregulars!'[4] I cried, recognising them at once. 'If I remember correctly, they found

[4] The Baker Street Irregulars were a group of street urchins, led by one called Wiggins, whom Sherlock Holmes recruited to help with his investigation because they could 'go everywhere, see everything, overhear everyone.' They helped with three investigations, the Study in Scarlet case, the Sign of Four investigation and the Crooked Man inquiry. Sherlock Holmes paid them a shilling a day. Dr John F. Watson.

Jefferson Hope's cab and traced the whereabouts of the steam launch *Aurora* in that other investigation of yours into the Sholto affair.'

Knowing Holmes' disdain for the softer passions, I did not add that it was during this latter case that I had met and fallen in love with Miss Mary Morstan, whom I was to marry later that same year.[5]

'Wiggins was the name of their leader, was it not?' I continued.

'Yes, and a more intelligent and resourceful youth one could not hope to find. The police would do well to recruit young men of Wiggins' calibre into their own force. It was Wiggins who made enquiries on my behalf into the gang of three among the members of London's underworld and came up with a positive identification.

'The couple posing as the husband and wife were, in fact, a brother and sister, George and Rosie Bartlett, a good-looking pair who, because of their stylish appearance, had worked as pickpockets in the West End, George acting as the "dip", Rosie as the "stickman", or

[5] Dr Watson met Miss Mary Morstan when she came to ask Sherlock Holmes to enquire into the disappearance of her father, Captain Arthur Morstan. Dr Watson fell in love with her and married her at some time between November 1888 and March 1889. It was a happy though childless marriage. She died during the Great Hiatus, when Sherlock Holmes was assumed dead but was travelling abroad. The date and cause of her death are unknown. There are several references to her in the canon. *Vide*: *The Sign of Four*, 'The Boscombe Valley Mystery', 'The Adventure of the Stockbroker's Clerk' and 'The Adventure of the Empty House'. Dr John F. Watson.

in her case the "stickwoman". As soon as George had "lifted" a wallet or a lady's purse, he would immediately pass them to Rosie who would hide them about her person. Thus, if by an unlucky chance, George was apprehended and searched, the stolen goods were never found on him and he was allowed to go free. No one thought of stopping and searching Rosie, who looked the very picture of a well-dressed, respectable young lady. And anyway, by the time the hue and cry had been raised, she had already disappeared among the throngs of shoppers or theatre-goers.

'Their partnership worked successfully for a number of years and then their luck changed. George fell and broke his wrist and, although it mended, it was stiff and was therefore no longer any use to him for "dipping". Consequently, they had to earn their living some other way. It was then that they came up with the idea of stealing from small jeweller's shops and recruited Whitey Johnson to act as their "stickman". As I have already mentioned, he was a genuine cripple, having been born with a withered leg. In the past, he had acted as a "fence" for them, when they had a gold watch or tie pin to dispose of. It is most likely that it was this connection with stolen jewellery which put the idea of the robberies into their minds in the first place.

'Johnson was also useful as a "stall" in obstructing anyone, in particular an irate shopkeeper, by limping out in front of him. No one would suspect him. The last person one would expect as being part of a gang of thieves was a cripple, although I must confess the part played by the crutch in their *modus operandi* did not occur to me until much later.'

He paused to raise an eyebrow at me.

'Are you any nearer to deducing it yourself, my dear fellow?'

'I am afraid not, Holmes,' I replied, a little crestfallen.

'Never mind. It may come to you later in a sudden flash of inspiration. To continue. The resourceful Wiggins was also able to give me the Bartletts' address in Notting Hill, an interesting piece of information in itself, for the first robbery had occurred in that very same district and all subsequent robberies had taken place within a mile radius. They evidently preferred to operate in familiar territory where they knew which alleyways and side roads to use if they had to make a quick escape.

'They were sharing a small house in a turning off Ladbroke Grove, a street in which nearly every other window contained a card advertising rooms to let, so I had no difficulty in finding lodgings which practically overlooked the Bartletts' residence. That room was, in fact, the first of several secret addresses I acquired where I could go to change my appearance when the need arose.[6]

'In this case, I passed myself off as a clerk, temporarily unemployed but respectably if shabbily dressed. My

[6] The fact that Sherlock Holmes had five secret addresses is mentioned in 'The Adventure of Black Peter'. Dr John F. Watson.

landlady, a widow with two young children, had no reason to doubt my story. Besides, she was too grateful for the few shillings I paid a week for my board and lodgings to ask any questions.

'I had insisted on having the bedroom at the front of the house from which I had a clear view of the comings and goings of the Bartletts and, within a little over a week, I had established their routine. We are all creatures of habit, Watson, and thank God for it because it made my task of keeping watch on my suspects all the easier. I knew the days and the times Rosie Bartlett went shopping or her brother left the house to visit the local public house. I also saw their visitors come and go, including Whitey Johnson, who called on them on a regular basis.

'I was also able to observe all three of them at closer quarters and make myself familiar with their appearances.

'Bartlett was a tall, slim man in his early thirties, with pleasant rather than handsome features, and a certain air of distinction about him. Dressed in the right clothes, he could easily pass himself off as a successful member of the lower middle classes: a head clerk in a solicitor's office, say, or a senior cashier in a bank.

'His sister Rosie was of a shorter stature but had the same upright deportment and confident demeanour, although her appearance was somewhat marred by a rather prominent nose. However, with her veil down to hide this feature, she and her brother could be taken for a respectable married couple, comfortably off and thoroughly trustworthy.

'In contrast to them, Whitey Johnson was a small, non-descript young man only in his mid-twenties and so pale and sickly in appearance that he put me in mind of a plant which had been grown in a cellar or a dark room, deprived of sunlight. It was this excessive pallor of his complexion which earned him the sobriquet "Whitey". There were, however, two remarkable qualities about him which marked him out as someone special. The first was his capacity not to be noticed. I have rarely known anyone who had his skill of inconspicuousness; a perfect qualification, of course, for a "stickman". He could melt away into a crowd like a raindrop in a puddle.

'His other talent was his quickness of movement despite his physical disability. Seeing him darting along on his crutch like a monkey swinging its way from tree to tree, one could understand why the Bartletts had recruited him into their gang. Not only could he disappear from the scene of the crime in an instant, he complemented them perfectly, their roles being, so to speak, public while his was entirely private; theirs to place themselves centre stage, his to vanish into the shadows.

'Johnson usually called at the Bartletts' on a Friday evening at half past seven, bringing with him a bag containing, I suspected, bottles of brown ale, for, on one occasion, I strolled past the house when he was there and saw through a gap in the curtains the three of them playing cards at a table under a lamp, the beer decanted into glasses which stood by their sides. At half past ten, he always left, swinging his way up the street on his crutch at that surprising speed of his. Apart from these regular *soirées,* Johnson appeared to have no other connection with the Bartletts. Intrigued by this strange little man and curious to find out more about his private life, I hired Wiggins to make enquiries on my behalf. To that end, Wiggins followed him one evening to a lodging house in Battersea where he lived alone. He apparently had no family or friends apart from the Bartletts.'

At this point, Holmes paused and gazed deeply into the fire, as if searching amongst the flames for an explanation for this uncharacteristic interest of his in Whitey Johnson whom he himself had referred to as 'inconspicuous'. But before I could remark on this unprecedented concern of his, for he rarely showed any feelings for his clients let alone any criminals who might cross his path, he roused himself from his reverie and resumed his account.

'On the Saturday afternoon of the week following Wiggins' little excursion to Battersea, Whitey Johnson arrived at the Bartletts' house; an unusual time for him to visit them. As I have explained, he invariably called on them on a Friday evening. As soon as I saw him enter the house, I was immediately on the alert, for I knew something out of the ordinary was about to happen. And I was correct. Ten minutes later, all three of them left the house and set off up the street. Pausing only to put on my shabby coat and bowler hat, part of my disguise as an out-of-work clerk, I followed them on foot to Ladbroke Grove where they hailed a cab. I did likewise, my hansom keeping a little distance from theirs on my instructions.

'Their destination was the North End Road in Fulham, a busy thoroughfare of shops, cafés and other business premises, including, I noticed, as my cab drew to a halt not far from theirs, a small jeweller's shop, its single window covered by a metal grille and the name Samuel Greenbaum painted on the board above it.

'Here the three of them separated, Johnson limping ahead to survey, I assumed, any alleys and side turnings which would serve as an escape route should one be needed. Rosie Bartlett also went her own way, sauntering along, her veil lowered, pretending to look in the shop windows but also doubtlessly surveying the neighbourhood on her own behalf.

'Bartlett, meanwhile, to my utter astonishment, entered the shop. It was a totally unexpected move on his part but one I could see the logic of when I thought about it. By doing so, he, too, could inspect for himself certain aspects of the premises in readiness for the actual crime which they planned would take place at some later date, for I was quite convinced this was not intended to be the actual robbery, merely a rehearsal for it. By this means, he could check, for example, if the proprietor worked alone in the shop or had an assistant; how agile the man might be when it came to a pursuit; what obstacles lay between the counter and the door; and how easily the door opened on to the street.

'I deliberately strolled past the shop and, glancing in through the glass panel in the door, saw Bartlett in animated conversation with the shopkeeper. They even shook hands on parting! It was then I realised what I was witnessing was an arrangement being made for Bartlett to call again at the shop on another day, in the company of his wife, to inspect some of the more valuable rings for her to choose from. In other words, the jeweller was unwittingly collaborating in the plan to steal his own property!

'I was convinced of the accuracy of my theory when, stepping into the shelter of a doorway, I watched Bartlett as he left the shop and saw him at closer quarters for the first time that morning. He was normally clean-shaven and never wore spectacles but on this occasion he was wearing gold-rimmed eye-glasses and a neatly-clipped brown moustache, the disguise he evidently intended wearing on the day the planned robbery would take place. These prior inspections of the proposed scenes of the crimes were an aspect of the case which Lestrade had not mentioned to me, either because he considered them of no importance or because the shopkeepers themselves had not mentioned them, which suggested they had not been interviewed by the police with sufficient vigour.

'I there and then resolved that whenever I had to

question witnesses I would spend as much time and effort as I could in drawing out of them even the most trivial-seeming facts to help with my investigation. Knowledge is everything, Watson. Even the smallest detail can be crucial in bringing a criminal to justice.[7]

'In the meantime, Bartlett had walked to the end of the street where he met up with his sister Rosie as well as Whitey Johnson and, having conferred together briefly, the three of them parted, Johnson hailing a hansom and driving off on his own, the Bartletts taking a separate cab. The reconnaissance was over and everything was now set for the actual robbery, which I was convinced would take place the following Saturday afternoon at about half past six.'

'What made you so sure, Holmes?'

'That was exactly the question Inspector Lestrade asked me when I called on him at Scotland Yard on Monday morning. My answer was to refer him to the facts. It was exactly at this time that Whitey Johnson and the Bartletts had made their survey of the territory with, I believed, good reason. As well as the premises they intended robbing, they would also wish to examine the neighbourhood in general. It was a busy commercial street containing a number of shops selling provisions in addition to the lines of market stalls set up along the kerb, a significant factor, I concluded. Now, many

[7] In 'The Boscombe Valley Mystery', Sherlock Holmes states that his methods of investigation are based 'upon the observation of trifles'. Dr John F. Watson.

workmen are paid their wages on a Saturday evening, in consequence of which they and their wives have money in their pockets to spend on food for their families as well as ale for themselves in the public houses, of which there were three in the immediate vicinity of Mr Greenbaum's shop. The pavements would therefore be crowded with people which would make Bartlett's escape that much the easier.

'As I have pointed out to you before, people, criminals included, are creatures of habit and all the other robberies had taken place late on a Saturday afternoon, a point which Lestrade himself made when he was discussing the cases with me. However, he failed to grasp the full significance of this fact, dismissing it as a mere whim on the part of the Bartletts, like the wearing of a lucky charm. But there was nothing superstitious in their attitude to thieving. They were professionals through and through, and therefore the choice of day and time was as deliberate as all other aspects of their strategy, from their use of disguise to the selection of their victims.

'It took some persuasion on my part to convince Lestrade of the accuracy of my theory but at last good sense prevailed and he agreed to fall in with my plans. Therefore, the next day, I made my own tour of inspection of the area in company with Lestrade, choosing the best places where he and his officers, six of them in plain clothes, might wait upon the events to come without making their presence known.

'I should add, in Lestrade's defence, that, once he had grown accustomed to my plan, he joined in it with enthusiasm; too much so at first and I had to persuade him that planting one of his men outside the jeweller's shop disguised as a blind beggar was more likely to draw attention to the man than divert it. Like the stall-holders and the street traders in general, beggars have their regular pitches and for a stranger to arrive amongst them would have immediately aroused resentment as well as suspicion.

'By six o'clock the following Saturday afternoon, the plain-clothes officers, suitably attired, were in place in the North End Road, mingling with the ordinary folk who were about their everyday business, like them looking in windows, going in and out of the shops, buying fruit and vegetables from the stalls, always keeping on the move as I had insisted but never straying too far from Mr Greenbaum's premises.

'Lestrade was among them, his sharp little eyes darting here, there and everywhere, anxious that all was going to plan, for his reputation at Scotland Yard depended on the success of this particular investigation, following his recent failure over the notorious Paddington Green murder case in which the killer had got clean away.

'I, too, sauntered to and fro, watching for cabs arriving, for I guessed the Bartletts and Whitey Johnson would not travel by omnibus, a slow method of getting about. And I was right, one cab halted a little way up the road and I saw Johnson emerge from it, carrying his crutch. Within moments, he had disappeared among the crowds.

'The Bartletts arrived shortly afterwards and immediately the game was set in motion. Arm in arm, the two of them strolled towards Greenbaum's shop, looking every inch a respectable couple, Rosie with her veil down, George wearing eye-glasses and the small brown moustache, his bowler hat set at a dignified angle. Pausing only to glance in through the window to ascertain the shop was empty of other customers, Bartlett pushed open the door and the pair of them entered to the discordant jangle of the bell above the lintel.

'I had agreed with Lestrade that, as we had no evidence against the Bartletts with which to charge them, their arrest and that of Whitey Johnson, their accomplice, would not take place until after the robbery. In the meantime, one of his men, a sergeant in plain clothes, and I would take it in turns to walk nonchalantly past the shop and, by looking in, as if casually, through the glass panel in the door, would keep watch on the progress of the crime and would flourish a pocket handkerchief at the exact moment when Bartlett had seized up the rings and was ready to make his get-away. In the event, it was I who gave the signal.

'As I glanced in during my second promenade past the door, I caught the scene for a moment, as if frozen in time like a tableau on a stage or a waxwork display at

Madame Tussaud's[8] depicting Larceny or The Criminal Caught in the Act. There was Mr Greenbaum, an inoffensive, white-haired little man reeling back from his counter, his features conveying shock as vividly as those of a Greek theatrical mask. There was Rosie Bartlett raising one black-gloved hand dramatically to her forehead as if on the point of losing consciousness. And to complete the trio, there was George Bartlett scooping up the velvet cloth on which the rings were laid out on the counter as he prepared to make his escape.

'Not wishing to impede him, for it was imperative to let him pass the stolen jewellery to his accomplice Whitey Johnson, so that he, too, could be gathered into our net, I walked on as if I had witnessed nothing, at the same time producing my pocket handkerchief and blowing my nose with a flourish. As I did so, I glanced rapidly about me, searching for Whitey Johnson among the passers-by. He was standing against the wall of a nearby public house, where the customers going in and out of the door would shield him from sight, his crutch under his left arm and his expression so mild and innocent that not even a hardened cynic would suspect him of loitering there with criminal intent.

[8] Madame Tussaud (d. 1850) was a Swiss lady who learnt the craft of modelling in wax in Paris. She came to London in 1802, bringing her collection of wax images of famous and infamous people to London where she first exhibited them at premises at numbers 57–58 Baker Street. The collection was later moved to Marylebone Road, near Baker Street Station. Dr John F. Watson.

'Bartlett, too, seemed no more suspicious than any ordinary man in a hurry about his business. Walking rapidly away, he brushed past Johnson as if accidentally. It was in that brief moment of contact that the cloth containing the rings, which was now gathered up into a bundle small enough to be hidden in the hand, was passed to Johnson in one swift, covert movement which a professional magician would not have been ashamed of. The next instant, Johnson had begun to limp hurriedly away in the opposite direction to Bartlett, who passed on down the street, mingling with the shoppers thronging the pavement.

'My target was Johnson and, accompanied by the plain-clothes sergeant, I made haste to catch up with him, for it was obvious he had to distance himself from the scene of the robbery as quickly as possible. But he had one important task still to complete and that was to conceal the stolen rings so that, should he be stopped and searched, nothing would be found on him.'

At this point in his narrative, Holmes paused and regarded me with a quizzical smile.

'Now, Watson,' said he, 'where do you suppose the rings were hidden?'

'Certainly not in his pockets,' I replied. 'Those would be the first places the police would search.'

'Well reasoned, my dear fellow! But if not in his pockets, then where exactly?'

'Somewhere on his person?' I hazarded, hoping for a further clue.

'In a manner of speaking,' Holmes replied in an infuriatingly casual manner.

'In his boots then?' I suggested, realising I was clutching at straws.

'Oh, come now, Watson!' he chided. 'Surely you are capable of making a leap of the imagination? I have given you all the information you need to reach the right conclusion. No? Then allow me to give you a little assistance. What was Johnson carrying?'

'Carrying?' I repeated, even more mystified, for Holmes had made no reference to anything Johnson might have had in his hand, such as a bag or some other receptacle.

Holmes' eyes were sparkling with mischief. It was evident that he was hugely amused not only by my obtuseness but the opportunity it gave him to tease me.

'Under his arm?' he suggested, smiling broadly.

Light suddenly dawned.

'Oh, the crutch!' I exclaimed.

'Well done, Watson!' he cried. 'And what was the crutch made of?'

'Aluminium, was it not?'

'Exactly so! A light-weight metal which is capable of being moulded into different shapes; in this particular instance, a hollow shaft with a cap on top of it which was concealed under the head of the crutch where it fitted into the owner's armpit. After he had discarded the velvet wrapping, all Johnson had to do was to release this cap and drop the rings one by one down the shaft of the crutch. Once that was done, he clipped the cap back into place and no one was the wiser. An ingenious hiding-place, was it not? If he was stopped and searched, who would think of looking inside such a piece of orthopaedic equipment? And was it not ironic that this same appliance which had been his lifetime's support, so to speak, should in more ways than one literally bring about his eventual downfall, as Lestrade pointed out? When one hears stories such as this, one cannot help thinking that Fate is not only inexorable but has its own rather bizarre sense of humour as well.'

'So you found the rings after Johnson was arrested?'

'Indeed we did. Johnson put up no resistance when the sergeant arrested him. In fact, he was remarkably sanguine, no doubt thinking that, as the jewels would not be found on him, he could not be charged with receiving stolen property. This confidence was considerably shaken when we accompanied him to the local police station where he found the other two members of his gang, George and Rosie Bartlett, who were already in custody. And it was altogether shattered when I took his crutch from him and, having removed the cap, tipped out a dozen or so valuable rings, the choicest items from Mr Greenbaum's stock.

'I let Lestrade take all of the credit and, as a result, his failing reputation at Scotland Yard recovered remarkably after the arrest of the Notting Hill jewel gang, as they came to be known.

'As for the gang itself, all of them were tried, found

guilty and sentenced to various terms of imprisonment, George Bartlett, the brains you might say behind the enterprise, receiving the heaviest sentence, Johnson the lightest as he had taken no active part in the robbery itself, only receiving the jewellery after it was stolen. His death in Pentonville prison seems a heavy price for him to pay for his misdeeds, for he was never a violent criminal, only a misguided one.'

He seemed genuinely saddened at the thought of Whitey Johnson's untimely demise, a display of sympathy which I have rarely seen him demonstrate even for his clients and certainly not for a member of the criminal classes.[9]

'By the way, Watson,' he added, his voice curt as if to prevent any softer feelings from manifesting themselves, 'I should prefer you did not publish an account of the case.'

He offered no explanation for this prohibition and the sight of his closed, fastidious profile discouraged me from pressing him to give one. I can therefore only hazard a guess at his motive, but my instinct told me it was for Whitey Johnson's sake, rather than his own, that he wished no written account to be preserved. It was clearly Holmes' wish that the sad little man with the withered leg whom Fate had treated in so cavalier

---

[9] In 'The Adventure of the Greek Interpreter', Dr Watson described Sherlock Holmes as a 'brain without a heart, as deficient in human sympathy as he was pre-eminent in intelligence'. Dr John F. Watson.

a fashion all through his life, including the manner of his death, should pass into decent obscurity, a behest I have obeyed. This account will, therefore, be placed among my private papers with all those other written records which, for one reason or another, will never be put before the public.

THE CASE OF THE MANOR HOUSE MYSTERY

It was shortly before my old friend Sherlock Holmes became involved with the strange affair of Mr Melas, the Greek interpreter,[1] that another extraordinary inquiry came his way. As in the Melas case, Holmes' brother Mycroft[2] played a significant role in the Manor

---

[1] Mr Melas was a Greek linguist who acted as interpreter for foreign tourists in London and also at the Law Courts. He was asked to interpret for Paul Kratides and his kidnappers. *Vide*: 'The Adventure of the Greek Interpreter'. Sherlock Holmes was introduced to the case by his brother Mycroft. See footnote below for further details. Dr John F. Watson.

[2] Mycroft Holmes was Sherlock Holmes' elder brother by seven years. Although ostensibly employed as a Government auditor, he was in fact a Government adviser on important issues. He was a founder-member of the Diogenes Club in Pall Mall, not far from his lodgings. *Vide*: 'The Adventure of the Bruce Partington Plans'. Dr John F. Watson.

House mystery, as I referred to the investigation in my notes, although I was not aware of his involvement until the inquiry was over.

It began, as had many of Holmes' cases, with a letter from a prospective client, asking for an appointment on the following morning to discuss a problem which his correspondent, a Mr Edward Maitland, described as 'an urgent matter of life and death'. But as he gave no further details, we were left in the dark as to precisely what the urgent matter might consist of.

'Although in my experience, the concept of the gravity of a situation differs widely from one person to another,' Holmes remarked philosophically. 'I remember once being asked by a certain actress, who features frequently in the gossip columns of the popular press, to find her missing lap dog, a King Charles spaniel by the name of Tootles.'

'And did you find it, Holmes?' I asked, much amused by the idea of my old friend, who prided himself on being the only private consulting detective in the world, becoming involved in such an absurd and trivial inquiry.

Holmes gave me a pained look.

'There was no need. From what the lady told me when I questioned her, it was quite clear the creature was on heat and I simply advised her to place a bowl of Tootles' favourite food on the doorstep. I was informed later that the animal returned that same evening, unharmed if somewhat dishevelled.

'We may find that Mr Maitland's problem falls into the same category as Tootles' and requires only the human equivalent of a bowl of boiled rabbit to solve it, although I must admit his handwriting has a sensible, well-formed quality about it which does not suggest an over-heated imagination.'

Holmes' analysis proved to be correct, for when Mr Edward Maitland was shown up to our sitting-room the following morning at the appointed hour, it was immediately evident from his appearance and demeanour that he was an intelligent young man of good sense and judgement. He was in his thirties, well-dressed and had a pleasant, frank air about him which was appealing.

Having been invited to sit down and state his business, he came straight to the point.

'In my letter to you, I deliberately withheld details of the matter which is troubling me, Mr Holmes, because I thought it better to explain it to you face to face. The business concerns my great-uncle, Sir Reginald Maitland, who is in his late seventies. You may have heard of him. Before he retired, he was a stockbroker in the City of London and was known among his colleagues at the Exchange as 'Midas',[3] because everything he handled seemed to turn to gold. As you may deduce from this, he is extremely wealthy.'

---

[3] Midas was the king of Phrygia, part of Anatolia, and was said to have married the daughter of Agememnon. According to Greek myth, he was granted his wish that everything he touched should turn to gold by the god Dionysus, a wish he came to regret when food turned to gold as he picked it up, as did his daughter when he embraced her. His name became a by-word for extreme riches. Dr John F. Watson.

'But not a fortunate man in other ways, I believe,' Holmes interposed. 'Did he not also have the reputation of attracting bad luck to himself?'

Maitland nodded in agreement, his expression sombre.

'Indeed he did, Mr Holmes, and some of that misfortune was of his own making. He was, and indeed still is, a very stubborn, opinionated man, who, over the years, has managed to quarrel with all who were once close to him, family, friends and colleagues. He never married but was once engaged, I understand, to a charming young woman who broke off the relationship because she found his behaviour quite intolerable. He quarrelled with his brother, my grandfather, and refused to have anything more to do with him or my father. However, for some reason, he seemed more sympathetic towards me and, on my father's death, sent me a letter of condolence. As a consequence of this, I met him from time to time for luncheon at his London club and, after his retirement, at his country house, Holbrook Manor, in Sussex.

'Recently, however, these visits have become more and more infrequent. Then a week ago, I received this letter.'

Taking a sheet of paper from his pocket, he passed it to Holmes who, having received Maitland's permission to read it aloud for my benefit, proceeded to do so.

It began abruptly.

'Sir. I consider your threatening behaviour totally

reprehensible. I refer, of course, to the anonymous letters you have sent me since your last visit. I therefore forbid you to enter my house ever again or to try to maintain any form of correspondence with me whatsoever. I have informed my solicitor and any attempt by you to transgress this prohibition will, if necessary, be dealt with in a court of law.'

'There is no closing salutation, merely a signature,' Holmes concluded.

Refolding the sheet of paper and handing it back to Mr Maitland, he remarked, 'An extraordinary missive! What is this anonymous correspondence your great-uncle refers to?'

'I found out about that only a few days ago. However, as soon as I received my great-uncle's letter, I became alarmed for his safety.'

'Really? On what grounds?'

'On the growing influence one of his servants is having on him – a man called Adams who is my late great-uncle's coachman. Adams has been in his employ for the past four years, ever since his previous coachman retired. I have good reason to believe Adams is behind this attempt to prevent my visiting my great-uncle.'

I saw Holmes lean forward in his chair, his eyes bright and his expression as alert and eager as that of a gun dog which has scented game.

'Pray continue, Mr Maitland,' said he.

'Adams is a plausible rogue who has contrived to worm his way into my great-uncle's confidence,'

Maitland went on. 'Although I have never liked the man – he is too ingratiating for my taste – I had at first no reason to mistrust him. He seemed a reliable servant, devoted to my great-uncle's welfare and anxious to please him. He tolerated his ill humour with exemplary patience, listened to his long accounts of his glory days on the Stock Exchange and was always prepared at the shortest notice to harness the horses and take him out for a drive in the countryside. In this manner, he gradually made himself indispensible until eventually, after my great-uncle dismissed his manservant, Jordan, for the theft of a pair of gold cufflinks, Adams was invited to take his place.

'I was only made aware of this change in Adams' position in the household when I visited Great-uncle Reginald about six months ago, not long after the man's promotion. To be frank, Mr Holmes, I was very uneasy at the time, but there was little I could do about it except to take my great-uncle's housekeeper, Mrs Grafton, into my confidence and express my misgivings to her. She is a sensible, trustworthy woman who has been in my great-uncle's employ for many years. What she had to tell me distressed me even further. She shared my distrust of Adams and in turn confided in me her suspicions that Adams had contrived Jordan's dismissal by stealing the cufflinks himself and concealing them in the manservant's room. She had seen Adams creeping about the house on several occasions but did not dare report it, as my great-uncle had such a high opinion of the coachman's trustworthiness. At my suggestion, she agreed to keep me informed about my great-uncle's welfare as well as Adams' behaviour and any changes which might take place within the household.

'When I wrote in return, I was to send my letters to the vicar's house, as we both agreed there was a strong possibility that Adams might examine the mail on its arrival and become aware of our correspondence or even destroy my letters before Mrs Grafton received them. It was therefore through her that I heard of several disturbing developments which had taken place at Holbrook Manor over the intervening weeks.'

'Such as?' Holmes prompted as Maitland hesitated, passing a hand over his face as if trying by this physical action to arrange his thoughts.

'Nothing that could be construed as of deliberately evil intent but which, in the light of what Mrs Grafton had already told me, increased my suspicions of the man. For example, there was the matter of the cancellation of several appointments with my great-uncle's physician, Dr McFadden. He had a fixed arrangement to visit my great-uncle every Friday morning to check his pulse and his heart and so on. On four occasions, Adams sent the gardener's boy to McFadden's surgery with a letter cancelling the appointment. It is possible Adams played no part in the situation. The letters were always in my great-uncle's handwriting and I know from experience that he was often very impatient with

McFadden's medical advice, especially that concerning his diet and his consumption of alcohol. My great-uncle enjoyed a glass of whisky and resented what he called the doctor's meddling in one of the few pleasures left to him.

'Which brings me to the matter of the whisky decanter. Mrs Grafton noticed that she had to refill it more frequently than in the past and suspected that either my great-uncle was drinking more than usual or Adams had access to his master's tantalus.[4] Once again, I was left with nothing tangible on which to base my suspicion; certainly nothing with which I could confront Adams. All I could do was keep up my correspondence with Mrs Grafton and continue visiting my great-uncle on the first Sunday of every month as I had done in the past.

'And then three weeks ago, Mr Holmes, I received the letter which I have shown you, forbidding me ever to enter the house again because of my "threatening behaviour", as my great-uncle calls it.'

'You are referring, of course, to the anonymous letters. Have you any idea what was in them?'

'I have indeed,' Maitland replied. Reaching once

[4] A tantalus was a wooden stand containing decanters of spirits, e.g. whisky, which could not be removed until a bar holding them in place was unlocked. It was named after Tantalus, a mythical king of Phrygia, who was condemned to stand for ever in Tartarus surrounded by food and drink which he could not reach. Dr John F. Watson.

again into his inside pocket, he drew out an envelope from which he extracted a folded sheet of paper which he again handed to Holmes, who scrutinised for several long moments in silence before passing it to me without any comment.

As far as I could see, it was a piece of ordinary, inexpensive white writing-paper such as one might buy at any stationer's. Its only remarkable feature was the message on it, which had been laboriously composed of words or single letters cut from a newspaper and stuck to the sheet.

It read: 'Beware! You are an old fool who deserves to go to Hell.'

It was undated and bore no name, not even initials.

'May I see the envelope?' Holmes enquired and, having been given it, he again looked at it in silence before passing it on to me.

Like the message, words and individual letters cut from a newspaper had been used to compose the address. Apart from this, I only noted that the envelope was of the same ordinary brand as the writing-paper and that it bore a West Central London postmark.

As I was examining it, Maitland was continuing, 'At my request, Mrs Grafton removed this letter from my great-uncle's bureau drawer and sent it to me with a note explaining that there were six more similar letters sent over the four weeks since my previous visit to Holbrook Hall. I should also add that my address in

London is in the West Central postal district. I can only assume my great-uncle, with Adams' encouragement, has come to the conclusion that it was I who sent the letters.'

'To what purpose?'

Maitland gave a wry smile.

'Exactly, Mr Holmes! What possible motive could I have for threatening my great-uncle in this way? On the other hand, Adams could have a very good reason for causing a rift between my great-uncle and myself. In the first place, I am now barred from seeing him again, thus preventing me from witnessing whatever devilry Adams has planned against Great-uncle Reginald. And secondly, I am the main heir to my great-uncle's estate. Should I be disinherited, I fear Adams will become the sole beneficiary.'

'Would Sir Reginald be foolish enough to cut you entirely out of his Will in Adams' favour?'

'He is a very stubborn man, Mr Holmes, who once he has taken against someone, for whatever reason, would never forgive that individual. My father is a good example of his intractability but there are other instances I could give you of friends and colleagues whom in the past he has discarded quite ruthlessly. You can understand now, I assume, why I referred in my letter to you of the urgency of the affair.'

'Indeed I can, Mr Maitland,' Holmes assured him grimly. 'And I give you my word that the case will receive my immediate attention. Before you leave, however, there are one or two further details I need to establish. To begin with, I assume Adams came with references?'

'I believe so. Mrs Grafton would be the best person to ask about this matter.'

'Of course. That brings me to my second point. Please give me the vicar's name and address so that, if need be, I can write to Mrs Grafton myself.'

'Of course. He is the Reverend George Paget and the address is The Vicarage, Meadow Lane, Holbrook, Kent. Both the vicar and especially his wife are on friendly terms with Mrs Grafton, who is a regular member of the church, and they understand some at least of the situation at the Hall. They will, I am sure, do everything they can to help you, should you apply to them.'

'May I keep the threatening letter and its envelope for the time being?' Holmes enquired.

On receiving Maitland's consent, Holmes rose to his feet and held out his hand.

'Then that is all for the moment,' said he. 'I shall write to you as soon as there is anything to report.'

After his client had left the room and we heard the street door close behind him, Holmes turned to me.

'I fear that Maitland is correct in thinking some devilry is afoot and that Adams is behind it.'

'You seem quite convinced of that, Holmes.'

'My dear fellow, it is as plain as the proverbial pikestaff. The anonymous letter confirms it.'

'Does it? I confess I do not see how. Anyone could have sent it. And if it is indeed Adams, how did he contrive to post the letters in London?'

'Oh, that is easily arranged!' Holmes said, waving a dismissive hand. 'He has an accomplice to whom he sent the letters and who in turn posted them in a pillarbox in the West Central district. I think we may find his co-conspirator also played another role in the affair. Which reminds me. I have an errand to carry out myself at the post office.'

'What role are you referring to?' I asked, bewildered.

But Holmes was busy putting the anonymous letter in his pocket before snatching up his hat and stick and making for the door. Moments later, I heard him whistling in the street for a cab.[5]

At the time, I assumed he had left the house in order to send a telegram to the vicar and his wife, requesting an interview, as indeed he had. But there was another reason for his hasty departure which I did not learn about until much later. He had gone to the Diogenes Club[6] to consult with his elder brother, Mycroft, whom

---

[5] Cabs could be summoned by blowing a whistle, one blast for a four-wheeler, two for a hansom. Some Londoners carried a special whistle with them for this purpose. Dr John F. Watson.

[6] The Diogenes Club was a gentlemen's club situated in Pall Mall. It contained a Strangers' Room, the only part of the premises where conversation was permitted. Mycroft Holmes was a founder member. *Vide*: 'The Adventure of the Greek Interpreter' and 'The Adventure of the Bruce Partington Plans'. Dr John F. Watson.

at that stage of the investigation I did not even know existed.

The telegram which Holmes sent that morning prompted a swift reply that afternoon from the Reverend George Paget. He wired to say that Holmes and I would be very welcome to call at the vicarage the following day where we could meet Mrs Grafton, and suggested we caught the 10.26 train from Victoria to Chichester, the nearest station to Holbrook, where he would meet us with the pony and trap.

The Reverend Paget, an elderly, white-haired cleric with a scholarly air, was waiting for us as arranged, and we set off on the three mile drive to Holbrook, down pleasant Sussex lanes which wound their way through cornfields, the wheat not yet ripe enough for harvesting. Everywhere the trees and hedgerows were in leaf and wild flowers spilled in soft and scented profusion from the wayside verges.

The conversation was as pleasant as the view and covered many interesting topics including early church music, one of Holmes' particular interests,[7] and rural life, about which my old friend expressed an unexpected enthusiasm to my great astonishment.

'I can think of nothing more agreeable,' he declared,

---

[7] Sherlock Holmes wrote a monograph on the polyphonic motets of Orlando Lassus, (d. 1594), a German composer who wrote mostly sacred music. The monograph, which was printed privately, was said by experts to be the last word on the subject. Dr John F. Watson.

'than to retire to a small farm and spend my declining years observing Nature in all its myriad forms.'[8]

He made no reference to the matter which had brought us there. Indeed, he had said nothing further on the subject even to me since he had returned from sending the telegram the previous day, and I was as mystified as ever by his assertion that the anonymous letter confirmed Adams' guilt. As for the vicar, he was of a cautious and retiring nature and his only reference to the matter in hand was to point his whip towards a large Queen Anne mansion standing in extensive grounds which we passed on our way to the village.

'Holbrook Manor,' he remarked.

Shortly afterwards we turned into the gates of the vicarage which was, like him, of a discreet nature, a high laurel hedge and heavy lace curtains protecting it from the public gaze.

Mrs Paget must have been even more retiring than her husband, for we did not meet her at all. Instead, we were shown directly into the vicar's study by a female servant where Mrs Grafton, Sir Reginald's housekeeper, was waiting to receive us, a little nervous at the prospect

---

[8] Although Dr Watson stated that Sherlock Holmes took 'no interest in Nature', as he grew older, Sherlock Holmes admitted that he 'yearned for that soothing life of Nature during the long years spent amid the gloom of London'. *Vide*: 'The Adventure of the Naval Treaty' and 'The Adventure of the Lion's Mane'. Dr John F. Watson.

of meeting two unknown gentlemen, one of whom was Sherlock Holmes, the great investigative detective.

But she was a sensible, down-to-earth woman, not easily daunted, and Holmes, who has a knack of putting ordinary people at their ease when he puts his mind to it, soon won her over.

'It was most kind of you to agree to meet us, Mrs Grafton,' he said, smiling benignly as he shook her hand. 'I greatly appreciate the trouble you have taken. And pray let me assure you that anything you say will be held in the strictest confidence both by me and my colleague, Dr Watson. Our sole purpose is to enquire into Sir Reginald's well-being so that we may reassure his great-nephew, Mr Maitland, who is my client in this affair. Now, to get down to business, madam. Were you able to carry out the instructions I gave you in my telegram to the Reverend Paget?'

'Indeed I was, Mr Holmes,' the lady replied and, opening the large black reticule she was holding in her lap, she took out a small bundle of envelopes, tied together with tape, which she handed to him. He examined them swiftly, first the postmarks on the envelopes and then the letters themselves which he removed, unfolded and hurriedly scanned.

For my benefit, he remarked, 'They are similar to the one we have already seen, the same postmark, the same threatening messages spelt out by the same method of using words and letters cut from a newspaper. And the same newspaper, as well, which confirms my theory.'

He said no more, returning the bundle to Mrs Grafton with the enquiry, 'No one will notice they are missing, will they?'

'I think not, Mr Holmes. They are kept out of sight at the back of the bottom drawer in Sir Reginald's bureau and, as he never uses the study in the morning, he is not likely to notice they have gone. As soon as I return to the house, I shall replace them in the drawer.'

'And the names and addresses of the referees?'

'They are here, sir,' Mrs Grafton replied, handing over a small sheet of paper. 'I copied them from the correspondence which was also kept in Sir Reginald's desk, in the top drawer in this particular case.'

'Excellent!' Holmes exclaimed, the compliment bringing a touch of colour to the good lady's cheeks. 'May I keep them?'

'Pray do so, sir.'

'May I ask what the Honourable Mrs Kelmore and Brigadier Charles Carraway had to say about Adams?' Holmes enquired, glancing down at the piece of paper.

'I did not dare to spend too much time reading their letters, Mr Holmes, let alone copying them out word for word. But I pride myself on having a good memory and can give you the gist of their contents. The Honourable Mrs Kelmore praised his honesty and loyalty, saying she was sorry that after four years, he had to leave her employ due to her own change of circumstances. The Brigadier, who acted as a character witness, stated he had known Adams for the past ten years and could highly recommend him to any prospective employer.'

'One last question before you go, Mrs Grafton. You obviously know Adams well. May I have a description of the man?'

Mrs Grafton seemed a little taken aback by this request, as I was, too. What possible purpose would it serve for Holmes to be told of Adams' appearance? But, after a moment's hesitation, she replied, 'He is, I should say, five and forty or thereabouts; of medium height and build; clean-shaven; dark hair and eyes; always very smartly dressed. Quite handsome, too, I suppose,' she added a little grudgingly. 'At least, I've noticed the ladies seem impressed by him and I'm not referring to just the female servants.'

'Any distinguishing marks? A mole, say? Or a scar?'

'Well, now you come to mention it,' Mrs Grafton said, looking a little flustered, 'there is something odd about his ears. The lobes are very small, sir, compared to most people's.'

She seemed embarrassed at having noticed, let alone spoken of, such a tiny, intimate detail, and Holmes was quick to restore her peace of mind as he escorted her to the door.

'Mrs Grafton,' he said solemnly, 'you would make an excellent private inquiry agent. Your powers of observation are quite outstanding. If, by the way, Dr Watson and I were ever to call at the Manor, you are to treat us as perfect strangers, you understand? I am sure with your undoubted talents you will manage that small deception with no trouble at all.'

We ourselves left soon afterwards, the Reverend George Paget driving us back to Chichester in time to catch the 2.57 train to Victoria.

The journey gave me the opportunity to put to Holmes several questions regarding the inquiry which until that moment I had not had the chance to ask him.

'I am a little puzzled, Holmes . . .' I began.

'About what, my dear fellow?'

'About Adams' testimonials. How was it possible that two highly respectable people, an Honourable lady and a Brigadier, were ready to supply him with references? Maitland was suspicious of him the moment he met him. Did they not also have reservations themselves about his character?'

'Oh, references are easily arranged!' Holmes replied with a nonchalant air. 'Adams or his accomplice acquired the sheets of headed writing paper from the referees' residences.'

'How?' I broke in.

'By buying them, of course, from the servants employed in the houses.' Holmes sounded a little impatient at my obtuseness. 'Any one of the servants, a housemaid or a footman, may be persuaded to part with a sheet of his employer's stationery for a fee, say, of half a crown. The writing paper is then taken to a "screever" and, before you ask what such a creature is, Watson, allow me to explain. A "screever" is an educated person, a clerk perhaps or even a lawyer, who is down on his luck and, again for a fee, is willing to write references to order. They are also employed by professional "cadgers" to write begging letters or bogus testimonials. They can be found in certain taverns or lodging houses and their fees vary, I believe, between sixpence to five shillings, depending on the length and complexity of the false documents.

'Should the references be taken up, the servant involved would have been paid an extra fee to intercept the letter before it reached its intended recipient so that the "screever" could write a reply in the referees' names.

'But that is by the way. What is significant about this aspect of the affair is Adams' obvious knowledge of the ways by which such deceits can be practised, which suggests this is not the first time he has carried out such a fraud. That is why I wanted a description of Adams, as I have no doubt that would have been your next question,' he concluded with a smile.

That had indeed been my intention and I was astonished by my old friend's apparent ability to read my very thoughts.

'Do you think you may be able to bring him to account?' I asked.

'I sincerely hope so, my dear fellow. Adams is almost certainly not his real name but I have no doubt that he, like a snail, has left behind a slimy track by which we can trace his past movements. That will be my first task on our return to London.'

He set out on this assignment soon after we had returned to our Baker Street lodgings, pausing only for a hasty luncheon of black coffee and bread and cheese, before plunging off once more down the stairs on his way, I assumed, to carry out his intention of investigating Adams' past.

I was used to this precipitate behaviour on Holmes' part and did not resent in the slightest the fact that he had not invited me to take part. Nevertheless, once he had gone and the flurry of his sudden exodus had died down, our sitting-room seemed so very quiet and empty that I, too, decided to look for a diversion elsewhere and, taking a hansom to my club, found Thurston[9] also alone and looking for company and so the two of us whiled away the afternoon playing billiards.

It was quite late when Holmes returned, tired but with a triumphant air about him which told me that his researches into Adams' past had proved fruitful.

'We have him *here*!' he cried exultantly, holding out the palm of his hand towards me before adding, 'And tomorrow the trap will shut on him!'

And with that his fingers snapped together to form a fist.

---

[9] Thurston, Christian name unknown, was a fellow member of Dr Watson's club, name also unknown, and the only man with whom Dr Watson played billiards. Dr John F. Watson.

We set off for Victoria the following morning to catch the same train we had caught the day before, but on this occasion we had company on the journey. As we walked down the platform towards a first class carriage, a middle-aged lady dressed in black and with a veil drawn down over her face approached us nervously.

Holmes had apparently met her before because he immediately introduced her to me in a rather dramatic manner.

'Watson, my dear fellow, I would like you to meet Miss Edith Cresswell or, to refer to her *alter ego*, Tisiphone, one of the Eumenides[10] who, if you recall your Greek mythology, hunted down and punished all those who had transgressed. Miss Cresswell has graciously agreed to perform the same service for us. Once we are on the train, I shall explain how I came to make her acquaintance and she will then repeat for your benefit what she knows about the unspeakable Adams.'

Once we had settled into our carriage and the train had set off, Holmes began his account.

'As you are aware, Watson, I already had very grave suspicions of Adams and strongly suspected that he intended to wheedle his way into Sir Reginald's good

[10] Tisiphone was one of the group of three goddesses of Vengeance in Greek mythology. In order not to arouse their anger, mortals referred to them as the Eumenides, the Kindly Ones. Dr John F. Watson.

books and make himself so indispensible that he might, at the very least, be left some money in his master's Will. I also suspected that he would, if the opportunity arose, so alienate Sir Reginald from his only living relative, his great-nephew, in order to supplant him as sole heir to the estate, a plot Adams had already put into motion with the use of the anonymous letters.

'I explained to you yesterday, my dear fellow, that it seemed to me highly likely that this was not the first time Adams had used these means to his own financial advantage. On thinking over this aspect of the affair, I suddenly remembered my—'

At this point in his account, he stopped abruptly and looked uncharacteristically flustered, a reaction I had never before witnessed on the part of my old friend, who was always in such complete charge of his feelings to the extent that, at times, I wondered if he were not entirely devoid of human emotion.[11]

However, he quickly recovered from this momentary break in his narrative, the thread of which he picked up again in his usual imperturbable manner.

'—informant telling me of a similar case that had happened to one of his colleagues ten years earlier. This colleague's wealthy grandmother, who was crippled by rheumatism, had taken into her employ a charming young man called Edwin Farrow, as a secretary who came with

---

[11] Dr Watson once referred to Sherlock Holmes as a 'brain without a heart.' *Vide*: 'The Adventure of the Greek Interpreter'. Dr John F. Watson.

excellent references and soon made himself indispensible to the old lady whom I shall call Mrs Knight. They played piquet[12] together, he took her out for walks in her invalid chair, he read aloud to her in the evenings. But Mrs Knight's female companion, who took care of the old lady's more personal needs, gradually grew more suspicious of Farrow. Money and jewellery went missing and, what was more sinister, Mrs Knight became more and more confused, as if she were taking some form of drug, although none was prescribed by her doctor.

'Her suspicions were confirmed when she found a small glass bottle in the dust-heap, which she took to the local chemist's. He analysed the few drops of liquid found in the bottom of the bottle and discovered that it contained morphia.'

At this point, Holmes paused and turned to Miss Cresswell, who had been sitting in silence, her veil raised, listening to my old friend's account, her plain and pleasant features quite calm, only her black gloved hands, which were tightly locked together in her lap, expressing the inner distress from which she must have been suffering.

'But it is your story I am telling, Miss Cresswell,' Holmes remarked. 'Perhaps you would care to take up the narrative yourself, if it would not cause you too much pain.'

---

[12] Piquet was a card game known under various names which originated in the fifteenth century. It could be played by two, three or four players. Dr John F. Watson.

'Thank you, Mr Holmes,' Miss Cresswell said gravely. 'There is, in fact, little more to tell. As soon as I received the chemist's report, I sent a telegram to my mistress's grandson, who arrived soon afterwards with his solicitor. I had sent Farrow on an errand to the village and, as soon as he had left the house, Mrs Knight's grandson and the solicitor searched Farrow's bedroom, where they found the missing money and jewellery hidden in his wardrobe. These were together with various pills and powders which no doubt he intended to give to Mrs Knight, for I strongly believe he had murder in mind once he had persuaded her to change her Will when she was under the influence of the morphia which he had secretly been giving her. This suspicion was confirmed by a piece of paper also discovered among Farrow's effects on which he had written down a rough draft of an alteration to her Will, leaving five thousand pounds to himself in gratitude for what he called his "kindness and devotion".'

At these last words Miss Cresswell almost broke down but, with commendable courage, she pulled herself together and continued.

'In the meantime, Farrow had disappeared. I think he may have returned to the house and seen the carriage in which the grandson and the solicitor had arrived standing outside the front door, which made him suspicious. Or my own conduct may have alerted him, for I confess I found it difficult to disguise my loathing of him when I had spoken to him earlier.

'The police were sent for and made a further search of his room. They also made enquiries in the district, hoping to discover his whereabouts, and heard of a man resembling him who was seen at the local station buying a ticket to London. That was the last that was seen of him to my knowledge.'

Her voice began to falter and she fell silent. Holmes, perceiving her distress, quickly took up the narrative once more.

'When I made enquiries of my informant,' he continued, this time making no hesitation over the word, 'I learnt that, by great good fortune, Mrs Knight's grandson was still in correspondence with Miss Cresswell and so I was able to call on her. Once I had explained my interest in the affair, she most generously agreed to fall in with my plans. For it was obvious when we compared the descriptions of Farrow and Adams that they were one and the same man, down to the peculiarity of the earlobes.

'Enquiries of Inspector Lestrade at Scotland Yard also confirmed the fact that, despite the lapse of time, the police were still anxious to arrest Farrow, alias Adams. They suspected him of not only carrying out similar frauds and attempted frauds on three other rich, elderly people, but the murder of a bedridden widow from whom he had netted the huge sum of twenty thousand pounds in her Will.

'By the way, Lestrade has alerted the Sussex constabulary by telegram and we will be met at the station by an Inspector Bulstone and his sergeant Cox, as well as two constables. The police will carry out the arrest once Adams has been identified by Miss Cresswell who, I must add,' Holmes concluded, turning one of his most engaging smiles on the lady, 'has shown the most exemplary courage in this sordid affair.

'I have also sent a telegram to Mr Maitland, Sir Reginald's great-nephew, who first alerted us to Adams' activities. He will already be at the manor house when we arrive. I thought that, as his great-uncle was a potential victim, he ought to be present to witness the *coup de grâce* as well as to take charge of his great-uncle's affairs once Adams has been removed from the house.'

As Lestrade had arranged, four members of the Sussex constabulary were waiting for us at Chichester station: Inspector Bulstone, a blue-eyed, fair-haired giant of a man with a soft local accent; his sergeant, Cox, short and dark, in complete contrast to his colleague, and two young, fresh-faced constables who regarded the three of us as we alighted from the London train with considerable curiosity, as if we had just arrived from a foreign country.

Bulstone had already commandeered two vehicles for our use, the station fly and an ancient four-wheeler, and we set off for Holbrook, Bulstone accompanying us in one vehicle, the others following behind in the second.

It was a beautiful early summer's day of unblemished blue skies and a soft breeze on which was carried the mingled scents of the countryside; of warm grass and wild flowers. After the heat and dust of London, it was indeed good to breathe in such delicious fragrances. I noticed that Holmes himself seemed to be indulging in these sensuous delights, for he sat with his eyes closed and his head thrown back in much the same attitude I have seen him adopt when listening to an opera by Wagner.[13]

I wondered again at the remark he had made the last time we had driven along this road about the pleasures of rural life, but dismissed the thought as fanciful. Holmes and London were inextricably linked and I could not imagine him in any other setting than among the busy streets and teeming multitudes of our capital city with all it had to offer in the way of excitement and stimulation.

The manor house, which we had only glimpsed before in the distance, proved to be a handsome eighteenth-century mansion of cream-painted stucco with tiers of glittering sash windows, each crowned with its own stone pediment. Our vehicle drew up under an imposing pillared canopy where Holmes, leaping out, ran up the steps to ring the bell.

Mrs Grafton, who had evidently been forewarned of our arrival by a message sent via the vicar, opened the door immediately and we entered a large hall,

---

[13] Wilhelm Richard Wagner (1813–1883) was a German composer. Sherlock Holmes was eager to arrive at a Wagner night at Covent Garden in time for the second act. *Vide*: 'The Adventure of the Red Circle'. Dr John F. Watson.

floored with marble and lined with pictures. More pillars supported a semi-circular gallery where the staircase, sweeping up towards the first floor, divided into two.

Hardly had we entered than Edward Maitland emerged from a doorway to our left, looking relieved to see us as well as anxious about the outcome of our visit.

There were hurried, low-voiced introductions and then, at a nod of the head from Bulstone, Mrs Grafton knocked on the door of the room from which Mr Maitland had emerged and disappeared inside.

We could hear voices; one a little louder than the others seemed to be protesting but, after a few anxious moments, the door re-opened and a man came out; Adams, I assumed.

Although I estimated he must have been in his middle forties, he appeared much younger, for there was a vivacious air about him, particularly in his movements and his smile, both of which I suspected had been deliberately assumed to give himself a boyish air. For all that surface vitality, however, he was suspicious of our unexpected arrival and kept his distance as he eyed us up and down, trying to calculate the reason behind our visit. His glance flickered first towards the four policemen, whose professional standing he seemed to guess despite their civilian clothes, for the muscles in his shoulders immediately grew tense. But his glance rested the longest on Holmes' face, as if he were more alarmed by the presence of this tall, lean-faced stranger with the piercing, cold, grey eyes than by anyone else. The veiled figure of Miss Cresswell seemed not to attract his attention, for she remained at the back of the group. It was only when Holmes spoke her name and she stepped forward, at the same time raising her veil, that Adams became aware of her.

The effect on him was dramatic. Ashen-faced, he staggered back, his eyes rolling wildly like a horse about to bolt as he looked about for a means to escape. But the two broad-shouldered constables barred his way to the front door, while the passage behind him which led into the house was blocked by Inspector Bulstone and his sergeant who had stepped briskly forward to cut off his line of retreat. He was, in short, cornered like a fox.

And like a fox, he was wily. Quickly recovering his composure, he demanded, 'What is the meaning of this intrusion? Unless you leave the house immediately, I shall inform Sir Reginald who will order you off the premises.'

I saw Holmes give a little smile as if amused by Adams' effrontery. Inspector Bulstone, however, was not impressed.

Having given Adams a glance heavy with disapprobation, he turned to Miss Cresswell.

'Do you recognise this man, madam?' he asked.

'Indeed I do,' she replied in a cool, clear voice. 'He is Edwin Farrow, who stole jewellery from my employer, Mrs Knight, and who deliberately drugged her with morphia, intending, I believe, to persuade her to change her Will.'

Bulstone cleared his throat and, taking a few steps forward, said in his best official voice, 'Edwin Farrow, I am arresting you for assault and for the theft of various valuables belonging to Mrs Knight.'

The conclusion to this drama followed as briskly as if it had been rehearsed. After Sergeant Cox had snapped a pair of handcuffs on Adams' wrists, the two constables seized him by the upper arms and he was bundled out of the house to be driven away to Chichester police station. There he was to await the arrival of Inspector Bulstone and his colleagues, who would escort him back to London where he would later stand trial, together with his accomplice, a certain Arthur Crossman, on various charges, including the murder of Mrs Godfrey Hamilton, an elderly bedridden widow, for which they were later hanged.

Holmes and I, together with Miss Cresswell, departed shortly afterwards, having taken our leave of Mr Maitland, who intended staying on at the manor house, caring for his great-uncle, until a suitable replacement could be found for Adams. The old gentleman was, we were assured, in good hands with both his great-nephew and Mrs Grafton to tend to him.

There remained two minor mysteries connected to the Manor House affair, the first of which Holmes was able to solve for me that very same day on our return to Baker Street.

'Tell me, Holmes,' I asked. 'Why did that first anonymous letter convince you so completely of Adams' guilt as soon as Maitland showed it to you?'

Holmes lowered the *Evening Standard* which he had opened in readiness to read.

'This, my dear fellow,' he replied briefly, shaking the pages of the newspaper at me.

'The *Standard*? But I do not see how . . .'

'Not the newspaper itself!' he exclaimed a little impatiently. 'The newsprint! I have made it my business to study the different types used by the daily press[14] and as soon as I saw that anonymous letter, I knew Maitland could not have sent it and that therefore Adams had to be guilty. Now, if you recall, it was formed from words and letters cut from one particular newspaper, which I recognised as the *Daily Gazette*,[15] a popular paper with a bias towards the more sensational scandals, hardly the choice of Maitland whose reading tastes almost certainly would have been more inclined towards *The Times* or the *Morning Post.* Hence my conviction that Adams, a much more likely reader of the *Gazette,* was guilty.'

And with that, he opened the paper with a vigour which told me that the conversation was over.

---

[14] Sherlock Holmes had made a study of the different styles of newspaper type faces. *Vide*: *The Hound of the Baskervilles.* Dr John F. Watson.

[15] The *Daily Gazette*, in the agony column of which Emilia Lucca's husband published messages to her, was a fictitious newspaper. *Vide*: 'The Adventure of the Red Circle'. Dr John F. Watson.

The second mystery regarding the case was one which, though it had puzzled me at the time, I had forgotten about until Holmes inadvertently reminded me of it.

One evening not long after the conclusion of the case, we were talking in a desultory manner about a number of topics ranging from the design of warships to the migration of birds when the subject turned to the question of how far an individual's character and aptitudes were decided by his ancestry and how far by his upbringing.

I made the point that I thought Holmes' peculiar gifts of observation and deduction were probably the result of systematic training on his part.

To my great astonishment, Holmes began to speak of his own ancestry and early life, a topic which he had never referred to during the years[16] I had known him. In particular, he put forward the theory that his artistic talents were probably inherited from his grandmother, who was the sister of Vernet, the French painter.[17]

On my asking how he knew this side of his nature was inherited rather than the product of his education, he came out with an even more astonishing statement which I will repeat using his own words.

---

[16] Dr Watson first met Sherlock Holmes in 1880. The case of the Greek Interpreter has been variously assigned to dates between 1882 and 1890. Dr Watson had therefore known him for between two to ten years. Dr. John F. Watson.

[17] According to Sherlock Holmes, the sister of Emile Jean Horace Vernet (1789–1863), the French artist, was his grandmother. *Vide*: 'The Adventure of the Greek Interpreter'. Dr John F. Watson.

'Because,' said he, 'my brother Mycroft possesses it in a larger degree than I do.'

He then went on to give me further details about this brother of his whom he had never mentioned before, speaking of his powers of observation which he asserted were superior to his own but which he lacked the energy and ambition to follow up. Later, during the investigation into the theft of the Bruce-Partington plans,[18] Holmes was to confide in me further details of his brother's background, how, although holding only a relatively lowly post as an auditor, Mycroft, because of his great capacity for storing and relating facts, had become indispensible to the Government and indeed, on occasions, actually was the Government.

On being introduced to Mycroft Holmes in the Strangers' Room at the Diogenes Club,[19] I was further astonished by the lack of similarity between the two brothers. My old friend is ascetic in appearance, with the lean, high-nosed features of a Red Indian. In comparison, his brother was so stout as to be positively corpulent, with a massive face and hands so broad and large that they put me in mind of a seal's flippers. Yet, on closer inspection, I was aware of certain likenesses

---

[18] An investigation by Sherlock Holmes into the theft of the Bruce Partington plans for a secret submarine from Woolwich Arsenal and the murder of Arthur Cadogan West, who witnessed the theft. *Vide*: 'The Adventure of the Bruce Partington Plans'. Dr John F. Watson.

[19] See footnote on p. 80. Dr John F. Watson.

between the two brothers, especially in the sharpness of their expression, which suggested they shared the same formidable mental powers.

It was shortly after the introduction was made that the other minor mystery concerning the Manor House affair was solved to my satisfaction. During the subsequent conversation, Mycroft Holmes referred to the case, mentioning the fact that Holmes had consulted him about it only the week before.

'It was Adams, of course?' Mycroft Holmes enquired, to which my old friend replied, 'Yes, it was Adams.'

At that moment, I made the connection. When Holmes had hesitated so uncharacteristically over the word 'my' when discussing the case with me earlier, he had not intended to refer to 'my informant', which he had so quickly inserted into his statement. Instead, he had meant to say 'my brother' or perhaps even 'Mycroft', the first syllable of which is the same as the personal pronoun.

This small deduction on my part gave me enormous satisfaction and I sat back to enjoy to the full the subsequent thrust and parry of the brothers over the identities of two men they observed through the window coming down the street.[20]

---

[20] When Sherlock Holmes introduced Dr Watson to his brother Mycroft at the Diogenes Club, Dr Watson was impressed by the brothers' ability to deduce many details about the lives and backgrounds of two strangers they saw from the window walking down the street, including their marital status and how many children one of the men possessed. Dr John F. Watson.

For a glorious moment, I felt I had something in common with this extraordinary pair of brothers whose powers of observation and deduction outrival those of any other experts in the country, if not in the whole world.

It is therefore with a touch of sadness that I must accept Holmes' prohibition over the publication of this account for the sake of Sir Reginald Maitland, who is still alive and whose reputation might be damaged should the truth be known. However, given the choice, I would have dearly loved to display before my readers my own small success in the field of deductive endeavour which at the time had given me so much personal satisfaction.

THE CASE OF THE CARDINAL'S CORPSE

I have remarked before in one of my published accounts[1] that the year '95 was a particularly momentous one for my old friend Sherlock Holmes. His increasing fame brought him a number of remarkable cases, including that of Wilson, the notorious canary trainer,[2] and the tragedy of Woodman's Lee, an account of which I have published under the title of 'The Adventure of Black Peter'.[3]

---

[1] This remark regarding the year 1895 was made in 'The Adventure of Black Peter'. Dr. John F. Watson.

[2] Dr Watson's account entitled 'The Case of the Notorious Canary Trainer' was published by Constable and Co. in 1990. Dr John F. Watson.

[3] The Adventure of Black Peter' was first published in *The Strand Magazine* in March 1904. Dr John F. Watson.

But perhaps an even more extraordinary investigation was that into the sudden death of Cardinal Tosca, which Holmes undertook at the express desire of his Holiness the Pope.[4]

It was in March, I recall, that an unexpected visitor, Father O'Shea, a Roman Catholic priest, arrived at our Baker Street lodgings. He was a plump, well-fed, rosy-cheeked man who, judging by the laughter lines round his eyes, was by nature an easy-tempered, jovial individual, although on this occasion his expression was more serious than was its wont, I suspected.

He was accompanied by an older woman, respectably dressed in black, whom he introduced as Mrs Whiffen and who kept a handkerchief tightly clasped in one hand as if she had had recourse to it recently and expected to have recourse to it again.

It was Father O'Shea who did the talking.

After apologising for having called without an appointment, he continued in his lilting Irish brogue, 'However, the case is so serious, Mr Holmes, that I felt obliged to waive the usual niceties and come straight to your door.'

'And what is the case, pray?' Holmes enquired, indicating two chairs where his visitors could seat themselves.

'It concerns the disappearance yesterday of Cardinal

[4] In 1895, the Pope was Leo VIII (1810–1903). He was also Pope when Sherlock Holmes investigated the theft of the Vatican cameos. *Vide*: *The Hound of the Baskervilles*. Dr John F. Watson.

Tosca of the Vatican,' the priest replied, at which Mrs Whiffen raised her handkerchief to her lips and began to sob quietly into it.

'Now, now, my good woman; no more tears, I beg you,' Father O'Shea admonished her gently. 'As I have told you before, you are not responsible for Cardinal Tosca's disappearance. And how can you tell Mr Holmes what happened if you sit there weeping like a willow in an April shower?'

Whether or not this bizarre image had some effect, I do not know but, on hearing it, she smiled faintly and put away her handkerchief to everyone's relief, including hers, I suspected.

'Now,' Father O'Shea continued briskly, 'first allow me to lay the facts before Mr Holmes here. And the facts, sir, are these.

'Cardinal Tosca arrived in London three days ago from Rome on private business, not connected with the church. Because of this, he chose to stay not at one of the official residences for visiting dignitaries of his rank but at St Christopher's House, a small private hotel in Kensington which is used by priests as well as lay members of the church when they come to London. Mrs Whiffen is the housekeeper at St Christopher's. My church, St Aloysius's, is close by and I act as parish priest for the staff of St Christopher's, including Mrs Whiffen and any guest staying there.

'When Cardinal Tosca failed to return to the house

yesterday, Mrs Whiffen quite properly came straight to me to report his disappearance and I, in turn, realising the gravity of the situation, immediately went with her to Scotland Yard, thinking it best to involve the police at the most senior level rather than the local constabulary. It was an Inspector at the Yard who recommended you, Mr Holmes, as being the best private consulting agent in the whole country and the most discreet.'

'Which Inspector was this?' Holmes enquired.

'Inspector MacDonald,[5] a Scotsman, judging by his accent, and a Presbyterian too, I should not wonder, but none the worse for being that, I suppose.'

I saw Holmes suppress a smile at this magnanimity on Father O'Shea's part.

'Of course,' the little priest was continuing, 'I had to seek permission from his Holiness the Pope for you to take the case, should you agree to do so, and, to that end, I sent a telegram to his Holiness yesterday and received an answer this morning granting his permission. All that remains is to obtain yours, Mr Holmes. So, sir, will you accept the case or no?'

---

[5] Inspector MacDonald, Christian name Alec, who came originally from Aberdeen, was a Scotland Yard officer from about 1888 and achieved national fame by 1914. He consulted Sherlock Holmes over the Birlstone case. He had a tall, bony figure, sandy hair, 'a dour nature' and a 'hard Aberdonian accent'. Sherlock Holmes, who was 'not prone to friendship', was 'tolerant of the big Scotsman' and referred to him by the affectionate nickname of 'Mr Mac'. *Vide*: *The Valley of Fear*. Dr John F. Watson.

'I will indeed, Father O'Shea,' Holmes replied. 'And now, Mrs Whiffen,' he continued, turning to the landlady who had sat in silence throughout Father O'Shea's rather lengthy introduction, 'perhaps you would be good enough to tell me the circumstances of Cardinal Tosca's disappearance. He has been missing, has he not, since yesterday?'

'That is so, Mr Holmes,' the lady agreed nervously, still twisting the handkerchief between her fingers. 'He left St Christopher's House soon after breakfast yesterday morning, saying he'd be back for luncheon at twelve o'clock sharp. But he never appeared, sir! He's never late for a meal and when it got to three o'clock, I knew something was wrong. So I went straight round to Father O'Shea at the church.'

She seemed about to burst out weeping again and to staunch any fresh outbreak of tears, Holmes hurried on, not giving her time to dwell on the painful details.

'What was he wearing when he left?'

'What any gentleman would wear in town, sir; a black frock coat and trousers, starched shirt, a silk hat and a black cravat.'

'Not clerical garb?'

'Oh, no, sir. Whenever the cardinal came to London private-like on his charitable affairs, he never wore clerical clothes.'

'Charitable affairs? What exactly are these, Mrs Whiffen?'

'I don't rightly know, sir. He never spoke of them to

me. All I know is, once a year he'd come to London to stay at St Christopher's for a week and he'd go out and about visiting these people he helped with his charity; poor people, I suppose, Mr Holmes, them as deserved help.'

'Yes, quite,' Holmes murmured and turned to Father O'Shea, who shrugged his shoulders and spread out his hands in an eloquent gesture suggesting his own ignorance of these *ex officio* activities on the part of the cardinal.

Holmes turned back to Mrs Whiffen.

'How long had Cardinal Tosca been engaged in this charitable work?'

'Beg pardon, sir?' she replied uncertainly, overawed at finding herself the centre of so much attention.

With admirable patience, Holmes rephrased the question.

'When did Cardinal Tosca first come to London on behalf of this charity of his?'

'Oh, years ago, sir; when he was a young man.'

'How many years precisely?'

Mrs Whiffen made some quick mental calculation.

'It was twenty-nine years ago, sir, in 1866. I remember him coming because I'd only started working at St Christopher's eighteen months earlier as assistant to the then housekeeper. It was also about the same time that he started . . .'

She broke off suddenly and, lowering her head, began to examine the handkerchief she was still holding with great attention, turning it over and over in her hands.

'The same time as he started what, Mrs Whiffen?' Holmes prompted her.

Looking decidedly flustered, the lady replied with an air of improvisation, 'Studying English, Mr Holmes. It seems he'd been sent to England by the Vatican especially to learn the language.'

At this point, Father O'Shea intervened with a frown of disapproval.

'And how did you come to find that out, may I ask?' he demanded of the lady. 'That sort of information was supposed to be confidential.'

Mrs Whiffen seemed close to tears again.

'Mrs Potter, the housekeeper, told me, Father,' she stammered apologetically. 'I don't know where she heard it.'

'But, knowing Mrs Potter, I can guess,' Father O'Shea said with a fine show of indignation. 'Listening at keyholes! I have never known a woman with a keener interest in other people's business nor a sharper ear for hearing conversations through closed doors! I used sometimes to wonder if she didn't sit outside my confessional, listening there as well to what the poor penitents had to say about their sins.'

Mrs Whiffen made no reply, only hung her head lower and subjected her handkerchief to further scrutiny. It was Holmes who eventually broke the silence. With the air of beginning the interview afresh, he asked, 'Now,

Mrs Whiffen, I should like a full description of Cardinal Tosca.'

Mrs Whiffen began to look more cheerful now that the conversation had moved from the embarrassing subject of how she had found out about Cardinal Tosca's private arrangement with the Vatican to the less controversial matter of his appearance, about which she could speak openly.

'Well, sir,' she began, 'he's of medium height and somewhat of that gentleman's figure,' she said, glancing across at me as she spoke.

'Well built and broad across the shoulders, would you say?' Holmes enquired with a mischievous twinkle in his eyes as everyone's attention was suddenly turned on me. 'However, I assume, unlike Dr Watson, he does not wear a moustache?'[6]

'Oh, no, sir!' Mrs Whiffen sounded scandalised at the suggestion. 'The cardinal is clean-shaven.'

'Colour of hair and eyes?' Holmes continued.

'Grey-haired, although rather more silvery than grey, I'd say; very distinguished, I always think. Eyes? Well, I've never liked to look too closely,' Mrs Whiffen admitted with a little nervous laugh, as though it would

---

[6] There are three references to Dr Watson's moustache. In 'The Adventure of Charles Augustus Milverton' it is described as 'modest', a second reference is in 'The Adventure of the Red Circle', and in 'His Last Bow', the last case Sherlock Holmes investigated, in which Dr Watson is described as 'a heavily built elderly man with grey moustache.' Dr John F. Watson.

be presumptuous of her to submit a priest of such eminence to so close a scrutiny.

Father O'Shea, who clearly did not share her scruples and was becoming restive at being excluded from the conversation, was quick to demonstrate his superior knowledge.

'Dark brown,' he put in decisively.

'Age?' Holmes suggested.

Now that he had gained the advantage, Father O'Shea was reluctant to relinquish it.

'In his middle fifties, I would estimate, Mr Holmes, and I pride myself on being able to judge within five years the age of any man, woman or child you might care to put before me. But remarkably well-preserved. And beautiful hands!' he added unexpectedly. 'Those of a real gentleman and, though I may be exaggerating just a wee, tiny bit, he had the bearing of a prince of royal blood.'

'Thank you both very much for such an excellent description,' Holmes said gravely, taking care to include Mrs Whiffen in this accolade, at which the lady blushed deeply at this brief moment of appreciation.

'Now, about Cardinal Tosca's charities,' Holmes began but was cut short by Father O'Shea, who held up an admonitory finger.

'I can tell you nothing about those,' he replied and added a little more sharply in case Holmes decided to question the lady herself, 'and neither can Mrs Whiffen. As I understand it, they are deserving cases which the cardinal has heard about during his visits to London over the years and whom he helps financially out of his own pocket. He is a very generous man but modest as well and never speaks of these private charities of his to anyone, unless it is to his Father Confessor in the Vatican. Speaking of which, you are quite sure about taking on the case, Mr Holmes?'

'I am indeed.'

'Then I shall immediately send another telegram to the Vatican informing his Holiness of your decision. And now if there are no more questions?'

Father O'Shea suddenly seemed anxious to leave and, having shaken hands with both of us, he bustled Mrs Whiffen out of the room.

'A fascinating case!' Holmes observed when the door closed behind them. 'A missing cardinal and a parish priest who, I suspect, knows more about this affair than he cares, or perhaps dares, to divulge.'

'You felt that, too, Holmes?' I remarked. 'What on earth do you suppose it could be?'

Holmes shrugged.

'We may never know. But at the moment, there are more substantial matters to resolve than some hypothetical secret from the past, and that is the present whereabouts of Cardinal Tosca. And for that to be discovered, we have to wait on MacDonald and his colleagues to find the answer.'

In the event, the solution came that very same afternoon more quickly than we had anticipated and was brought, not by the Inspector but by a messenger of his, a red-faced constable in civilian clothes who arrived post-haste in a four-wheeler and presented himself in our sitting-room, very out of breath, to announce that, on instructions from Inspector MacDonald, we were to accompany him without delay.

To Paternoster Yard, Spitalfields, it seemed, according to the address the constable gave to the cab driver who was waiting downstairs in the street.

'I assume a body has been found,' Holmes remarked as we clambered inside the four-wheeler, which set off at a brisk trot.

The constable looked startled.

'You know about the dead man, sir?'

'I know of a missing person,' Holmes replied. 'I deduce from the urgency of Inspector MacDonald's summons that it is probably a criminal matter and that the man is almost certainly dead; possibly even murdered. But Spitalfields! That is the last place in London I would have expected his body to be found.'

I could understand Holmes' reservation over the address when, having driven us through a poor district of London to the east of Liverpool Street station, the cab set us down at the entrance to Paternoster Yard, a large cobbled area overlooked on three sides by the high, soot-stained brick walls and broken windows of a derelict factory, closed off from the yard itself by a pair of tall, black-painted doors, their tops bristling with iron spikes.

The yard was deep in mud and strewn with malodorous rubbish including what appeared to be a bundle of old clothes, roughly covered with sacks, which was lying in a corner formed by the angle of two walls and over which Inspector MacDonald and two uniformed officers were standing guard. A self-important, plump, little man in civilian dress, with a leather medical bag set down on the ground beside him, who was making an examination of the corpse, was, I assumed, a police surgeon called out to certify death before the body was taken away for a post-mortem.

As we entered the yard, the tall, sandy-haired figure of MacDonald disengaged himself from this group and came over to join us.

'Our missing cardinal?' Holmes asked in a low voice.

MacDonald pulled a wry face.

'I am afraid so, Mr Holmes. He answers the description given to me by Father O'Shea and Mrs Whiffen. And besides, I found these in his pocket.' Holding out his hand, he displayed a gold crucifix on a heavy chain and a ring set with a dark red stone on a gold band. 'Not the usual objects most people would carry in their pockets,' he continued. 'But, man, what a devil of a place for a Christian, let alone a cardinal, to find his last resting place!'

'Indeed!' Holmes agreed grimly. 'When was he discovered?'

'About two hours ago. A man was walking his dog

when it bolted into the yard after a rat. When he went to fetch it back, he found it sniffing excitedly at that pile of old clothes, as he at first thought it was. When he looked closer and saw it was a dead body, he told the local constable, who in turn told his inspector, until finally the information was passed on to me at Scotland Yard.'

'And what was the cause of death?' Holmes continued when MacDonald had finished his account. 'Has that been established yet?'

He had asked this last question in his normal voice and, overhearing it, the police surgeon bustled forward to be introduced and to shake hands.

'Mr Holmes!' he exclaimed, puffing out his cheeks with pleasure. 'I have heard of you, sir, and your famous detective skills. May I say how delighted I am to make your acquaintance?'

'What of the dead man?' Holmes asked, cutting short this eulogy.

'Ah, the *corpus delicti!*' the doctor replied, flourishing the Latin tag like a silk handkerchief. 'No external injuries visible, so cause of death is uncertain but I may be able to ascertain that at the post-mortem. Of course, he may have died of natural causes such as a heart attack. As to the time of death,' he continued, taking out a gold pocket watch and examining it in the same ostentatious manner, 'it is now twenty minutes past three o'clock. At a rough estimate, he has been dead for about twenty-eight hours.'

'Which would place his death at approximately eleven o'clock yesterday morning,' Holmes put.

'Exactly so, sir!' The little doctor seemed impressed with the speed with which my old friend had made the computation.[7]

'Thank you. You have been most helpful,' Holmes said gravely, shaking the man's hand in a dismissive manner, for he showed every sign of remaining while Holmes and MacDonald made their own examination of Cardinal Tosca's body, which was lying on its back, its legs straight and its arms folded across its chest as if whoever had placed it there had gone to some trouble to lay it out properly.

As soon as the police surgeon had taken the hint and departed, Holmes crouched down over the corpse with the eager air of a terrier at a rabbit-hole, taking care to avoid certain marks in the mud near to where it was lying which consisted of a number of footprints overlapping one another and, more clearly defined, two parallel grooves about three quarters of an inch wide and two feet apart. At that early stage, he touched nothing but his keen gaze moved swiftly over the dead man's face and clothing. At the same time, he kept up a running commentary on his observations, as much for his own benefit, I felt, as for ours.

---

[7] While travelling to Devon on the Silver Blaze investigation, Sherlock Holmes was able to calculate in his head the speed of the train from the time it took to pass the telegraph posts which were set sixty yards apart. Dr John F. Watson.

'He is undoubtedly the missing cardinal,' he remarked. 'The clothes and features exactly match the description we were given.' Picking up one of the plump white hands, he turned it over in his own. 'Father O'Shea spoke of his beautiful hands and he was right to do so. They are carefully looked after and suggest a man unused to physical labour. One can also see the mark on this finger where he normally wore the ring, a symbol of his clerical status. No other marks on his hands and face, which suggests he was not attacked by an assailant or tried to defend himself. The surgeon may be correct in suggesting he died of natural causes.

'Now for the clothing. No blood that I can see, nor any tears in the fabric. But *hello!* What have we here?' he suddenly exclaimed. He had rolled the body on to its right side and was running his hand over the frock coat the dead man was wearing, and had evidently felt something inside an inner pocket which proved to be a leather pocket book. Opening it up, he revealed a wad of paper which, when unfolded, revealed ten five-pound bank notes.

'Interesting!' Holmes commented. 'Why should the cardinal be carrying so much money on his person? Well, it proves one fact at least. If he was murdered, robbery was clearly not the motive.'

Having handed over the pocket book to MacDonald, Holmes returned to his close scrutiny of the dead man's clothing and began examining, with the aid of his magnifying glass which he always carried with him in his pocket, the right sleeve of the dead man's coat, to which some coarse yellow grains were clinging, before moving his attention down the corpse towards the lower garments.

'Nothing on the trousers that I can see,' he continued. 'Now for the feet. And what have we here? More fascinating debris, by Jove! Why, the cardinal's boots are a veritable mine of crucial evidence.'

Opening his own pocket book, he took out several small envelopes of the type he always carried on his person and, using the blade of his penknife, he carefully scraped samples of that debris he had referred to into the little paper receptacles. As far as I could see, it consisted of more of the yellow grains he had found on the sleeve as well as some grey, gritty substance and a white, powdery paste which was compacted into the arch between the heel of one of the dead man's boots and the sole. Having sealed the envelopes, he replaced them in his pocket book.

It was at this point that MacDonald, who had stood silently watching Holmes as he set about collecting this evidence, now moved forward.

'I think you will nae need me to point out the two lines of parallel marks on the ground,' he remarked.

Holmes looked up at him.

'Indeed, friend Mac. I had already observed them. From the distance between them, I would guess they were caused by the wheels of a hand-cart. I would also hazard, judging by the place where they stop, close by the body, that the cart was used to transport the dead man here from wherever it was he died. Note also the footmarks round the corpse,' he added, pointing a long finger to an area where the mud was heavily trampled. 'Two men, would you not agree? And here,' he went on, 'you may see the fainter traces of the wheels as the two men pushed the cart away; fainter because it was then empty and, without the weight of the body, the wheels were not pressed down so hard on to the muddy surface.'

Head lowered, he set off to follow the tracks back to the entrance, MacDonald and I close upon his heels. At the point where the yard opened out into the street, he paused again to point downwards.

'And here, if you look closely, gentlemen, you will see the wheel marks veer off to the left, suggesting the owners of the cart must reside in that direction.'

Although the tracks were particularly difficult to discern, being only faintly impressed on to the mud and moreover trampled over by the comings and goings of MacDonald and his colleagues as well as the police surgeon and whoever had discovered the body in the first place, it was still possible to see, now that Holmes had drawn our attention to them, the double row of wheel tracks turn off to the left before vanishing from sight altogether on the cleaner surface of the public footpath.

'To sum up what we have already discovered,' said

Holmes as we turned back into the yard, 'we can, I believe, safely assume that, while it was not necessarily murder and that robbery was not a motive, two men were concerned with the disposal of Cardinal Tosca's body in Paternoster Yard and that the two men were in a line of business that involved the moving about of certain materials, more of which I think you will find on the back of the cardinal's coat once the body is turned over.'

'You are referring, are you not, Holmes, to the various substances you have collected from his boots?' I asked.

'I am indeed, my dear fellow.'

'Which are?' Inspector MacDonald interposed.

Holmes gave an enigmatic smile.

'That, my good Inspector, I will have to ascertain when I have performed various chemical tests on them,' he replied with an evasive air. 'As soon as I know the results, I will, of course, inform you.'

And with that, he shook hands with MacDonald, beckoned to me and, stepping out briskly into the street, hailed a passing cab.

He made no further reference to the case on the journey to Baker Street, nor during the next few hours after our return when he closeted himself in the sitting-room with his chemical apparatus and proceeded to subject the contents of the little paper envelopes to a series of tests. Experience had taught me not to ask questions when he was absorbed in the investigation of a case and, after twenty minutes of sitting silent by the fire with only the *Evening Standard* for company, I admitted defeat and left the house for my club, where I passed the time more agreeably playing billiards with an old acquaintance of mine, Thurston.[8]

When I returned to my lodgings, Holmes was absent, although the evidence of his recent activities was apparent in the jumble of test tubes, litmus paper and bottles of chemicals which still littered his chemistry bench. There was no note, however, of where he had gone or when he proposed returning and I was left to kick my heels for three quarters of an hour before I heard the street door slam and footsteps bounding eagerly up the stairs.

'Get ready to leave, Watson!' he cried. 'I have a cab waiting below!'

'To go where, Holmes?' I enquired, wondering, as I scrambled into my coat and seized up my stick, what destination Holmes needed to set out for with such urgency when he had only that very moment returned to the house.

'You will shortly see, my dear fellow,' he replied over his shoulder as he set off down the stairs which he had so recently mounted. 'And no questions, Watson! I refuse to answer any questions. I know what you are going to ask and the answers will be made as clear as daylight very shortly.'

---

[8] See footnote on p. 88 regarding Thurston. Dr John F. Watson.

As if to emphasise this prohibition, he dominated the conversation on the journey to an address, Makepeace Court, which was unknown to me, talking in such a sprightly manner on a variety of subjects from Gothic architecture to the study of philology[9] that I could do nothing except listen to him, fascinated by this monologue, for, when Holmes is in one of his high-spirited moods, he can be a scintillating companion. However, from time to time, my thoughts strayed to those forbidden questions which still occupied my mind: What had he discovered during his chemical tests which had led to this exuberant state of mind? Where had he gone during his absence from Baker Street? And what was the significance of Makepeace Court, our apparent destination?

At the same time as I listened to Holmes and pondered these questions, I also glanced occasionally at the passing scenery, trying to ascertain our whereabouts and, after a while, I began to recognise some of the streets we were driving through. One in particular seemed especially familiar and it was only when the hansom clattered past an opening between

---

[9] In 'The Adventure of the Devil's Foot', Sherlock Holmes was advised by his doctor, Dr Moore Agar, to take a complete rest. Consequently, he and Dr Watson travelled to Poldhu Bay in Cornwall where they rented a cottage. While there, Sherlock Holmes took the opportunity to study the ancient Cornish language which he concluded was akin to Chaldean and had been derived from Phoenician traders who had visited Cornwall in the past to buy tin. Dr John F. Watson.

some dingy houses and I caught a glimpse of a painted sign affixed to the wall which read 'Paternoster Yard', that I realised we had returned to Spitalfields and to the scene of our earlier examination that afternoon of Cardinal Tosca's body. But on this occasion we did not stop but drove on for another quarter of a mile or so down shabby little streets of workmen's cottages interspersed with taverns, pawnbroker's, second-hand dealers and, from time to time, terraces of once-elegant eighteenth-century houses, the former homes of prosperous silk weavers, now sadly dilapidated, until eventually the cab drew to a halt outside another entrance, not dissimilar to Paternoster Yard, where we alighted.

It led, however, not into the filthy recesses of that earlier setting but into a smaller but more orderly open area in which the various materials used in the building trade were neatly stacked, timber in one corner under a lean-to shelter, bricks and slates in another, and, on the far side, gravel and sand under a tarpaulin next to a handcart tipped up on its front edge, its shafts pointing upwards, with the name Jas. C. Buskin & Son painted on its sides and the word 'BUILDER' written in larger letters below.

The same name and occupation was displayed on a board over the doorway of a single-storey building to our left. It appeared to serve as an office as well as a store, for, through the open door, I caught a glimpse of a tall, old-fashioned wooden desk and stool in front of the window and, further back in the darker nether regions were shelves, containing, I surmised, more perishable building materials such as tins of paint and sacks of cement kept under cover from the weather.

Our arrival was not unnoticed, for hardly had we set foot inside the yard than a man emerged from the rear of this building and came towards us.

He was a broad-shouldered, grey-haired man with a walrus moustache, wearing shabby working-clothes of boots, waistcoat, corduroy trousers, very worn and stained about the knees, and a flannel shirt without a collar, the sleeves of which were rolled up to reveal powerful forearms. His manner was aggressive and unwelcoming.

'Mr Buskin?' Holmes enquired with a pleasant smile.

''Oo wants to know?' the man demanded belligerently.

'My name is Sherlock Holmes,' my old friend replied in the same pleasant manner, 'and this is my colleague, Dr Watson. We have come on behalf of the police to enquire into the sudden death of Cardinal Tosca, whom I believe you are acquainted with.'

The effect of this remark on Mr Buskin was immediate and dramatic. With a loud cry, he staggered back a few steps, his face grey, one hand going up to clutch at his throat as if gasping for air. Fearing he might be about to suffer an apoplectic seizure, I hurried forward and, grasping him by the arm, supported him into the low building where I found an upturned crate, on to which I was able to lower him.

His outcry had alerted a younger man, his son, I assumed, who until that moment had been out of sight in a storage area at the back of the office and who ran forward.

'Holloa! What's going on?' he called out, his pleasant, rather plump features expressing acute anxiety.

I glanced round as I bent over his father.

'Fetch some water!' I ordered him abruptly.

The young man took one horrified look at his father's face and, seizing up a cup which was standing on the desk, he dashed the dregs of tea which it had contained on to the floor before running out into the yard to fill it at a standing tap and bringing it back to me.

''E's not going to die, is 'e, like . . . ?' he began and then broke off suddenly before he had completed the question.

I was more concerned with my patient's condition than with the significance of the unfinished query, although Holmes must have taken heed of it, for, as I saw Mr Buskin, to my relief, recover sufficiently to sip a little water from the cup I held to his lips, Holmes had turned with a stern expression to the younger man.

'Like your visitor who came here yesterday morning?' he enquired.

The younger man's face went white as he cast a terrified look at his father, who was now struggling to sit upright.

'Tell him, Jack,' he ordered in a hoarse voice.

But even with this parental permission, the son seemed incapable of speech and it was Holmes who took up the narrative.

'Yesterday morning a visitor came to see you and your father, a wealthy Italian gentleman who had helped you and your family financially for many years. I am correct, am I not?' He waited for an affirmatory nod from the young man before continuing, 'At some point during the visit, your visitor suddenly collapsed and died.'

Again Holmes paused but this time Jack Buskin made no gesture to confirm the truth of Holmes' statement; he merely ran his tongue over his lips. Only Buskin senior made any response. He groaned aloud and I felt him put all his weight on my arm as he struggled to rise to his feet.

'Holmes!' I called out in warning.

Perceiving the older man's distress, Holmes said quickly, 'I shall stop there, Mr Buskin. I should not wish to cause you any further concern.'

But Buskin senior was adamant.

'No, go on, sir!' he cried, making a beckoning gesture with one arm as if urging Holmes to step forward. 'I'm glad the truth is coming out at last.'

'Then with your permission, I shall continue,' Holmes replied and resumed his account. 'I do not know what caused your visitor's death but I am sure it was natural, a heart attack possibly or a stroke.

But whatever the reason, you and your son were left in a dreadful dilemma. You had a dead man on your premises whose address you did not know and whose identity you were unsure of. I think I am correct there. Mr Buskin, under what name did you know the Italian gentleman?'

'Signor Morelli.'

'And did you know his occupation?'

''E said 'e 'ad a business in Rome; something to do with church buildings, as I understood it.'

'I see,' Holmes said gravely, his expression perfectly bland. 'And now we come to the nub of the matter – how Signor Morelli became acquainted with you and your family in the first place.'

I saw Buskin senior glance across at his son, a humble, placatory expression on his face and, when he spoke, he addressed his remarks to his son, not Holmes.

'I'd always 'oped I'd never 'ave to tell you this, Jack, but the story's got to come out now that Signor Morelli's dead. The truth is me and my wife was not your mother and father, although we brought you up from when you was a baby and loved you like our own son. Signor Morelli was your real father and my late sister, Lizzie, was your mother.'

At this point in his narrative, Mr Buskin, who seemed on the verge of breaking down, fell silent and covered his face with one large, calloused hand.

It is never an agreeable sight to see a grown man

reduced to tears, certainly not someone of Mr Buskin's large and powerful stature, and I was considerably relieved when Buskin junior dragged another crate to the side of his erstwhile father and, seating himself upon it, placed a protective arm about the older man's shoulders.

'Now, Pa,' said he, 'for you'll always be Pa to me, don't distress yourself. Whatever 'appened in the past is over and done with. All that matters is that you and me are together and always will be. Now I know Mr 'Olmes 'as to make enquiries on be'alf of the police or whoever it is 'e's acting for, but I'm sure 'e's enough of a gen'leman to come back another time when you feels up to talkin' to 'im. Isn't that so, Mr 'Olmes?'

'Of course,' my old friend began but Buskin senior cut him short.

Drawing himself up, he said with great dignity, 'It's kind of you to offer, Mr 'Olmes, but the truth 'as got to be faced and better now than later, says I. And the truth is this.

'Thirty years ago, my sister Lizzie was in service in a boarding-house somewhere in London, although I can't remember the address. She was a lovely looking young woman was Lizzie, not quite seventeen, and she caught the eye of this Italian gentleman who had been sent to London to improve his English. Anyway, to cut a long story short, he fell in love with Lizzie and I'm sure you and your friend there, being men of the world, don't need telling what happened. Signor

Morelli went back to Italy and Lizzie found she was carrying his child. There was nothing to be done. We had no address for him and Lizzie wouldn't tell us the name of the 'otel where she'd met 'im; not that it would have done any good because, as soon as the 'otel owner found out about the baby, Lizzie was dismissed with no references.

'Well, Lizzie had the baby, a little boy, and you won't need me to tell you 'oo he is now. But things went wrong with her soon after the baby was born and Lizzie died of a fever. My mother couldn't bring the child up herself. She was widowed and in poor 'ealth. So we talked it over and decided it was best if me and my wife took the baby on as ours. We'd been married about three years but didn't have no children of our own, a big disappointment to both of us. So we raised him as our own.

'Then two years after Lizzie died, Signor Morelli turns up again in London. God knows 'ow he found out where we was living, but I was working then for a builder in Wapping and he arrived one evening out of the blue, looking for Lizzie. When we told him she had died after having his baby, he went as white as a ghost. He gave us money to 'elp pay for the child's keep. I didn't want to take it, Mr 'Olmes, because it seemed wrong some'ow to be paid for looking after a child we loved and looked on as our own. But times was 'ard and the money was very welcome. Anyway, after that, he came back every year to see the child and pay for his keep. It was a generous sum; so generous that I was able to put a bit aside and, after a few years, I'd managed to save enough to buy this little business in Spitalfields. But there was one condition. We was to go on pretending the child was really ours and we wasn't to let on to anyone 'oo the real father was.'

'Did you never ask yourselves why he should insist on this?' Holmes asked.

Buskin senior looked abashed.

'Of course, we did, but we understood he was from a rich family and he didn't want them to know he'd fathered a child out of marriage. And to be honest, Mr 'Olmes, it suited us as much as it suited him. 'E'd turn up 'ere once a year, stay for a couple of hours and give me the fifty pounds which, now that Jack's left school and 'as been working 'ere with me, we ain't needed. So I've been putting it aside so that if 'e ever wants to get married and set up on 'is own, there's a tidy little nest egg to get 'im started.'

'But you didn't keep the money Signor Morelli brought the other day?' Holmes pointed out.

Buskin looked affronted by the question, as if the answer should have been obvious.

''E dropped dead afore he could pass it over and it didn't seem proper to go through 'is pockets and 'elp myself to it, even though I knew 'e'd 'ave it on him, same as usual. Anyway, we was more concerned with what we was to do with 'im. We couldn't go to the police. They might think we'd murdered 'im. And besides, who was going to believe our story about an Italian gen'leman givin' us money. So we put 'im on the 'and-cart and covered 'im with some sacks and, when it was dark, we pushed the cart down to Paternoster Yard where we left 'im, laid out decent-like. It was all we could do for 'im. We didn't know where 'e lived so we couldn't let 'is family and friends know.'

'But why Paternoster Yard?' Holmes asked.

'Well, sir, it was quiet and bein' a dead end – no disrespect intended to Signor Morelli – no one 'ardly ever used it. We thought by the time the body was found, things might 'ave gone quiet-like.'

His voice trailed away miserably as if, having put into words, probably for the first time, the unspoken hope that, like dirt swept under a carpet, the whole matter might somehow also disappear, he was made aware of the foolishness of such an expectation.

Buskin senior cleared his throat and, drawing himself upright, he looked Holmes in the face.

'I know me and Jack done wrong, sir, by not telling no one about 'im and just leavin' 'im there like a bundle of old clothes,' he said. 'It's been on my mind ever since. So what can we do to put things right? Shall I go to the police or will you go for me? If it's a matter of a fine, I'll pay up on the nose.'

There was a long moment's silence, so intense that I could hear quite clearly the sound of wheels and horses' hooves passing up and down the main thoroughfare beyond the entrance to the yard. While it lasted, the two Buskins stood side by side at attention, like soldiers awaiting the judgement of a superior officer.

I was unable to look at them because their expressions, so pitifully submissive and yet at the same time oddly dignified, made me feel humbled by their willingness to accept whatever punishment Fate, in the person of Holmes, might mete out to them. I ventured a sideways glance at my old friend to see if he also was affected by the Buskins' self-abasement.

He was staring fixedly down at the toes of his boots, his face quite imperturbable.

And then suddenly, as if coming to an abrupt decision, he looked sternly at the two Buskins standing there side by side and said in a clipped voice, 'Leave it with me! Do nothing yourselves. I myself will arrange matters on your behalf.'

With that, he turned on his heel, so quickly that he cut short the Buskins' exclamations of gratitude and left me no choice but to hurry after him.

'What will you do, Holmes?' I asked when at last I caught up with him in the street.

'I have already told you. Nothing!' he retorted impatiently.

'Nothing? But surely, Holmes . . .' I began in protest.

'I repeat. I shall do nothing. What more can I say? If I report this business to the police, there will be no question of paying a mere fine, as Mr Buskin so sanguinely expects. They will be arrested and charged, if not with murder, then most certainly with the failure to report a death and with the concealing of a body, both of which can carry a prison sentence. Is that what you want, Watson? To see the Buskins, two decent, hard-working men, behind bars, their business, and probably also their lives, ruined?'

'Of course not, Holmes!' I protested, much taken aback by the ferocity of his reply. 'But what will you tell Inspector MacDonald and Father O'Shea?'

'That I have nothing to tell them,' Holmes replied. 'In short, that I have failed. For all my much-vaunted skills and the evidence of the builder's materials on the dead man's clothes, I was unable to find the yard where those materials originated and therefore I cannot say where he died or who was with him at the time of his death or who carried his body to Paternoster Yard. In other words, the investigation was a total failure on my part, a deception which you will support me in, Watson, if you value our friendship.'

And with that, he raised his stick and hailed a passing hansom, in which we returned in mutual silence to Baker Street.

There is very little more to tell.

Inspector MacDonald and Father O'Shea were separately informed of Holmes' apparent failure, an admission which both of them accepted, on the Inspector's part with a degree of scepticism, for I saw him give my old friend a long, searching glance of disbelief.

On Father O'Shea's part, I thought I detected unexpected relief.

'So that is the end of the matter,' he declared, trying but failing to entirely suppress a small, gratified smile and, as he walked out of the room, he looked positively cock-a-hoop. I found this response quite extraordinary until Holmes explained that it was highly likely that Lizzie Buskin had been a servant at St Christopher's House where Cardinal Tosca, then a young priest, had met her and fathered her child, for which she was dismissed. If Father O'Shea was already the parish priest at the nearby church of St Aloysius, he might have been aware of the situation which, at the time, was hushed up.

It seemed to me a little far-fetched until Holmes pointed out that it would account for Father O'Shea's reluctance at the time my old friend interviewed him to discuss Cardinal Tosca's charitable works as well as his poorly-disguised relief at Holmes' apparent failure.

As for Cardinal Tosca's body, it was transported back to the Vatican where it was duly buried with, I assume, all the rites and ceremonies suitable for a priest of such high standing.

As for myself, I have become reconciled to the fact that this account can never be published which, all things considered, is perhaps the best outcome after all. For while Holmes' reputation suffered a temporary set-back at his apparent failure, it was soon restored by his success over his next investigation, the case of the Devonshire Scandal and the supposed murder of a member of the House of Lords by his butler, which occupied the newspaper headlines for the next three months.

THE CASE OF THE ARNSWORTH AFFAIR

'Now there's a name from the past,' Holmes exclaimed, laying aside the *Morning Post* to address me.

'What name?' I asked.

'The first one listed in the obituaries,' Holmes replied, handing me the paper folded back to the correct page. 'The lady in question was before your advent as my chronicler, Watson, when I was still in practice at Montague Street.'[1]

Putting down my coffee cup, I glanced at the item. It referred to the death the previous day of Dowager Lady Edith Arnsworth of Arnsworth Castle in the County of Surrey, aged seventy-three. The funeral would be private.

I was about to enquire who Lady Arnsworth was and

[1] See footnote on p. 45. Dr John F. Watson.

what part, if any, she had played in Holmes' past when he anticipated my question. Getting up from the table, he reached down his encyclopedia[2] from the shelves in one of the chimney alcoves and passed it silently to me, already opened at the relevant entry which consisted of several newspaper cuttings carefully pasted on to the page. Leaving me to peruse them on my own, he went into his bedroom, which adjoined our sitting-room, where I heard him rummaging about.

The first cutting referred to the castle itself and had obviously been clipped from a journal devoted to descriptions of the lives and backgrounds of the rich and famous.

'Arnsworth Castle,' it stated, 'the home of the Arnsworth family, is a magnificent fourteenth-century building standing in over ten acres of parkland and pleasure gardens. It is encircled by a moat and access to the house is gained by a long stone bridge of over forty arches. Although extensively altered in the Tudor period, it still retains many of its original features, including the battlemented west tower, from the top of which the visitor may enjoy splendid views over the surrounding countryside.

'The castle is said to be haunted by the ghost of the

---

[2] There are several references to Sherlock Holmes' encyclopedia, sometimes referred to as his 'commonplace book'. In the 'Adventure of the Sussex Vampire', Dr Watson speaks of it as 'the great index volume', 'the accumulated information of a lifetime'. Dr John F. Watson.

second earl, Philip de Harnsworth, who was murdered by his brother Ffulke during a quarrel over the inheritance. The house is also reputed to have several secret rooms and passages. Extensive dungeons and cellars below the castle house the family collection of weapons and instruments of torture.

'The castle is open to the public only when Sir Grenville Arnsworth and his family are absent in Scotland during the shooting season. For permission to view, application should be made to the Steward, Mr Lionel Monckton, at the Castle Lodge.'

It was followed by an obituary notice from *The Times* for 12th July 1824, referring to the death of Sir Grenville together with a long account of his life, largely spent, it seemed, on the hunting field and only very occasionally in the House of Lords, much of which I merely glanced at.

The next three clippings received the same cursory treatment, as they were concerned with Sir Grenville's heir, Sir Richard Arnsworth, including an account of his marriage to Lady Edith Godalming at St Margaret's, Westminster in 1849, the birth of their only child and sole heir, Gilbert, in 1853, and the death of Sir Richard in a hunting accident in 1872 when Gilbert inherited the title, the castle and the considerable family fortune.

I was about to turn to the next much longer and more interesting-looking cutting, pasted separately on its own page and preceded by a dramatic heading of which I only had time to catch a few words – 'Tragic', 'Nobleman' and 'Mysterious' – when Holmes re-entered the room, dragging behind him the tin trunk in which he kept his records and mementoes of past cases.[3]

Crossing the room to my chair and perceiving that I had not yet read this last item, he snatched the volume away from me unceremoniously and, slamming it shut, returned it to the bookshelves.

'I say, Holmes!' I protested at this cavalier treatment.

'I am most sincerely sorry, my dear fellow,' Holmes rejoined. 'But swift action was called for. Had you read that last cutting, my own account of the case would have been totally ruined and, as you know, I must be allowed my dramatic moments. And now, Watson,' he continued, taking his seat by the fire and handing me a small package tied up with tape, 'you shall hear about the Arnsworth case from my own lips rather than from the pen of some inky newspaper hack. In that package, you will find likenesses of the two main protagonists in the case, the Dowager Lady Edith Arnsworth, now deceased, and her son, Gilbert Arnsworth. I acquired them at a sale of family effects a few years ago.'

I loosened the tape and, unwrapping the brown paper cover, revealed two photographs mounted on thick paste-board, one of a woman in her sixties, I judged, the other a young man in his mid twenties.

---

[3] Sherlock Holmes kept all the documents and mementoes of past investigations in this tin trunk, such as the case of the *Gloria Scott* and the Musgrave Ritual. He brought it with him from his lodgings in Montague Street when he and Dr Watson moved into their Baker Street rooms. Dr John F. Watson.

The woman, dressed in black silk elaborately swathed and ruffled, was sitting very upright against a photographer's backcloth of painted trees, one hand grasping the arm of a high-backed chair which was throne-like in its proportions and carved embellishments. Her features were handsome, the fine bone structure of the face suggesting that noble blood had coursed through her veins and those of her ancestors for many generations. Only her expression spoilt the general effect. It was cold, proud, arrogant; the look of a woman who has an unforgiving heart and little love for her fellow human beings.

I put it to one side, thinking that I should not want to have crossed swords with her, and took up the second photograph, that of her son.

The contrast was dramatic.

Whereas she sat erect, he lounged in a low chair, legs crossed, one arm resting negligently on a small round table at his side; and while her expression was one of indomitable pride and patrician haughtiness, his was of a vain, foolish complacency. It was true he shared with her a certain handsomeness of physiognomy but, in his case, the features were weak, as if the sinews beneath the flesh lacked support, giving a general effect of languor. His clothes and hair reflected this same foppish affectation in their cut and style.

'I would appreciate your opinion of them, Watson,' Holmes suggested in a tone of genuine interest.

'Lady Arnsworth looks formidable while the son appears a weakling. Was he spoilt as a child?'

'My dear fellow, you have scored a bullseye! Well done! There are times when you are astonishingly perspicacious!' Holmes exclaimed.

Although the compliment was a little back-handed, I smiled to show my pleasure at it as Holmes continued, 'Lady Arnsworth doted on her son. Her marriage was, I imagine, unsatisfactory, her husband being more interested in dogs and horses than his wife. Consequently, she poured all the passion she possessed and, believe me, Watson, under that iron exterior, she was a woman of strong emotions, into her son. As a result, Gilbert grew up thoroughly spoilt; a rich young man who was denied nothing.

'He inherited not only the title and the fortune but also most of his character from his father, who was himself excessively self-indulgent. In his case, it was his hunters and his fox-hounds on which he lavished his money. Gilbert Arnsworth's preference was for another type of filly – actresses and what the French, with their charmingly euphemistic use of language, refer to as *poules de luxe*.

'Like his father, Gilbert also had a taste for strong liquors and fine wines and it was during a debauch in a hotel bedroom in London with one of his fillies that matters went terribly wrong. There was a quarrel, about what I do not know, which resulted in Gilbert strangling the young lady, whose professional name, according to the newspapers, was Nanette Pearl, although her real name was, more prosaically, Annie Davies. The body was discovered the following morning by the chambermaid. In the meantime, Gilbert had fled the scene and disappeared.

'The police were, of course, summoned and our old friend Lestrade was put in charge of the case. Although at that time I had been in practice as a private investigative agent for only a few years,[4] Lestrade had already called on my assistance on two or three occasions when an inquiry of his had proved difficult. It was so in this particular investigation.

'It had started well. The night porter at the hotel where Gilbert Arnsworth had stayed and where the murder had been committed was alerted to the fact that something might be amiss when, at half past two in the morning, a young man came running down the stairs, his clothes dishevelled and in a state of considerable alarm. Although at that time the murder had not yet been discovered, the porter was suspicious enough to follow the young man into the street where he saw him hail a four-wheeler.

'Now the porter had worked at that particular hotel for several years. It was in a turning off the Haymarket[5]

---

[4] It is generally believed that Sherlock Holmes set up as a private consulting detective in 1874 and had met Inspector Lestrade by the end of 1880, when he asked Sherlock Holmes to help him with a case of forgery. Dr John F. Watson.

[5] The Haymarket, a turning off Piccadilly, was a notorious area for prostitutes and for cheap hotels in the side streets nearby, such as Windmill Street, where they took their clients. Dr John F. Watson.

and was regularly used by the ladies of the night and their clients. Consequently cabs, both hansoms and four-wheelers, were always in demand as these customers came and went, and the porter had come to know a number of their drivers by name as well as sight. So, once the murder had been discovered, the porter was able to give Lestrade not only a description of the young man who had run down the stairs but also the name of the cab driver who had driven him away. It did not take the Inspector long to trace the cabby and learn from him that he had taken the suspect to the gates of a large estate in Surrey where his passenger had paid him off. The cabby had good reason, of course, to remember his client, for not only was it unusual to drive a passenger that distance but the fare was enormous. His description of the young man and the location of the estate enabled Lestrade to establish the suspect's identity as Gilbert Arnsworth and the destination as Arnsworth Castle.

'As it seemed likely that Arnsworth had gone to ground in his ancestral home, Lestrade began his enquiries there and immediately came up against a wall of flint, in other words, the Dowager Lady Arnsworth. She was adamant that her son had not returned to the house and also denied any knowledge of where he might be. In fact, she challenged Lestrade to bring his men and search the castle from top to bottom, an offer Lestrade took up the following day. With a posse of ten uniformed men, he had the place searched from the top of its battlements to its dungeons.

'"It was a thorough search, Mr Holmes," Lestrade assured me when, a few days later, he called on me at my Montague Street lodgings. "Knowing the place was famous for its secret chambers, we tapped walls and the backs of cupboards, listening for hollow sounds which might suggest there was a hidden cavity; we inspected floorboards to make sure none could be lifted easily; we looked up the chimneys. Because it's such a warren of a place with Heaven knows how many chambers and passages, we hung towels or sheets out of the windows of every room after we had searched it[6] so that we could tell, after we had finished, if we had missed any. But we hadn't. Every window had its white marker to show the room had been searched."

'"But you found nothing?" I asked him.

'"Not a sign, Mr Holmes, although . . ."

'At this point Lestrade began to look distinctively uncomfortable.

'Now I know in the past I have criticised the police for their lack of imagination,'[7] Holmes broke

---

[6] A similar event is said to have happened at Glamis Castle in Scotland, the home of the Bowes-Lyon family, which included the late Queen Mother, and the Earls of Strathmore. According to a family legend, a 'monster' was said to be locked away in a secret room in the castle. On one occasion, members of the family and their guests searched all the rooms, hanging towels and sheets out of the windows to indicate which rooms had been inspected. Apparently, no 'monster' was found. Dr John F. Watson.

[7] Sherlock Holmes makes this criticism of Inspector Lestrade in 'The Adventure of the Three Garridebs'. Dr John F. Watson.

off to explain to me, 'but for once Lestrade showed the first faint glimmer of any sensitivity which might be described as perceptive or intuitive. I believe the sensation surprised and bewildered him by its novelty, for he went on to add in a faltering manner:

'"All the same, Mr Holmes, I had the feeling that Lord Arnsworth was hidden somewhere in that house. I can't explain it any better than that. It was nothing more than this impression; no proof; no evidence. It was like that creepy sensation you sometimes get that someone behind you is staring at you. You know what I mean?"

'"Of course I do!" I hastened to assure the poor man, for he was looking quite distressed at this, to him, quite irrational instinct on his part. "How would you like me to help you, Inspector?" I went on to ask, for it was obvious he had called on me with some positive request in mind. His face immediately cleared.

'"Well, Mr Holmes, I wondered if you would agree to come with me to Arnsworth Castle to make a second search? I have warned her Ladyship that I might have to return and she has reluctantly agreed."

'"But not with ten of your officers," I stipulated, for I had no intention of tramping about the castle accompanied by Lestrade's no doubt keen but heavy-footed colleagues. "You may bring two, in case an arrest has to be made, but no more."

'Lestrade agreed to this condition and also to a date for the visit. Consequently, two days later we travelled by train to Guildford in Surrey and from there took a cab to Arnsworth Castle.

'It is a magnificent building, Watson; the product of the combination of two quite different architectural styles – the medieval represented by the imposing battlemented west tower and the curtain walls of massive stone, still preserved in some places; and the more domestic Tudor design exemplified in the beams and red brick of the rest of the building.

'It was a perfect day in early autumn and the castle in all its magnificence was mirrored in the still water of the moat, where its reflection seemed to float like a double image of itself painted on glass.

'We rattled over the long bridge with its many arches, described in the magazine article you may have read, my dear fellow, and then through an imposing gateway entrance into a large cobbled courtyard where Lady Arnsworth's butler was waiting to conduct us through a series of hallways and passages, all hung with tapestries and portraits of Arnsworth ancestors and guarded by suits of armour. Eventually, we were shown into a small drawing room where, despite the warmth of that autumn day, a bright fire was blazing in the hearth. In front of the fire, an elderly lady was seated in a high-backed chair, not unlike the one in the photograph, surrounded by family heirlooms in the way of silver and porcelain, fine rugs and heavy furniture in blackened oak, polished to a high gloss.

'Lady Arnsworth gave the impression of having been

carefully preserved along with all the other household treasures. Her skin was the colour and texture of old parchment while her hair, artfully coiled and plaited on top of her head in the style of a coronet, had the same silvery sheen as the large pewter plates on display nearby on an Elizabethan court cupboard. She sat very upright, her hands, with their sparkling rings, folded in her black silk lap, and, without moving her head, she followed our progress from the door towards her chair with considerable disfavour.

"'Who is this man, Inspector?" she demanded, looking straight at me.

'Lestrade awkwardly introduced me. It was clear she had no intention of shaking hands with me, for her own hands remained clasped in her lap. It was also clear that she had never heard of me; not surprising, I suppose, Watson, for in those early days I was unknown except to a very few people in Scotland Yard and a limited circle of acquaintances I had made through my former Varsity colleagues, including that handful of clients whose cases I had already taken up.[8]

---

[8] Sherlock Holmes' early cases included the *Gloria Scott* inquiry, which was his first case, and the Musgrave Ritual inquiry, his third case. Both these cases he recounted to Dr Watson, who later wrote up and published accounts of them. Sherlock Holmes also referred to other cases, the Tarleton murders, the case of Vamberry the wine merchant, the old Russian woman, the singular affair of the aluminium crutch, which is included in this collection, and the case of Ricoletti and his abominable wife. *Vide*: 'The Adventure of the Musgrave Ritual'. It is not known which was his second case. Dr John F. Watson.

'But she apparently accepted me as one of Lestrade's minions, for she did not look at me again and, when she spoke, she addressed her remarks to Lestrade.

'"Although I do not approve of your examination of my property, certainly not for a second time, Inspector," she said coldly, "I suppose I am obliged by law to give my permission. However, I repeat the assertion I made on your first visit: you will not find my son in this house. As before, Norris will accompany you."

'At this she nodded abruptly to the butler who had remained, standing just inside the door, which he then opened to usher us out.

'As we shuffled in an embarrassed silence out of the room, two aspects of the encounter struck me. The first was the manner in which she had phrased her reference to her son's suspected presence in the house. She had not categorically denied it. Instead, she had referred to it more obliquely by stating that Lestrade would not find her son, thereby avoiding a direct lie. This equivocation convinced me that her son was indeed concealed somewhere in the building. The second was her insistence on the butler accompanying us. This pleased me. Lestrade had already told me that, during the initial search of the castle, Norris had been with them the whole time. It crossed my mind that, rather than being struck by some irrational conviction that Arnsworth was concealed in the house, this feeling might have been suggested to Lestrade by some involuntary movement made by a member of the household, the effect of which the Inspector himself had not been fully aware of and which he had later ascribed to his own intuition. Norris could well have been the unwitting source of such a sensation. If Arnsworth was indeed hiding in the castle, who would be most likely to know this, apart from Lady Arnsworth, but the family butler?

'I therefore decided to keep a close watch on Norris for any small changes in his demeanour which might lead me to the suspect.

'I will not bore you, my dear fellow, with a detailed account of our search of the castle. At the time, it seemed interminable. We began at the top of the building and worked our way down, much as Lestrade had done on the first occasion and, as he had described, there were dozens of rooms, some large and well-furnished, others little more than cubbyholes containing nothing but dust. We did not, as Lestrade had done, hang sheets and towels out of the windows, although I could understand his concern to mark off each chamber as it was searched, for the place was like a labyrinth. And all the time, Norris accompanied us.

'He was a tall, heavy-shouldered man with a long, lugubrious face, the colour of lard, which was difficult to read, for it registered no emotions whatsoever, not even the smallest flicker of impatience or weariness as he followed us from room to room or stood waiting as we made our searches. Only his eyes showed any sign of animation and even that was limited to a sideways movement when Lestrade or one of his officers stepped too near a table or a cabinet on which were displayed ornaments or other small valuables which could have been knocked over or spirited away into a pocket. But no other feature so much as twitched.

'However, I kept him under very close observation, trusting to my own instinct that eventually he would unwittingly betray his young master's whereabouts. But nothing happened.

'After about three hours of searching the upstairs rooms, we descended to the ground floor where we stood grouped together a little uncertainly in the main entrance hall, the walls of which were lined with a curious collection of weapons – swords, sabres, shields, flintlock pistols and halberds arranged into intricate designs of chevrons, triangles and concentric circles.

'Lestrade hesitated over which room we should inspect next and I guessed from his manner that he was trying to postpone the inevitable moment when the drawing room would have to be searched for a second time and he would be forced into another encounter with the formidable Lady Arnsworth.

'To help him make up his mind, I turned to Norris.

'"Where does that passage lead to?" I asked, pointing to an archway to the right which led into a dim gallery hung with ancient banners and lined, like the hall, with suits of armour.

'His response to my question was so controlled that, had I not been watching him closely, I could have missed it altogether. He became even more impassive if that were possible. Even his eyes remained fixed, staring straight ahead at the wall opposite as if he had suffered a cataleptic seizure, and when he spoke his voice had the expressionless tone of an automata.

'"To the family chapel, sir," he replied, not looking at me but keeping his gaze fixed forwards.

'At that moment, I knew exactly where Gilbert Arnsworth was hiding.

'"Let us search there first," I said to Lestrade and, giving him no time to protest, I led the way down the passage.

'It ended in a heavy oak door, strapped with iron and furnished with a large metal ring as a handle. It was weighty and difficult to open but with the help of one of the constables, I managed to force it back and we stepped inside the chapel.

'It was a long, rectangular chamber with a high vaulted ceiling supported on stone pillars. Although the fabric of this part of the building was probably of the same early date as the west tower and the other medieval features, it had clearly been refurbished at some later date, at which time the oak pews with their heavy carvings and red velvet cushions had been installed, as well as the magnificent reredos of green marble and gilded wood placed against the east wall.

'The altar, which stood beneath it, was a comparatively modest fitting compared to its elaborate backdrop, for it consisted of nothing more than a simple table hung with a green velvet cloth, trimmed with gold braid, and bore only a silver cross and a pair of elegant branched silver candle-sticks. On the steps of the altar stood two tall white marble vases containing lilies.

'We halted just inside the door and I was aware of the response of both Lestrade and Norris. The butler stood like a statue; not even his eyes so much as blinked and his profile, when I glanced sideways at it, might have been chiselled from the same stone with which the chapel was constructed. In contrast, Lestrade's uneasiness was all too obvious in the small movements of his head and hands and in his rapid, shallow breathing, as if he had run a long distance.

'I knew immediately why he was showing such signs of distress and why he had not discovered Gilbert Arnsworth the first time he had searched the chapel. The good Inspector was intimidated by the atmosphere of religious sanctity about the place, manifested in the scent of flowers and beeswax, and in the silence that hung like a shadowy veil over the altar and its green and gold reredos. It had inhibited him from making a thorough search of the place. I was also convinced that, when Lestrade was in the chapel on that first occasion, or perhaps even in the passage leading up to it, Norris had made some slight, involuntary movement which had given Lestrade that apparently irrational conviction that Arnsworth was hiding somewhere in the building.'

'But not necessarily in the chapel?' I interrupted Holmes' narrative to ask.

'Obviously not, or he would have given orders for the place to be thoroughly searched,' Holmes replied. 'But Lestrade is a conventional man, subject to all the restraints which that implies, one of which is the fear of behaving inappropriately in a sanctified place, and that *tabu* overrode all other considerations.

'Luckily, I do not suffer from the Inspector's inhibitions and, once I was convinced that I had discovered Gilbert Arnsworth's hiding-place, I proceeded to flush him out, using the same method which I was later to put to good effect in the Bohemian scandal case, namely the use of fire.[9]

'The lesson of that inquiry, as I think I explained to you at the time, is that when a woman thinks her house is on fire, she will rush to the rescue of whatever she values most – her baby, in the case of a married woman, her jewel box if she is unmarried. As you know, Irene Adler immediately hurried to the secret recess in which she had concealed the photograph of herself and the King of Bohemia.

'In the Arnsworth affair, the same principle applied,

[9] In 'A Scandal in Bohemia', Sherlock Holmes arranges for Dr Watson to throw a smoke rocket into the drawing room at Briony Lodge, Irene Adler's house, and in her eagerness to save the photograph of herself and the King of Bohemia, she unwittingly revealed its hiding-place. Sherlock Holmes used the same ruse in the adventure relating to the Norwood builder, Jonas Oldacre, whom he flushed out from the secret room in which he was hiding by setting light to some straw and making him believe the house was on fire. Dr John F. Watson.

except in that case the suspect had more to save than a mere photograph – his life, or so he thought. The fear of being trapped in a hiding-place during a fire would have caused most men, unless they had the courage of a lion, and Gilbert Arnsworth was not among their number, to make a bolt.

'Before setting out that morning for Arnsworth Castle, I had taken the precaution of concealing in the pocket of my ulster a box of vestas[10] together with a long taper made from twisted brown paper which I had liberally smeared with tar. It was the work of a moment to light it and hold it above my head, shouting "Fire!" at the top of my voice as I did so. Black smoke poured from it in a choking cloud.

'There is a saying about all Bedlam breaking loose, an eventuality I have never witnessed, but I imagine it must be very similar to the scene my action provoked.

'Norris dashed forward, showing a remarkable turn of speed for a man normally so stately in his bearing, and tried to seize the taper from me, assisted by Lestrade who, judging by his expression of scandalised outrage, must have imagined I had gone mad, while the two constables hung back, mouths agape at this scene of

[10] The original vesta match was invented by William Newton in 1832 and consisted of a wax taper, the tip of which was coated with a friction composition which caught fire when rubbed against a rough surface. But safety matches were first produced in 1855 in Sweden, using red phosphorus, a much safer chemical than white phosphorus, which gave off a poisonous vapour. The match was tipped with an oxidiser which was struck against a special phosphorus strip on the side of the box. Dr John F. Watson.

unexpected pandemonium, for both Lestrade, Norris, as well as myself, were shouting as we struggled together.

'In the midst of all this noise and confusion, I noticed that the green and gold cloth which hung over the altar had begun to move as if an unseen hand was trying to fumble its way through the covering.

'I immediately flung down the taper and began to stamp it out, as I did so pulling on Lestrade's arm and pointing towards the altar. As the two constables took over the task of trampling out the last fragments of smouldering brown paper, the Inspector and I, together with Norris, watched as a crouching form emerged from under the folds of fabric. A moment later, the figure of Gilbert Arnsworth stood upright and confronted us.

'I recognised him at once from the description which the night porter at the hotel had given to Lestrade and which Lestrade had passed on to me; also from his physical likeness to his mother. They shared the same haughty bearing and handsome patrician features, spoilt in his case by a dissolute air, although, as we stared at each other in those first few seconds of disclosure, his face expressed mainly shock and terror.

'Despite this, he was the first one of us to recover. Before I or Lestrade or either of his officers could stir so much as a finger, he was off like a hare, spurred on no doubt by a desperate need for self-preservation, vaulting over the pews as he made a wild rush for the door which had been left open.

'Lestrade and I were hampered by the fact that we were still interlocked by our earlier struggle over the taper with Norris and it took us several seconds to free ourselves. Being younger and fitter than the other two, I was the first to disengage myself, but I was not prepared for Norris's intervention. As I pushed past him to make my own dash for the door, he thrust out a leg causing me to trip and to lose my balance momentarily. It was only a matter of seconds before I recovered but it was long enough for Arnsworth to reach the door and pass through it, slamming it shut behind him. By the time I had wrenched it open and reached the passageway, there was no sign of him, although from the doorway, I had a clear view down this corridor as far as the main entrance hall, which Arnsworth could not have reached in those few seconds' advantage he had over me. And yet he had disappeared as if by magic.

'Now, my dear fellow, I know I have repeated to you before that old maxim of mine that when you have eliminated the impossible, whatever remains, however improbable, must be the truth. No doubt you have grown tired of hearing it. But that does not lessen its validity. As I stood there contemplating the empty passage, logic told me there was only one explanation which had nothing to do with the supernatural. Arnsworth must have escaped through a hidden opening of some kind in the passageway itself, although none was immediately apparent.

'However, halfway down on the right hand side stood a suit of armour, behind which hung a long curtain of heavy red velvet as if to serve as a backdrop for the figure. I noticed that the hem was swaying to and fro as if in a light draught, but there was no current of air that I could feel and everything else in the passage, the hanging lamps and the banners arranged crossways on the walls, remained motionless. Therefore, with Lestrade at my heels, I sprinted towards the curtain which I pulled to one side, revealing an ancient oaken door which stood ajar and, with its iron straps and studding, was very similar to that leading into the church.

'This one, however, led on to a winding staircase, as I discovered when I pulled it fully open. It was, I surmised, the door to the west tower.

'Up I went and round I went, following the tight spirals of the stone steps – a giddying sensation, especially as the staircase was so narrow that my shoulders brushed the walls on either side. At intervals, windows, little wider than slits, let in some much-needed fresh air and afforded me glimpses of the moat and the surrounding gardens, diminishing in size the higher I went until I could look down on the tops of trees and the sheet of water in the moat lying as flat and as still as a mirror in which were reflected the blue sky and the white, drifting clouds.

'After what seemed like an eternity of climbing ever upwards, the staircase ended at a small semi-circular landing with a low door which I pushed softly open and, crouching down, emerged at the top of the tower with Lestrade behind me.

'Gilbert Arnsworth was not expecting us. The thickness of the stone must have deadened all sound of our footsteps and it was only when Lestrade cried out as he stumbled over the threshold of the little door that Arnsworth was alerted to our presence.

'He was standing at the far side of the tower, gazing out at the distant view of woods and fields and, by his lounging stance, I guessed he was confident that he had escaped detention. At Lestrade's exclamation, he spun about to face us, his expression one of shocked disbelief and that kind of rage which a small child might exhibit when he is unexpectedly frustrated.

'Throughout his life, Gilbert Arnsworth had been denied nothing and I believe he had come to expect that this fortunate state of affairs would continue, whether his own behaviour warranted it or not. In his own eyes, he was like a god, immune from all punishments and disasters to which ordinary mankind is subject. The sight of Inspector Lestrade, accompanied by the two constables who had joined us, advancing upon him, intoning those sonorous, doom-laden words "Gilbert Richard Grenville, ninth Earl of Arnsworth, I am arresting you on the suspicion of murder," as he produced a pair of handcuffs from his pocket was not to be borne.

'I saw him back away, his eyes fixed on Lestrade's

face as if mesmerised by the awful solemnity of the occasion, and then the spell broke and his glance darted back toward the stone battlements and the distant view.

'I read his thoughts, Watson, as clearly as if they had been written on his face, but before I could shout out a warning he had turned and, with a great cry which drowned out my own exclamation, he had vaulted on to the narrow coping where he stood for a moment outlined against the blue sky, arms outstretched, before he dived down into space.

'Lestrade and I, together with the two constables, rushed to the battlements and peered over them just in time to see his body plunging downwards like a great sea-bird, into the moat as if hunting for its prey within its very depths.

'God knows what was in his mind. Did he still believe in his invincibility? Was he convinced that he would surface safely and could swim to the further side and make his escape?

'If he did, he was tragically deceived. There was no sign of him apart from the ripples which spread out across the water to touch the grassy banks and, within a few moments, they too had disappeared and the surface once more lay as smooth and as still as glass.

'The uniformed officers recovered his body later with the help of two of the gardeners. The rest, as they say, is history, not all of which was recorded correctly.

'The new Earl of Arnsworth, Gilbert's cousin Eustace,

inherited the title and moved into the castle, while the Dowager Lady Arnsworth took up residence in the Dower house which was situated at the far side of the estate. As you know from my newspaper archives, she has since died. Gilbert Arnsworth's death was attributed to a tragic accident, while at the inquest on Annie Davies a verdict of murder by a person or persons unknown was returned. As far as I know, no connection was ever made between the two deaths.'

'"Persons unknown"!' I protested. 'That is not justice, Holmes!'

My old friend shrugged his shoulders and gave a small, cynical smile.

'Not moral justice, perhaps, Watson; but legal justice all the same. There was no hard evidence against Arnsworth, only a strong suspicion. Neither the cab driver nor the night porter were ever asked to identify him as the young man seen running from the hotel in the early hours of the morning, nor as the client who engaged the cab which drove him to the gates of Arnsworth Castle. Besides, what does the death of a prostitute count against that of a belted earl? Shall you write up the story, my dear fellow?'

I paused to reflect for a moment. Although I felt a keen responsibility to place the facts of the case before my readers and to redress, if only a little, the imbalance of the scales of justice between the rich and powerful and the poor and weak, I knew in my heart I would never publish an account of the case. For, as Holmes had pointed out, there was no final proof of Gilbert Arnsworth's guilt, only a very strong suspicion, and I myself would be committing an injustice by suggesting otherwise.

I shall therefore place this account among my other unpublished papers, trusting that future research into the case may at last provide that evidence which will prove Arnsworth's guilt, so that the truth may finally be laid before the public.

THE CASE OF THE VANISHING BARQUE

Looking through my notes, I see that 1889 was a particularly busy year for my old friend Sherlock Holmes. In addition to those cases such as the mystery of the five orange pips or the Reigate squire, accounts of which I have laid before my reading public, there were others which, for various reasons, I withheld publication. These include the inquiries into the Paradol chamber, the Amateur Mendicant Society, the adventures of the Grice Patersons on the island of Uffa, the Camberwell poisoning case and, finally, the investigation into the disappearance of the British barque, the *Sophy Anderson,* in which I played a small part and of which I have kept the records.

The inquiry began, I recall, one morning in April of

that year, some time after my marriage to Miss Mary Morstan[1] and my return to civil practice. I was on my way home from visiting a patient in the Baker Street area when, on the spur of the moment, I decided to call on Holmes, whom I had not seen for several weeks. As I turned into the familiar road, I saw a stocky, heavily-built man on the opposite pavement walking in the same direction as myself but more slowly, for he frequently halted to glance up at the numbers on the doors before consulting a piece of paper he held in his hand.

His appearance was so striking that I decided to play the game with which Holmes often amused himself as well as me, that of judging an individual's character and profession by his clothes and his demeanour.

The man in question was in his fifties, I estimated, and even at a cursory glance it was easy to guess from his pea jacket and peaked cap that he was a sailor. His rolling gait and weather-beaten face bore out this impression.

---

[1] In 'The Adventure of the Five Orange Pips', Dr Watson dates the case to 1887, in consequence of which those unrecorded cases mentioned in the account, i.e. the loss of the British barque, the *Sophy Anderson*, should also be dated to that year, along with the case of the Camberwell poisoning. However, in 'The Adventure of the Five Orange Pips', Dr Watson refers to his wife and from this as well as other evidence in the canon, it can be established that his marriage to Mary Morstan must have taken place between November 1888 and March 1889. Therefore many commentators date the Five Orange Pips inquiry to 1889. All these cases must therefore have taken place in 1888 or 1889. Dr John F. Watson.

I hurried ahead of him, eager to reach Holmes and lay my deductions before him so that, by glancing out of the window, he could confirm my conclusions. I was so eager, in fact, that I took the stairs two at a time and, bursting into the room, seized my old friend by the sleeve and drew him across the room. The man was now directly opposite the house, staring straight across the street at it.

'Look, Holmes!' I cried. 'I am right, am I not, in thinking the man is a sailor who has spent most of his life at sea?'

'You are quite correct, my dear Watson,' Holmes replied, looking down appraisingly at the man. 'He is indeed a sailor. But more to the point, what *sort* of sailor is he?'

'I do not quite understand,' I began, rather chastened by Holmes' response.

'Come now. Is he an able seaman, for example? Or a naval officer? Or perhaps a stoker? One must be precise about such details. My own assessment is that he is a merchant seaman, someone of rank, probably a mate rather than a captain, that he has sailed extensively in the southern latitudes and that he is left-handed.'

Seeing my expression, he burst out laughing.

'It is really quite simple, Watson. His bearing tells me he is a man used to authority but of a lower order. He lacks the demeanour of an officer of high rank. His skin is tanned but the wrinkles round his eyes are paler on their inner surfaces, suggesting he has spent considerable time with his eyes screwed up against bright sunlight. As for his left-handedness, that, too, is obvious. He is holding the piece of paper in his left hand. He is also a potential client,' he added, 'a deduction for which I claim no credit at all for the man has, at this very moment, crossed the street to our front door.'

As he spoke, there came a peal on the bell and, seconds later, the sound of heavy, deliberate footsteps mounting the stairs, and the man in question entered the room.

Seen at closer quarters, he bore out those particulars of his appearance which Holmes had specified but which I had failed to notice. His bearing did, indeed, have a stamp of authority, while the network of fine lines about his eyes showed the paler skin which lined their inner surfaces which Holmes, with his amazingly keen eyesight, had already remarked on.

However, what he had not apparently noticed and which I, as a medical man, immediately discerned, was the unhealthy flush about our visitor's face and the difficulty he had in regaining his breath after mounting the stairs. If ever I saw a man suffering from heart disease, it was he.

In addition to these physical symptoms, there was an aura of profound melancholy about him which seemed to sit upon him like a large, heavy weight, bowing his shoulders and making his movements slow and cumbersome.

At Holmes' invitation, he lowered himself ponderously

into an armchair, bringing his two great hands, which put me in mind of shovels, to rest one on each knee. He had already removed his cap, revealing close-cropped grey hair and a deeply furrowed brow.

'I'm sorry to call on you like this, Mr Holmes, without writing to you first to fix an appointment,' he said in a gruff voice which had an unmistakable North country accent, 'but I had to speak to someone about the affair and I daren't go to the police with my tale.'

As he spoke, he glanced dubiously in my direction under heavy eyebrows, a look which Holmes intercepted.

'This is my colleague, Dr Watson,' he said briskly. 'You may speak as frankly in front of him as you would to me. Now, sir, tell me about this affair which I see is causing you great disquiet. But first, I would like to know a little about yourself, including your name. You are a seafaring man, are you not?'

'Indeed I am, sir. As for my name, it's Thomas Corbett and I'm the mate on board the *Lucy Belle,* a four-masted barque which trades mostly between Newcastle and the Far East.'

At this point in his narrative, he hesitated and I saw him clasp his two huge hands convulsively together.

'Leastways, sir, that is the name the ship has carried for the past three years. Before that, she used to sail under a different name.'

Although I was considerably taken aback by this last statement, as well as confused about exactly what it might imply, Holmes seemed to understand, for he gave a little inclination of his head.

'And what was her original name, may I ask?' he enquired.

'The *Sophy Anderson,*' Corbett replied, his voice husky with emotion as if he were naming a dead child.

'If I recall correctly, she sank with all hands, did she not?'

'Aye, sir; or so it was believed. She was supposed to have gone down in January three years ago off the coast of the Outer Hebrides when she was making for Glasgow from Valparaiso carrying a cargo of nitrate.'

I saw Holmes' features sharpen and he murmured under his breath as if to himself, 'Ah, an insurance fraud!'

Corbett heard him, for he replied, his expression grave, 'Aye, it was sir, and one I bitterly regret taking part in.'

'Tell me about it,' Holmes said, settling back in his chair and directing a sharp, attentive glance in Corbett's direction.

'That I will, Mr Holmes. But first I must explain a little about the circumstances behind it. The *Sophy Anderson* was built on the Clyde in 1876 and was owned by a small shipping company, called the White Heather Line, based at Glasgow, which ran three or four other barques. The owners were a pair of brothers, Jamie and Duncan McNeil, and the captain was Joseph Chafer, a relative of the McNeils by marriage.

'It seems the McNeils owed a lot of money and were close to going bankrupt, which was why the scheme was put in place. The plan was this. The *Sophy Anderson* would pick up a cargo of nitrate from Valparaiso but no passengers on the return voyage. Months before this, the crew had been carefully looked over and anyone Chafer thought couldn't be trusted to keep his mouth shut over the plan was turned off and a new crew member taken on his place. You see, they wanted men who would be willing to disappear, so to speak, as if they really had been lost at sea, and would take up new lives and new names. So they had to be men with no families to question their whereabouts. They'd be paid, of course, with a cut of the insurance money.

'When the scheme was put to me, I agreed to it like a shot. My wife's been dead these many years and my only child, Tom, named after me, had died when he was twelve, so I had no close family to worry what had become of me. A sum of several hundred pounds, my share of the insurance money, would come in very useful. I was getting close to retiring age, you see, Mr Holmes, and I had this dream of owning a little farm somewhere south where it's warmer, in Cornwall maybe, but near the coast so that I could still be in sight and sound of the sea. As for the details of the plot, the claiming of the insurance money and the re-registering of the *Sophy Anderson* under a new name, I left all that to the McNeil brothers. For that was the idea, Mr Holmes. She'd go on trading as the *Lucy Belle* but not from those ports where the *Sophy* had traded in the past, like Liverpool, Glasgow or London. That way, the vessel would still be making money and the men would earn their usual wages, plus their share of the insurance which, taking into account the value of the ship and its cargo, would add up to a fair sum, more than most of them would see in a year's sailing.

'Like I said, we took on a cargo at Valparaiso but no passengers and set sail for Glasgow on January 17th and, with a good wind behind us, in 128 days we were in sight of the small island of Duncraig to the south west of the Outer Hebrides. Chafer and I knew the island well because we'd taken shelter there from a storm several years before. It's an uninhabited island with steep cliffs rising straight from the sea on its western coast, a treacherous shoreline for any mariner who doesn't know the tides and currents. But to one who does and has the courage to take a ship between the rocks, there are several sheltered inlets where a vessel can lie up for weeks out of sight of other shipping. And to give Chafer his due, he didn't lack for neither skill nor courage. So with my help and the rest of the crew's, Chafer took the *Sophy Anderson* into one of those inlets, where we dropped anchor.

'When we'd loaded up the nitrate, I'd taken on board extra stores at Chafer's orders in the way of lengths of timber and tins of paint, and, once we were safely anchored, the whole crew set about changing the look of the ship, painting her dark blue down to the water-line instead of grey and giving her a white line round the hull. The ship's carpenter, Morrison, also changed the trim round the edge of the deck housing which, too, was painted white. We renamed her as well, the *Lucy Belle*, which was written in dark blue letters along her prow.

'When all that was done and the paint was dry, Chafer called us all up on deck and made a speech welcoming us aboard the *Lucy Belle* and wishing us God speed on all her voyages. He then re-christened the vessel in a little ceremony, pouring a tot of rum over her fo'csle. When that was done, every man jack of us from me, the mate, down to the least on board, young Billy Wheeler, a deck-hand, was handed a glass of rum and his new papers and the old ones were torn up and burnt there on deck in an old iron cooking pot. More rum was handed round and we went from one to the other getting used to our new names and those of the rest of the crew. Chafer's was Michael Lofthouse, mine Joseph Nully, but I only use it when I have to. It don't seem to sit easy on me like my old one, Thomas Corbett.

'I think the handing out of the new names and the getting rid of the old ones made everyone realise there was no turning back. Like the papers, we had burnt our bridges and it was too late to change our minds. Some took it hard, especially Billy Wheeler, the young deck-hand. I was told later that on his last trip to Glasgow he'd met a lass he fancied but that was all finished and done with now.

'Anyways, whatever the reason, he drank too much

of the rum and lost his nerve. Or perhaps he found it. He ran up and down the deck telling everyone that when we got to Rotterdam, the port we was to make for after we'd got under sail again, he'd sign on with another vessel and make his way back to Scotland. "I want to go home!" he kept shouting. As for the insurance money, it could be dropped in the sea, as far as he was concerned. He wanted none of it.

'Well, Mr Holmes, what with him running about and shouting like a madman, it was like putting a spark to a powder keg. Several of the men, including Morrison, the ship's carpenter, set about him like madmen themselves and began hitting him, not just with their fists but with anything that came to hand. I think I know what was in their minds. They, too, were wondering if they'd done the right thing and at the same time they were fearful that Billy might blab and then not only would the fraud come to light but their part in it. They'd lose their share of the money and perhaps finish up in gaol. By the time me and Chafer managed to drag the men off Billy, he was lying on the deck, his face and head covered in blood.

'Chafer knelt beside him and felt for the pulse in his neck. Then he stood up and said in a loud, harsh voice, "Now listen up, my lads. Billy's dead. There's nothing we can do for him except set him adrift."

'The sound of his voice and the sight of Billy's dead body brought the men to their senses. They drew back and one of them, Newton, started to speak, the tears standing out in his eyes.

'"We didn't mean to . . .' he began, but Chafer cut him short. "Shut your mouth and get below," he ordered him. "Find a length of canvas and some rope."

'When Newton came back, he and another man wrapped the body in the canvas and tied it up. They were lifting it to carry it over to the side ready to tip it overboard, when I stepped forward.

'I don't know what made me do it but I couldn't let them chuck him into the sea like a dead sheep. He was fifteen, Mr Holmes; a pleasant lad, always laughing and joking. Many a time he'd put me in mind of my dead son with his fair hair and blue eyes. I just couldn't see him thrown overboard with nothing to mark his going.

'When I first went to sea, my mother gave me a silver St Christopher on a chain, which I'd always worn round my neck for good luck on my voyages. I took it off and, just as they had lifted the body up on to the rail and had it balanced there, I put my hand through the folds of the canvas and laid it on his chest.'

At this point, Corbett broke off his account and stared fixedly down at his huge hands, which he was kneading together as if trying to squeeze the life out of them. Then just as suddenly, he lifted his head and looked directly at Holmes.

'He was still alive, sir!'

'Are you sure?' Holmes asked sharply.

'As sure as I'm sitting here. I felt his chest rise and fall under my hand. I looked across at Chafer, who was standing by the rail ready to give the order to throw

Billy overboard. He looked back at me, Mr Holmes, and he knew, sir! Oh, yes, he *knew* all right! He stared me straight in the eyes and then he drew one finger across his throat, meaning "I'll kill you if you don't keep your mouth shut."'

'About Wheeler still being alive?'

Without speaking, Corbett nodded his head in agreement. Then, swallowing hard, he continued, 'The next second, Chafer looked away to give the order and Billy had gone overboard. It all happened so quickly, Mr Holmes, I didn't get a chance to stop them.'

A terrible silence fell over the three of us as we pictured the scene, Holmes and I in our imaginations, Thomas Corbett all too vividly in his memory.

Then Corbett continued in a husky voice, 'I've thought of what we did that day thousands of times since and gone over and over in my mind what I could or should have done. I've tried telling myself that, if we'd kept him aboard, he wouldn't have lived. The injuries to his head were too severe. He'd've died sooner or later. But thinking that don't make it any better. The truth is, sir, we committed murder and it's been lying on my conscience ever since like a stone. That's why I've come to you, Mr Holmes. I can't bear the burden no longer and I want you to ease my soul by reporting what happened to whoever needs to be told. I'm willing to make a full confession and take whatever punishment the law thinks fit for me.'

'That is highly commendable of you but it is easier

said than done, Mr Corbett.' Holmes said in a brisk, matter-of-fact manner which I thought a little brusque under the circumstances, although Corbett seemed to accept my old friend's comment, for he lowered his grizzled head in a humble, compliant manner.

'I'm in your hands, sir,' he said in a low voice.

Holmes took a turn or two up and down the room, deep in thought, eyes lowered and arms folded tightly across his chest. Then, spinning round, he confronted Corbett, his mind clearly made up.

'Before I go any further with this matter,' said he, 'first let me establish the facts of the case and, in order to do that, I need to learn from you what happened after Billy Wheeler was put overboard. You continued on your way, I assume?'

'Yes, we did, Mr Holmes. Once we were clear of Duncraig, we threw some debris into the sea – bits of wood, some rope, a lifebelt with the name *Sophy Anderson* painted on it – so that anyone finding it would think the vessel had gone down with all hands. Then we set course for Rotterdam. We had all the necessary papers to show the officials there, for the McNeil brothers had already registered the ship as the *Lucy Belle* with a shipping company based in Panama. No one questioned the papers. The McNeils had already set up a buyer in Rotterdam for the nitrate we were carrying, so we unloaded it and took on a cargo of coal which they'd also arranged in advance. We then set sail for Bergen where we sold the coal and took on another cargo. And so it went on for the next three years, going to and fro between the Baltic and the Dutch ports where we'd never traded before and where the crew was not known, as well as the Far East where we were likewise strangers.

'In the meantime, a passenger ship had picked up the debris we had thrown overboard and the *Sophy Anderson* was duly posted missing by Lloyds, presumably lost at sea with all hands. Later, the insurance money was paid out and all seemed sealed and settled but I couldn't put it out of my mind. In fact, Mr Holmes, as the years have gone by, it's got worse, not better.'

'And where is the *Lucy Belle* now?'

'In the Port of London. We were on our way from Bremen to Shanghai when one of the crew fell down a companionway and broke his leg and we had to put in there to get him to a doctor. Chafer went off to find a replacement for him and I took him by cab to the London hospital in the Mile End Road. While I was there, I got talking to one of the porters and, without telling him what it was all about, I asked him if he knew of a detective, not a policeman, who could look into a private matter for me. It was him who mentioned your name. "Go and see Mr Holmes," said he "at 221B Baker Street. He's the best in the business."

'Indeed!' murmured Holmes, raising his eyebrows. 'A hospital porter, your said? Was his name Reynolds, by any chance?'

Corbett looked abashed.

'I didn't ask his name, I'm afraid, Mr Holmes, but he was a little man with as much hair on his head as a billiard ball.'

Holmes threw back his head and laughed heartily at this description.

'Excellent, Mr Corbett! You have caught Reynolds exactly!' Seeing my baffled expression, he turned briefly to me in explanation. 'I met Reynolds two years ago. A lady, a Mrs Dawlish, wanted me to find her husband who was missing. To cut a very long story short, I found him in the London hospital, thanks to Reynolds' co-operation. The man had been knocked down by a hansom and had lost his memory temporarily as a result of head injuries.'

Turning back to his client, he added, 'Pray continue, Mr Corbett.'

'There is not much more to tell, sir,' he replied. 'I took a cab straight here from the hospital to ask for your help. There may not be much time to spare, Mr Holmes. At this very minute, Chafer is looking about for a new crewman to replace the one who's broken his leg. It's his intention to sail early tomorrow morning with the high tide. If it's possible, I'd like to have this business settled before we leave. God knows when we'll be back in London. Perhaps never.'

'I take your point, Mr Corbett,' Holmes said gravely. 'But before I agree to act in this matter, I must explain the serious nature of the situation. We are dealing here with murder on the part of Chafer, the ship's captain, for, if your account is correct, and I assume it is, then he gave the order for Billy Wheeler to be thrown overboard knowing he was still alive. Then there is the part played by those members of the crew who attacked the young man, against whom charges of grievous bodily harm could be brought. In addition, there is the question of your own responsibility in the affair. Supposing the case came to court with you as witness against Chafer? A clever counsel could argue that you, too, knew Wheeler was alive and yet did nothing to prevent his death by drowning.'

'I had no chance, Mr Holmes!' Corbett broke in, the sweat standing out on his brow. 'On my oath, he was thrown over the rail before I could stop it from happening!'

'On your oath!' Holmes repeated. 'That is another important point to consider, Mr Corbett, before you decide to take action. It is your word against Chafer's that Wheeler was still alive. There are no other witnesses to that fact. Chafer, who is obviously no fool, will swear to the contrary – should a trial be held – that when he felt for the carotid artery in Wheeler's neck, there was no pulse. The man was undoubtedly dead. Who is a jury most likely to believe, you or Chafer? Are you prepared to take that risk? For whatever way the decision goes, you are certain to suffer. If the vote goes against Chafer, then it is murder in which you are implicated. And if the verdict goes the other way, then you could be charged with perjury and, even if it does not come to that, your reputation will be ruined. What shipping company would be willing to take you on as mate when the imputation is you lied on oath against a senior officer? Apart from all that, there is matter of the insurance fraud in which every one of you is involved. Have you thought of that?'

As Holmes put the question, I saw Corbett's right hand make a small, involuntary movement towards his chest as if, by physically reaching for the region of his heart, he wanted to reassure himself that the decision he was about to make was the right one, despite the strain it would cause him, an action which confirmed my earlier supposition that the man was suffering from some chronic, and possibly life-threatening, cardiac condition. His reply was a further ratification, if any were needed.

'Mr Holmes,' said he in the tone of a man who has come to a decision, 'I've carried this burden for nigh on four years and I have no wish to go to my grave with it still on my conscience. Whatever the outcome, I want the truth known at last.'

'Very well, Mr Corbett!' Holmes replied, his voice as resolute and vigorous as his client's. 'Then there is only one problem left to be solved.'

'And what is that?' Corbett asked.

'The matter of proving Chafer's guilt. As I have already pointed out, it is a question of your word against Chafer's as to whether or not Wheeler was still alive when he was thrown overboard. From what you have told me about the captain, I doubt very much if he would ever confess the truth of his own volition. What is needed therefore is a witness who is prepared to support your account of the events on board the *Sophy Anderson* the day Wheeler was murdered. Is there any among the crew who was present on deck and saw what happened?'

Corbett was silent for a moment, rubbing his chin.

'Well, there's Harry Deakin, the ship's cook,' he said at last. 'He was there at the time.'

'He saw the attack on Wheeler?' Holmes asked sharply.

'He did, sir. In fact, he tried to stop it but he was outnumbered.'

'And he was there when Wheeler's body was wrapped in the canvas?'

'He was, sir.'

'And saw you put the St Christopher on Wheeler's chest?'

'Aye. He helped me fold the canvas back so that I could get my hand in. And I'm pretty sure he saw Chafer make that cutting motion across his throat because, after he made it, Deakin looked hard at me as if to ask what was going on. But nothing was said either then or later.'

'No matter. If Deakin would be willing to make a statement, that would be enough corroboration to persuade a jury you are telling the truth. Is Deakin still on board the ship?'

'Aye, he is, Mr Holmes.'

'Could he be persuaded to speak up for you in court if need be?'

Corbett looked doubtful.

'I wouldn't like to swear to that, Mr Holmes. Deakin likes a quiet life and he's afraid of anyone in authority. If it came to choosing between me and Chafer, he'd be more inclined to pick the captain or, at best, refuse to say anything.'

'Then he must be forced to speak up on your behalf,' Holmes replied.

'But how?' Corbett asked with a hopeless air.

Without replying, Holmes got to his feet and strode up and down the room several times, before swinging back to face Corbett.

'Who has left the crew since Wheeler's murder, preferably someone who is himself dead?' he demanded.

Corbett seemed bewildered by the question.

'Well, there's Tommy Brewster, a deck-hand. He was killed when he fell from the rigging last February on a voyage to . . .'

'Never mind the details. Was the man literate?'

'Literate?' Corbett stammered, his bewilderment increasing.

'Could he read and write?'

'Aye, sir. He could.'

'Splendid!' Holmes exclaimed, rubbing his hands together with satisfaction. 'Now only one problem remains. Can you arrange for Dr Watson and myself to come aboard the *Lucy Belle* without arousing any suspicion?'

'Yes, I could, sir, provided it's after dark. If you could get yourselves up to look like seamen and make your way to Picott's Wharf in St Katherine's dock by ten o'clock tonight, I'll be on deck with a lantern. I'll wave it three times when the coast is clear for you to come up the gang-plank. Is there anything else I can do?'

'Yes. Make sure Deakin is on board. Perhaps you could also arrange for a cabin to be available for Dr Watson and myself, equipped with paper, pen and ink. And now, Mr Corbett, I wish you good morning. We shall meet again at ten o'clock.'

'But your plan . . . ?' Corbett began as he rose to his feet. However, his protest was to no avail. Shaking hands firmly with him, Holmes conducted him to the door.

'Yes, what *is* your plan, Holmes?' I asked when he had returned to his chair.

But I fared no better than his client.

'You will find out tonight, my dear fellow,' he replied with a smile. 'All I will tell you for the moment is that what I propose using is one of the oldest tricks in the world and, if Harry Deakin is deceived by it, as I have every reason to suppose he will be, then we will have a witness to testify to all that Corbett has told us. I suggest you call here again at nine o'clock tonight. And, by the way, make sure you bring your revolver.'

And with that, he picked up the *Morning Post* and, giving it a shake, retired behind its open pages.

Feeling dismissed, I, too, left the house to return to Paddington, where I was kept busy for the rest of the day with my medical duties. Although the practice was not yet a large one, having been neglected by the previous owner,[2] I was determined by sheer diligence and hard work to make a success of it.

However, despite my professional preoccupations, whenever I had a spare moment my thoughts turned to Holmes' parting remarks. What was this trick he had mentioned, I wondered. And why was he so sure it would deceive Harry Deakin, whom he had never met?

I also had certain arrangements of my own to make with regard to the coming appointment with Holmes later that evening. Without wishing to alarm my wife unnecessarily, I did not speak of his advice to bring my revolver with me but mentioned only an inquiry in which he had asked me to take part. My dear Mary, the most generous and understanding of women, raised no objections. In fact, she urged me to go.

'You deserve a change,' she said. 'You have been working far too hard recently and are looking quite pale. An evening spent with your old friend will do you the world of good.'

The only other person who had to be consulted was my neighbour Jackson,[3] a fellow doctor, with whom

---

[2] The practice was in Paddington and had belonged to a Mr Farquhar, an elderly gentleman who suffered from St Vitus Dance. Because of this, the practice had declined and Dr Watson had to work hard in order to build up his list of patients. *Vide*: 'The Adventure of the Stockbroker's Clerk'. Dr John F. Watson.

[3] Jackson, who was also a doctor, was a neighbour of Dr Watson in Paddington. They had an arrangement to look after one another's practices when the need arose. *Vide*: 'The Adventure of the Crooked Man'. Dr John F. Watson.

I had a reciprocal arrangement to act as locum should the need arise. Having gained his agreement to be on call that evening, I set off by cab for Baker Street, my heart beating high at the prospect of the adventure to come. For, although I was happily married and would not have changed my life for all the money in the world, I must confess that there were times when I missed that tingle of excitement which taking part in any of Holmes' investigations always roused in me. Part of it was the intellectual stimulation of such occasions but mostly it was the thrill of the physical challenge which stirred the blood, and I could not help smiling as I felt the comfortable weight in my pocket of my army revolver, a relic of my days in Afghanistan serving with the 66th Berkshire Regiment of Foot.[4]

Holmes was waiting for me in my old Baker Street lodgings with our disguises in the form of pea jackets and peaked caps, very like those which Corbett had been wearing and, once we had we put these on, we took a cab to Picott's wharf.

It was a damp, overcast night with low clouds and therefore there was very little light from either the moon or the stars. Once we had passed from the well-lit streets of west London into the meaner byways of the East End, the only illumination was the subdued yellow gleam of the street lamps which glistened fitfully on the wet pavements and the brick façades of buildings. Even

[4] See footnote to p. 20. Dr John F. Watson.

the passers-by seemed diminished by the weather and slunk furtively along like sad ghosts, huddled in mufflers and shawls against the chill night air. The only bright islands in this sea of murky darkness were garishly-lit taverns and public houses which shone like beacons,[5] beckoning the inhabitants of the dingy streets to their warm, glittering interiors.

After travelling along Leadenhall Street for some distance, the cab turned right into a labyrinth of narrow side streets behind St Katherine Docks, until at last it drew up at an arched stone entrance from which a cobbled lane gave access to the wharf. It was poorly lit by a single gas lamp fixed to the brickwork by an iron bracket and, by this dim glow, we made our way between high walls of blackened brick towards the river Thames, led by our ears and noses rather than our eyes, for, although we could see little, we could smell the unmistakable odour of river mud mingled with the fainter tang of the sea and hear the heavy, rhythmic, liquid slop of water against wood and stone.

By that time, the drizzle had turned into a fine rain which lay over the scene like a sombre wash over a pen and ink drawing so that everything, the wharf, the vessels, the river itself, seemed to blur and run into one another, the dark hulks of the ships at anchor melting into the river, the tall masts and rigging merging with

---

[5] In 'The Adventure of the Naval Treaty', Sherlock Holmes refers enthusiastically to the new board schools as being 'the beacons of the future'. Dr John F. Watson.

the sky. As for the river itself, it had turned into a dark, sliding mass, like thick oil, in which the glow from the ships' lanterns was smeared into long, shifting patterns of light.

We felt our way gingerly along the wooden planking of the wharf, so sodden with rain that the sound of our footsteps was deadened as, stepping carefully round casks and barrels and over ropes which lay like coiled serpents in our path, we approached the vast bulk of the *Lucy Belle* which towered above us, the lower part of its four masts just visible before the upper sections and the rigging were swallowed up by the lowering darkness.

There were few lights aboard the ship and no sign of any human activity. Indeed it had the ghostly air of a vessel abandoned by its crew after some terrible tragedy at sea, and I instinctively reached into my pocket to feel for my revolver as a talisman against some unknown danger.

It was a moment of foolishness which quickly passed Moments later, we heard a distant bell strike ten o'clock and, on this signal, the yellow gleam of a lantern sprang up on the darkened deck above us, hung motionless for a second and then gently swung from left to right and then back again.

This was our signal and we groped our way forward towards the gangplank, which we mounted slowly, for it was treacherous underfoot, until at last we reached the top and were hauled on to the deck by Thomas Corbett, who loomed out of the blackness to meet us.

He led the way towards the stern of the ship to a flat-roofed wooden construction housing the passengers' accommodation and down some steps into a dimly-lit passage lined with doors, one of which he opened before ushering us into a cabin furnished with a bunk bed and a number of lockers, as well as a small table and a chair screwed to the floor. As Holmes had requested, a pen, inkwell and several sheets of paper were lying on the table, above which a lantern was hanging from the ceiling, swinging gently with the movement of the ship and casting glinting lights and shadows over the polished mahogany and brass fittings with which the cabin was equipped.

Thomas Corbett waited until we had settled ourselves, Holmes on the chair, I on the edge of the bunk, before announcing, 'Since you seem satisfied with the arrangements, Mr Holmes, I'll fetch Harry Deakin to speak to you.'

Holmes nodded to show his agreement and, as Corbett left, we divested ourselves from our seamen's outer garments, Holmes first producing from the pocket of his pea jacket a large envelope containing a sheet of stiff paper covered with legal-looking writing that had an official seal of red wax affixed to the bottom, stamped with what appeared to be the impress of a coat of arms.

Having laid this sheet of paper alongside those provided by Corbett, he looked across at me and chuckled.

'Here, Watson, you see stock in trade for performing the old trick I mentioned to you.'

'But where on earth did you get that letter?' I asked.

'From a dealer in Charing Cross Road who sells second-hand books and old legal documents. If you examine the one I have here, you will see that it is connected with the lease of a property drawn up many years ago.'

'But suppose Deakin realises what it is?'

'He will not be given the opportunity to look at it, my dear fellow, as you will shortly see. Ah, here he is now!' He broke off as there came a knock on the door and Corbett ushered in a nervous-looking, middle-aged man, the very antithesis of the conventional image of a ship's cook. His features were thin and melancholy, his stature small, and his general air was one of wary suspicion as he stood just inside the door, his eyes darting between Holmes and myself before shifting down to the table where the papers were laid out.

'Mr Deakin?' Holmes asked, his voice as clipped and austere as a prosecuting counsel's. The man nodded.

'Mr Harry Deakin?' my old friend persisted.

'That's me, sir,' Deakin replied in a hoarse voice.

The impact of this opening move was evident in Deakin's demeanour. He seemed to shrink in upon himself and shifted from one foot to another in a manner which suggested extreme unease.

'I have reason to believe,' Holmes continued in the same terse voice, 'that three years ago you served as cook aboard the barque the *Sophy Anderson* and that . . .'

At this point he broke off briefly to consult the document with the wax seal as if to confirm his facts before continuing '. . . and that you made the acquaintance of a deck-hand called Billy Wheeler, who later was attacked in a brawl on board the same vessel.'

The effect of this statement on Deakin was immediate and dramatic.

'That's a flaming lie!' he shouted, starting forward so violently that, thinking he was about to attack Holmes, I jumped to my feet to seize my revolver. But Holmes waved me back with a masterful gesture of his hand.

'Is it indeed a lie? Well, we shall see,' he told Deakin, tapping with a long index finger on the official-looking document. 'You will no doubt recall Tommy Brewster, the deck-hand who was killed by a fall from the rigging? Then let me inform you that the year before that accident, Brewster made a statement to a lawyer about those events aboard the *Sophy Anderson* and the death of Billy Wheeler. So there is no use your denying the facts. I have them here in black and white, signed and sealed. Do you still deny that such an incident took place?'

At once, all the fire went out of Deakin, who seemed to shrink in upon himself, his shoulders bowed and his expression one of utter defeat and despair.

'I ain't denying nothing, sir,' he mumbled. 'It all 'appened as Tommy says but I swear on my mother's 'ead I ain't guilty of Billy's death. I never touched 'im.

It were the others 'oo set on 'im and beat 'im. I tried to stop 'em but what good was one man against five?'

'You were also a witness to other events on that same morning, I believe?' Holmes continued, scanning the document as if reading from its contents. 'You saw, did you not, Captain Chafer feel for a pulse in Wheeler's neck and then pronounce him dead?'

'I did, sir,' Deakin replied in the tone of a man who realises he is defeated.

'And you witnessed the mate, Thomas Corbett, placing a St Christopher medallion on Wheeler's chest?'

'I saw that, too, sir. I'elped 'im put it there.'

'You also saw Corbett look across at the captain?'

'Aye, sir.'

'What did Chafer do when Corbett looked at him?' Deakin ran his tongue over his lips before replying. 'The cap'n drew a finger across 'is throat as if with a knife,' the man replied without any prompting.

'Indicating what?'

Again Deakin hung his head, refusing to meet Holmes' eyes.

'I don't foller you, sir.'

My old friend flung himself impatiently back in his chair.

'Do not trifle with me, my good man!' he cried. 'You know perfectly well the meaning of the gesture. It suggests that the person whom it is intended for, Mr Corbett on that occasion, should keep silent or he would have his throat cut, does it not? Does it not, Deakin?' he repeated, his voice rising.

The wretched man glanced up briefly.

'Aye, it does, sir,' he agreed softly.

'In other words, Chafer was threatening to murder Corbett?'

'I suppose so, sir.'

The words were dragged out of Deakin.

'There is no "suppose" about it,' Holmes retorted.

He paused for a few seconds but, receiving no further response from Deakin, he pressed on.

'Do you know what Corbett was supposed to keep silent about?' When Deakin shook his head dumbly, Holmes looked down at the document in front of him, his eyes scanning it as if he were looking for a particular passage. Then, raising his head, he looked directly at Deakin, his gaze fixed and implacable.

'Then allow me to inform you, Mr Deakin. The truth which Chafer was so anxious Corbett should not divulge was this: Billy Wheeler was still alive when he was wrapped in that canvas shroud and put over the side of the ship. In plain words, he was murdered!'

For several seconds, there was a dreadful silence which seemed interminable and then, without uttering a word, Deakin's head fell forward and he began to weep. It was a pitiful sight to witness. I doubt if Deakin had wept since he was a child and the tears were wrung out of him in a series of harsh cries, more like the death throes of an animal in torment than a human being.

I was considerably relieved when Holmes, getting up from his chair, came across to whisper to me, 'Find

Corbett and tell him to signal again with the lantern.'

As I left the cabin, I glanced back to see the tall figure of my friend standing over the crouched form of the ship's cook, his arms folded and an expression on his lean features as hard and as implacable as if they had been carved from granite. He put me in mind of some grim statue, personifying Vengeance itself.

I had no difficulty in finding Corbett. He was anxiously pacing up and down in the passageway outside the cabin and, as soon as I gave him Holmes' instructions, he seized his lantern and made for the companionway which led up to the deck. I followed at his heels, wondering who or what the second signal was intended for.

It soon became clear. As soon as Corbett had swung the lantern, several human forms emerged from various hiding-places among the shadows below on the wharf and began to mount the gang-plank. At their head was the unmistakable figure of Inspector Lestrade, dressed in unofficial tweeds, his sharp, sallow features turned up towards the light of the lantern, his dark eyes glinting suspiciously. Behind him tramped half a dozen uniformed men, their black waterproof capes reflecting the light like the oily surface of the Thames.

Lestrade seemed as surprised to see me as I was to see him.

'What's going on here, Dr Watson?' he demanded.

'Did not Holmes explain matters to you?' I countered.

'No, he did not. He called at Scotland Yard this

afternoon when I was out and left a message asking me to come here with half a dozen men at half past ten this evening on what he called a very serious matter. What is this matter, may I ask? And it had better be serious. I don't take kindly to requests to take myself and a posse of my officers out on a wet night to the back of beyond unless it is a very serious matter indeed. If it wasn't Mr Holmes who asked, I'd've stayed at the Yard in front of the office fire.'

'I think you had better wait and ask Holmes himself,' I replied, a little uneasy at Lestrade's obvious annoyance. 'This gentleman, by the way, is Mr Thomas Corbett, the mate of the vessel the *Lucy Belle,* or rather the *Sophy Anderson*.'

'Make up your mind, Dr Watson,' Lestrade snapped, nodding briefly at Corbett to acknowledge his presence. Realising the situation was too complex to explain to Lestrade in a few sentences, I led the way towards the passengers' accommodation.

Leaving the six uniformed officers outside the door, only the three of us entered the cabin. Even so, there was hardly room for all of us and Corbett and I were crushed against the bunk bed while Lestrade approached the table where Holmes and Deakin were standing, Holmes looking bright-eyed and confident, Deakin cowed and nervous.

'Ah, Lestrade!' Holmes exclaimed as the Inspector came towards him. 'I am sorry to call you out on such an inclement evening. Allow me to explain the situation.'

This he proceeded to do in a few concise sentences while Deakin shuffled his feet and hung his head in shame and Lestrade's mouth dropped open in amazement at the account.

'So you see,' Holmes concluded briskly, 'what we have here is a case of murder as well as fraud on a massive scale. And this is what I propose should be done so that the case may go to court. Thomas Corbett is willing to give evidence on oath to those counts of murder and fraud which I have just reported. That evidence will be corroborated by Harry Deakin, the ship's cook, from whom I have just taken a statement,' Holmes continued, picking up a sheet of paper from the desk and brandishing it in the air. 'I now suggest that Mr Deakin signs it in your presence, Lestrade, after which I shall add my signature as witness.'

The little ceremony was carried out in silence as Holmes gave the pen, already dipped in ink, to Deakin who, awed by the gravity of the occasion, signed his name with a trembling hand before Holmes, recharging the pen with ink, added his own signature with a flourish and handed the statement to the Inspector.

'And now, Lestrade,' he concluded, laying down the pen, 'I suggest you arrest Chafer and charge him with the murder of Billy Wheeler. The rest of the crew involved in the assault on the young man and the insurance fraud may be rounded up later. But I do most earnestly advise you to put a guard on the gang-planks so that none of the crew can escape. Meanwhile,

Mr Corbett, the ship's mate, will show you the way to the captain's cabin.'

Much bemused by Holmes' masterly control of the situation, Lestrade, who under the circumstances had no other option, followed Corbett out of the cabin and we heard the tramp of their feet and those of the accompanying uniformed officers proceed along the passage on their way to arrest Chafer, Deakin taking the opportunity to scuttle out after them like a frightened rabbit released from a trap.

'You see what I mean about the oldest trick in the world, Watson?' Holmes remarked as the door closed behind them.

'You mean, of course, Brewster's supposed statement?' I replied.

'Of course, my dear fellow. If you want someone to confess, all you have to do is declare you have irrefutable proof of his guilt. Unless the suspect is unusually hardened and, in my experience, he is most often not, then he will invariably crumble and confess all. It often works. There is a story, probably apocryphal, of telegrams being sent to various members of a gentlemen's club stating quite simply, "Flee the country. All is discovered." It is claimed that half a dozen of them did exactly that.

'You may also have noticed that it was not necessary to lie directly to Deakin. I simply asked him if he knew that Tommy Brewster had made a statement about the events on board the *Sophy Anderson* before he died.'

'At the same time drawing his attention to the legal document,' I pointed out.

'Oh, that is perfectly acceptable under the rules of the game,' Holmes replied with a shrug and a smile. 'Any conjurer or stage magician uses exactly the same ruse when performing a trick. He makes sure the audience's eyes are directed towards what he wants them to observe. Anyway, whatever the method employed, it has been a good night's work, do you not agree? I suggest we return to Baker Street and celebrate its conclusion with a whisky and soda in front of the fire.'

Of course, it was not the end of the affair. After months of investigation on the part of the police in rounding up all the original members of the crew of the *Sophy Anderson* who could be traced and who had agreed to the insurance fraud and been present at the murder of Billy Wheeler, they as well as the main participants in the events were sent for trial at the Old Bailey and were sentenced to various terms of imprisonment, including the McNeil brothers who had set up the scheme in the first place. Because of his direct participation in the murder, Captain Chafer was sentenced to be hanged.

Thomas Corbett, like most of the others, was found guilty of conspiracy to defraud and was given ten years in gaol.

It is with mixed feelings that I have to report that he did not live to serve out this sentence. Eighteen months later he died of a heart attack while in prison; a sad end for a man of such courage and honesty but probably one he himself would have wished for.

In recognition of these qualities of his, I have decided not to publish this account but will place it among my other papers in my despatch box, a decision, I feel, which would also have met with his approval.

THE CASE OF THE GUSTAFFSON STONE

I

It was not long before my marriage that my old friend Sherlock Holmes was asked to enquire into a matter involving one of the crowned heads of Europe. It was of such delicacy that, although Holmes himself has referred to it obliquely in public on two occasions,[1] I

[1] There are two references to the King of Scandinavia in the canon. One is in 'The Final Problem', in which Sherlock Holmes speaks of the financial benefit he had received from 'recent cases', in one of which he had been of assistance to the Royal Family of Scandinavia. The other is in 'The Adventure of the Noble Bachelor', in which Sherlock Holmes remarks to Lord St Simon that, in taking on his case, he is 'descending the social ladder' as his last client was the King of Scandinavia. There was, in fact, no King of Scandinavia, only of the united kingdoms of Norway and Sweden which were ruled over by Oscar II (1829–1907). After Norway's independence in 1905, Oscar II ruled over Sweden only. The fictitious king of Scandinavia's daughter, Clotilde Lothman von Saxe Meringen, had been engaged to the King of Bohemia. *Vide*: 'A Scandal in Bohemia'. Dr John F. Watson.

believe the time is not yet ripe for a full account of the case to be published, a decision with which Holmes heartily concurs.

I shall therefore place this record in my despatch box along with those other written accounts which, for various reasons, may never see the light of day, even though I know from the many letters I have received that there is considerable curiosity among my readers to know the full details of the case, roused, I might add, by those two references I have already mentioned.

It was, I recall, a pleasant morning in early autumn[2] when Holmes received a letter introducing him to the case. Considering the illustriousness of our correspondent, as we only later discovered, it was a curiously anonymous missive, bearing no coat of arms or other insignia to indicate the identity of the individual concerned, not even an address. However, the quality of the writing paper and envelope suggested it was someone of wealth and discernment.

Having read through the single sheet of paper and raised a quizzical eyebrow at its contents, Holmes passed the letter to me.

The handwriting was clear, educated and bold, the message short and to the point.

'Dear Mr Holmes,' it read. 'Having heard excellent

[2] This is the autumn of 1888, as Dr Watson married between that autumn and the spring of 1889. Dr John F. Watson.

reports of your skill as a private consulting agent, I beg your assistance in a case of great importance.

'As I am in London for a limited period only, I should be exceedingly obliged if you could find the time to see me this morning at 11 a.m.

'As the matter is of great delicacy, I trust I can rely on your discretion.'

In contrast to the legibility of the letter itself, the signature was almost indecipherable but, on close scrutiny, appeared to be Erik von Lyngstrad.

'A German gentleman?' I suggested as I returned the letter to Holmes.

'Perhaps,' he conceded with a shrug. 'We shall find out in an hour.'

'So you intend to see him, despite the shortness of the notice?'

'I think so, Watson. No other client has presented himself. Besides, I am curious to find out what this matter of extreme delicacy involves.'

'An *affaire de coeur*?' I suggested.

Holmes burst out laughing.

'My dear Watson, you are an incurable romantic! But you may well be correct. Shall you stay and find out?'

'If I may,' I replied a little stiffly for, to be frank, I was somewhat annoyed by his amusement at my expense. However, curiosity soon overcame any chagrin on my part and, taking the *Morning Post,* I sat down by one of the windows from where I could watch the street while glancing through the newspaper. Holmes had settled down with *The Times* and so we passed the next hour in companionable silence until the sound of a cab drawing up outside the house alerted both of us to the arrival of his client.

A few moments later, there came a ring at the front-door bell, footsteps were heard mounting the stairs and the boy in buttons[3] ushered in a tall, well-built gentleman with a noble, upright bearing and finely modelled head whose clipped moustache and beard gave him the air of a senior army officer.

There was a military air also in the brisk, authoritative manner in which he shook hands with Holmes and myself and announced his name as Count Erik von Lyngstrad.

Here was a man, I felt, who was used to commanding others.

'May I introduce my colleague, Dr Watson?' Holmes continued. 'I should be much obliged, sir, if, with your permission, he remains during our interview.'

'Indeed! Indeed!' Count von Lyngstrad agreed, bowing in my direction with a little formal click of his heels which also suggested military training as well as a Continental background. His voice was deep and his English excellent, containing only a very faint foreign accent, the origin of which I could not quite place.

The formalities over, the three of us seated ourselves,

---

[3] See footnote to p. 12. Dr John F. Watson.

Holmes in a chair set a little apart from his client's and in such a position that he had his back to the window, which afforded him a clear view of the Count's features while leaving his own in shadow. His expression was curiously immobile, a facial rigidity I had noticed before when his mind was most engaged. But behind those lean features which had the inflexibility of a Red Indian chief's, I knew his thoughts were working at speed like a steam locomotive under pressure.

Placing the tips of his fingers together, he leant back in his chair.

'In your letter,' he began, 'you refer to a matter of extreme delicacy. Let me assure you on behalf of myself and Dr Watson that not a word of what you tell us will pass beyond these four walls.'

The Count bowed his head in acknowledgement of Holmes' guarantee.

'Thank you, Mr Holmes,' he replied. 'It was partly because of your reputation for discretion that I have decided to consult you. Not on my own behalf,' he added hastily, 'but on the part of a very old and dear friend of mine.'

Holmes' features maintained the same grave, listening expression.

'I understand,' was all he said in reply. 'Pray continue, sir.'

Count von Lyngstrad hesitated as if not sure where to begin and then, after a moment's silence, he took up his account.

'About two months ago, this friend, whom I shall refer to as Herr Braun, was called to the bedside of an elderly and very sick uncle of his who wished to make a death-bed confession. It seems that six months earlier, the uncle, a gentleman of impeccable reputation, had taken a valuable jewel from among the family heirlooms and had used it as collateral to meet a debt of honour. The loan was only temporary and, within a month, the uncle was able to pay back the borrowed sum with interest and to retrieve the jewel, which he replaced in the family strongbox. The crisis appeared to be over.

'However, when he had first handed over the heirloom to the money-lender, the uncle, whose instinct told him not to trust the man too implicitly, had marked the piece of jewellery with a tiny scratch which would be invisible to anyone not aware of its presence. On examining the jewel when it was returned to him, he found the scratch was not there and he realised he had been tricked. The heirloom was not the original gem but a copy.

'This discovery came as a final blow after a period of great distress, for it was a close member of his own family who had accumulated the large debt which the uncle had felt obliged to repay. In consequence, the uncle suffered a stroke which left him partly paralysed and bedridden. Fearing another stroke would kill him, the uncle sent for his nephew to confess the loss of the family heirloom, the nephew being the titular head of the family and therefore the guardian of all the family property.'

It was apparent that the Count, who up to that moment had related the facts in a straightforward and unemotional manner, had now reached a point in his narrative which caused him personal concern.

Resuming his account again, he continued more hurriedly, 'As I have already said, all of this happened about two months ago. As soon as I learnt . . .'

The personal pronoun fell into the ensuing silence like a stone into a pool of still water. I was aware that I started up in my chair instantly alert, while Holmes, who has better control over his emotions than I, moved not a muscle but remained as motionless as a statue. As for the Count, I observed a faint flush infusing his handsome features before, quickly recovering his composure, he said with a smile, 'Ah, gentlemen, I am afraid I have let the cat out of the bag, as you English so charmingly express it. I am, of course, the nephew in question.'

'And the uncle?' Holmes enquired, raising an eyebrow at his client, who appeared about to continue his account.

The Count smiled again.

'You are very quick, Mr Holmes. I had intended to pass over the uncle without further explanation. In fact, there was no relationship between myself and the elderly gentleman, except that between a master and an old and trusted servant. The man is now dead and I am anxious that his reputation should remain as unsullied as it was before all this tragic business concerning the family jewel. No one else knows about its loss and I would prefer that it remained a secret known only to us.'

'Of course,' Holmes agreed. 'Pray continue.'

'Very little remains to be told. As soon as I realised the jewel had been replaced by a fake by the money-lender, I made certain to find out all I could about him. His name is Baron Kleist.'

'Ah, Baron Kleist!' Holmes exclaimed as if the name were familiar to him. Rising to his feet, he went to a bookshelf in one of the chimney alcoves. Taking down his encyclopaedia of reference,[4] he carried it back to his chair where he quickly turned to the entries under the letter *K* and began to read out loud.

'"Baron Kleist. Antecedents unknown, although he claims descent from a cadet branch of the Hapsburgs. Immensely rich. Fortune derived mainly from dealing in currency, jewellery and *objets d'art* on an international scale. Also a money-lender and a blackmailer. It is rumoured he was responsible for the suicide of the Duchesse de Nantes and the Member of Parliament, William Pepper. Also suspected of forgery. Has no settled abode but moves freely between the major capitals."' Holmes closed the book with the comment, 'A notorious character of whom much is suspected

---

[4] See footnote to p. 140. Dr John F. Watson.

but nothing proved. Unfortunately, I have never made his acquaintance but I understand he is at present in London. There was a small item two days ago in the *Morning Post.*'

'Then if you agree with my plans, Mr Holmes, you may soon have the pleasure of meeting the Baron,' Count von Lyngstad replied. 'I have made enquiries and I am told he is at present staying at the Hotel Imperial[5] in Piccadilly, and has been in contact with a certain American millionaire, Cornelius F. Bradbury, who is due to arrive in England in a week's time and who is a collector of rare items of jewellery, particularly those with an historic connection. It is my belief that the Baron is intending to sell my family heirloom, which is in the form of a pendant, to Mr Bradbury and that he has come to London for this very purpose, bringing the jewel with him.

'This is where your services are called for. I have already had some enquiries made and I have no doubt that the pendant is kept in a small strongbox which the Baron always carries with him and which, I understand, he keeps in his bedroom, preferring not to entrust it to the hotel's safe. Your task will be to remove the real pendant and replace it with the fake one without the Baron's knowledge. This way, the Baron will suspect nothing, the fake jewel can be sold to the American

---

[5] I have not been able to trace a hotel of this name in Piccadilly and therefore suggest it is fictitious. Dr John F. Watson.

collector and a scandal of international proportions will be averted. Moreover, if the Baron should be aware of the substitution, he may seek his revenge and I have no wish to risk making such an enemy.'

'You are indeed wise,' Holmes said gravely. 'Should his enmity be aroused, Baron Kleist has the means to finance and organise an implacable vendetta which could include murder. It is rumoured that Petro Cecconi, a member of the powerful Mafia family, ran foul of the Baron and was stabbed through the heart one evening as he left a restaurant in Rome, although, at the time, the murder was attributed to a falling-out between the Cecconi family and another Mafia gang, the Badaglio clan. I believe Baron Kleist travels everywhere with a bodyguard?'

'Two, in fact, Mr Holmes. My own inquiry agents tell me that one guard accompanies him wherever he goes, while the other, Igor, a Russian gangster, remains in the hotel suite to guard the strongbox should the Baron leave the building for any reason. They are ostensibly manservants but both are armed and are, according to my informants, experts in the martial arts. I should add that my own agents are also staying at the Imperial in a suite of rooms, number twenty, adjoining the Baron's at number twenty-four. If you take up the case, you will very likely meet them. One is named Oscar. He is a tall, fair-haired young man. The other, Nils, is short and dark and, being less conspicuous, is mostly engaged in shadowing Baron Kleist.

'I understand from Nils that the Baron intends to go to the opera on Friday night with a young actress of his acquaintance and will afterwards dine with her at Claridge's hotel.'[6]

'May I ask how your informant knows this?' Holmes broke in to ask.

The Count gave a smile.

'How very perspicacious of you, Mr Holmes!' he remarked approvingly. 'Besides being an expert in the art of shadowing, Nils can also lip read. He managed to get close enough to the Baron one afternoon at the hotel reception desk when he was making arrangements for two seats to be booked at Covent Garden for Friday evening and also for a table to be reserved, again for two, at Claridge's for later that same evening. As for the identity of the young actress, Nils has seen her in the Baron's company on several occasions since his arrival in London. A few discreet enquiries on his part established her identity. Are there any more questions you would like to ask, Mr Holmes?'

'Not for the moment, Count von Lyngstrad,' Holmes replied. 'Pray continue.'

'As I was saying, it is unlikely the Baron will return to the Imperial until the early hours of Saturday morning. It therefore seems an excellent opportunity

---

[6] Claridge's hotel was situated in Brook Street, Westminster. J. Neil Gibson, the 'Gold King', stayed there. *Vide*: 'The Problem of Thor Bridge'. Sherlock Holmes asked Martha, his agent, to report to him there. *Vide*: 'His Last Bow.' Dr John F. Watson.

for you to substitute the fake jewel for the real one. It will not be easy, Mr Holmes. You will have to find some means to get into the Baron's bedroom past Igor, who will remain in the suite to guard the strongbox. You will then have to open it and relock it once the substitution has been made so that the Baron's suspicions are not aroused.

'I should perhaps warn you at this stage that the strongbox in which the jewel is kept is no ordinary container secured by a key. It has been specially made and is fitted with three separate locks, each requiring its own key, and is, I understand, kept in a leather grip which is itself locked and which is placed inside the wardrobe in the Baron's bedroom.'

'Also locked, I assume?' Holmes asked with amusement.

'Almost certainly,' Count von Lyngstrad replied, smiling in return.

'May I ask why your agents are not themselves carrying out the substitution?' Holmes continued. 'From what you tell me, they seem highly professional.'

'At gathering information, yes. However, their skills do not extend as far as picking locks or slipping past bodyguards. That is why I have turned to you.

'How you carry out the substitution is entirely your decision. But however you contrive it, the reward will be substantial, I can assure you. And now for the jewel itself; or rather the Baron's excellent copy of it, made I believe by Bieberbeck, the Viennese expert who supplies substitute jewellery for those members of the aristocracy who have been forced to sell the family heirlooms. It is said Princess Magdelena von Ullstein's famous tiara is one of Bieberbeck's copies.'

Reaching into his inner pocket, he took out a small jeweller's box covered in blue and gold tooled leather which he set down on the table before opening it to reveal its contents lying on the white satin lining.

It was indeed a pendant, but to my untutored eye it seemed a crude object with nothing of either beauty or value about it, for it was merely an oval stone of a brownish-yellow colour, about an inch and a half in length, roughly engraved with the head of a bearded man with narrow, fierce-looking eyes and high cheekbones. The stone itself was enclosed in a broad gold frame bearing some strange, angular letters. There was a loop at the top of it to which was attached a chain made of coarse gold links so that, I supposed, it could be worn round the owner's neck like a locket.

It looked undoubtedly old but, apart from that, had no other merit at all, as far as I could see.

However, Holmes' response on seeing it was quite the opposite to mine.

I heard him draw in his breath in amazement, at the sound of which his client cast a keen glance in his direction. But my old friend had already regained control of his features and the face he presented expressed nothing more than a mild interest.

'I see,' he remarked non-committally. 'Well, Count

von Lyngstrad, I will do my best to arrange the substitution, but I can promise nothing.'

'I am staying at the Northumberland hotel,[7] should you wish to contact me,' the Count said. Rising to his feet, he held out his hand to each of us in turn.

'I am most grateful, gentlemen,' he added, giving the same courteous little bow and click of his heels with which he had greeted us, before leaving the room.

Hardly had the door closed behind him than Holmes let his true feelings find expression.

Smiling broadly, he clapped me on the shoulder.

'My dear Watson, we have been honoured with an inquiry of some importance!' he exclaimed.

'Have we, Holmes?' I asked, casting a dubious eye at the pendant in its little box which the Count had left lying on the table. 'I cannot myself see the significance of the pendant. In fact, it does not look at all valuable to me.'

'No?' He sounded dumbfounded. 'Then let me ask you a question. Have you heard of the Alfred jewel?'[8]

---

[7] Sir Henry Baskerville stayed at the Northumberland hotel, which was situated in Northumberland Avenue, not far from Trafalgar Square. Dr John F. Watson.

[8] The Alfred jewel dates from the reign of King Alfred the Great (871–899) and bears the inscription '*Aelfred mec heht gewyrcan*' – 'Alfred ordered me to be made'. It is made of gold and cloisonné enamel and carries the figure of a man, covered with a piece of transparent rock crystal, thought to be a representation of Christ. Its function may have been that of a book pointer. Discovered in 1693 four miles from Athelney where Alfred founded a monastery, it is at present in the Ashmolean Museum in Oxford. Dr John F. Watson.

'I think so, Holmes. It is connected with King Alfred, I assume.'

'It is indeed. Now what value would you place on it?'

'I have no idea but as it is famous as well as very old, I suppose it must be worth a great deal of money.'

'It is priceless, my dear fellow, even though its intrinsic value is minimal, for it consists merely of some crystal and enamel plus a little gold. Its true value lies in its uniqueness as well as its age and its historical connection. A collector such as Cornelius Bradbury would be willing to pay a fortune to acquire it.'

Bending down, he picked up the pendant which the Count had left on the table and held it towards me on the palm of his hand.

'This is, of course, only a copy,' he continued, 'but were it the original it would, like the Alfred jewel, be priceless.'

After a pause in which he looked at me keenly, he added in a solemn tone, 'What you are looking at, my dear Watson, is the Gustafsson Stone.'

I could think of nothing to say in response and, after a moment's silence, Holmes remarked, 'I see you have not heard of it.'

'I am afraid not, Holmes,' I said humbly.

'Then let me enlighten you. The Gustafsson Stone is a sixth-century jewel which once belonged to Gustaf Gurfson, a Viking leader who is hardly known in England but is famous throughout Scandinavia as a national hero. The head etched into the stone, which by the way is amber, is supposed to be a portrait of him. You see these strange letters engraved on the gold frame? These are runes and are said to spell out his name. There is something else about the Gustafsson Stone which adds to its uniqueness. It is part of the crown jewels of the kingdom of Scandinavia.'[9]

Holmes, who has a taste for the dramatic,[10] paused again to give me the opportunity to respond appropriately to this startling statement and this time I was more prepared than on the earlier occasion.

'Good heavens, Holmes!' I exclaimed. 'Then Count von Lyngstrad must be the King of Scandinavia!'

'Precisely, Watson,' Holmes agreed coolly. 'I congratulate you on your powers of deduction. Count von Lyngstrad is indeed King Erik of Scandinavia. Now, having settled the matter of the real identity of our client, we must now turn our attention to a less easily solved aspect of it, namely: how are we going to contrive to exchange this copy of the Gustaffson Stone with the original without alerting the Baron and his bodyguards? Have you any ideas, Watson?'

'I am afraid not, Holmes.'

'Neither have I. But they will come, Watson. They will come.'

With that, he rose from his chair and left the room.

---

[9] See footnote to p. 201. Dr John F. Watson.

[10] In *The Hound of the Baskervilles*, Sherlock Holmes admits, 'Some touch of the artist wells up within me, and calls insistently for a well staged performance.' Dr John F. Watson.

Returning shortly afterwards, he stretched himself out on the sofa and stared fixedly at the ceiling, his eyes hooded, as if inspiration were to be found up there upon its white-washed surface.

Recognising the symptoms and realising that Holmes would be lost in whatever world he had drifted into through the needle of the syringe,[11] I, too, rose and, quietly letting myself out of the house, hailed a cab and set off for my club and the consolation of a game of billiards.

---

[11] There are several references in the canon to Sherlock Holmes' unfortunate habit of injecting himself with a ten per cent solution of cocaine. He also used morphia on occasions. *Vide*: *A Study in Scarlet*, 'A Scandal in Bohemia', and 'The Adventure of the Five Orange Pips'. Dr John F. Watson.

II

By the time I had returned to our lodgings, Holmes had fully recovered and was overflowing with high spirits and impatience at my absence.

'Where on earth have you been, Watson?' he demanded. However, before I could reply, he had swept on. 'While you were away, I have devised the most brilliant scheme. So come along at once, there's a good fellow! Let us not waste any more time!'

'But where are we going, Holmes?' I asked as I hurried after him down the stairs.

'To inspect the lie of the land, of course!' he said dismissively over his shoulder, as if that should have been obvious.

Our destination, it seemed from the address he gave to the cab driver, was the Hotel Imperial where Baron

Kleist was staying and I wanted to ask Holmes if he thought this was a wise decision but, having seen him before in this mood, I knew it was better to hold my tongue and simply follow where he led.

The Hotel Imperial, a large, white, porticoed edifice, its façade decorated with half pilasters and elaborate cornices, was situated in Piccadilly overlooking Green Park. A uniformed doorkeeper saluted and held the doors open for us as if we were royalty as we passed into a magnificent entrance hall lined with mirrors and palm trees in huge brass pots. A grand staircase swept up in front of us to the upper floors.

However, we turned to the left into a large lounge furnished with small tables and tapestry-covered sofas and armchairs.

'Coffee, do you not agree, my dear fellow?' Holmes asked, seating himself on one of the sofas and, as he gave the order to a soft-footed waiter who had suddenly appeared before us as if conjured up out of the air, I lowered myself on to one of the armchairs.

'What are we doing here?' I asked in a low voice, hoping to encourage him by example into adopting a more discreet attitude, for he was glancing about him with obvious interest.

'As I have already told you, Watson. Like troops before battle we are carrying out a preliminary inspection of the enemy's position. And there is no need to whisper, my dear fellow. There is nothing more likely to draw attention to oneself than a furtive manner. And now,' he continued, lowering his voice a little to my great relief, as the waiter, having reappeared to serve our order, withdrew, 'I want you to glance about in a casual manner as you drink your coffee. For example, if you look over to your right, you will observe a dark-haired man reading *The Times* and, like us, taking a discreet interest in what is going on about him. You have observed him, Watson?'

'Yes, I have Holmes,' I replied in an admiring tone, for, had Holmes not pointed the man out, I should have not noticed him at all, for there was nothing remarkable about him. Indeed, he was so ordinary in both his appearance and behaviour as to be virtually invisible.

'That, I believe, is none other than Nils, one of our client's agents whom he mentioned was staying at the Hotel Imperial. The other, Oscar, the more conspicuous-looking of the two, is presumably keeping discreetly out of sight until his services are called for. And if you look over to the far side of the lounge, you will see a pair of double glass doors. These lead into the main restaurant from which, I believe, one can gain access to the famous Winter Garden at the back of the hotel, while on the far side of the reception desk are the doors leading into the Smoking Room, the Writing Room and the Ladies' Drawing-room. You look bemused, my dear fellow. Why is that?'

'I do not understand why all of this is necessary. You are, I assume, not thinking of making use of the Ladies' Drawing-room by any chance?'

'Not unless it is absolutely necessary,' Holmes replied solemnly and then, on catching sight of my expression, he gave a low chuckle. 'I am merely making sure of all the exits beforehand in case we need to make a run for it. I can assure you, my dear fellow, that the Ladies' Drawing-room will be my very last point of retreat.'

He broke off suddenly and, putting down his coffee cup, announced in a low voice which carried an undertone of excitement, 'I believe the situation is about to unfold, Watson. Our friend Nils is getting ready to make a move. No, no! Pray do not turn in his direction. You will give the game away. If you look to your left, you may watch the developments much more discreetly.'

With a nod of his head, he indicated the double glass doors on the other side of the room which led into the restaurant, one leaf of which had been left half open and which, like a mirror, reflected the opposite side of the coffee lounge and part of the foyer. Without needing to turn my head, I could see in its polished surface Nils, the Count's unobtrusive agent, in the act of folding up his copy of *The Times* and, placing it under his arm, begin to rise to his feet.

'He has scented his prey,' Holmes remarked with a chuckle, leaning back in his chair. Although to any casual observer he was apparently quite uninterested in what might be happening behind him, I was aware that, even though his eyes were half-closed, he was watching with close attention the restaurant door and the events being reflected in it.

While he was speaking, the images had shifted. Nils was now fully upright and was examining a handful of small coins he had taken from his pocket, as if searching for a suitable tip to leave by his coffee cup. At the same time, a man's figure advanced into the focus of the door's reflection.

He was a tall, well-built man in his mid-fifties, I estimated, and had apparently just descended the staircase which led to the upper floors.

'And there is the prey: Baron Kleist himself,' Holmes added, his eyes still hooded and his lips barely moving.

I sharpened my own focus on the new arrival, excited at being afforded my first glimpse of the man whose reputation as an international forger and blackmailer was notorious and whom Holmes was committed to outwitting on behalf of his royal client, the King of Scandinavia.

He carried his bulk and height with the confident air of a man whose wealth and status entitled him to the deference of others. His clothes also suggested money and social standing, for they were impeccably cut by the best tailors – English, I suspected – his morning coat fitting smoothly across his broad shoulders, his trousers of exactly the right length to the nearest fraction of an inch. His spats, too, were exquisite and his boots shone like black glass. But although the general effect was one of a wealthy gentleman-about-town, there were details about his appearance which failed to live up to this image. The gold watch and chain he was sporting was just a little too lavish; so, also, was the orchid in his button-hole, while he handled his gold-topped cane with just a touch too much ostentatious flourish.

He was handsome in a rather florid manner, the colour in his broad, flat cheeks indicating self-indulgence and high-living, a suggestion which was borne out by the small, well-padded mouth under his carefully trimmed mustachios. But it was his eyes which revealed his true nature. He had halted at the reception desk to speak to the clerk on duty, who was bowing and smiling profusely in his anxiety to please. As he stood there, ignoring the man's obsequiousness, the Baron turned his head to survey the foyer and the coffee lounge.

Even at a distance, I was aware of the quality of that scrutiny. It was hard, cold and implacable, like a snake's, and had the same fixed, bright, reptilian intelligence.

Here, I thought, was a clever, calculating man who would make a formidable opponent, and I felt a clutch of fear at my heart.

Involuntarily, I glanced across at Holmes, wondering if he, too, was aware of the Baron's dangerous potentiality.

He was still leaning back in his chair, his eyes half-closed, but he was now wearing a beatific smile as if the thought of the forthcoming mission to outwit the man was affording him pleasurable anticipation.

In the meantime, the reflections in the glass were shifting once more as the figures in the dumb-show changed their positions. As if anticipating the Baron's next move, Nils was bending down over the coffee table to place some coins by his empty cup. At the same time, a third figure whom I had not been aware of until that moment stepped forward into the frame from his position a little distance from the reception desk. He was a young, stockily-built man, dressed all in black like a manservant, but it was immediately apparent that his role was not that of a conventional gentleman's gentleman. There was an air of menace about his movements and the manner in which he carried his hands loosely in front of him half-formed into fists like a pugilist entering a boxing ring ready for the contest.

This newcomer, I realised, was one of the Baron's two bodyguards, the one who, as Count von Lyngstrad had remarked, followed him everywhere. He fell in a few yards behind the Baron, who had turned away and was crossing the foyer towards the hotel entrance.

Hardly had the pair of them vanished out of sight than Nils made his own move. Strolling casually, as if he had all the time in the world, he too made his way towards the great swing doors which the uniformed commissionaire was holding open for him, disappearing in turn through them into the noise and bustle of Piccadilly.

Judging it was safe to turn my head, I glanced directly towards the foyer, empty now of both the Baron, his bodyguard and Nils, the King of Scandinavia's unobtrusive little agent, but not deserted, for there were plenty of other people arriving and leaving all the time, a situation which I was aware Holmes was watching with keen interest. Sitting alert and upright now in his chair, his eyes were following these comings and goings, particularly those of the new arrivals.

Suddenly, he announced in a low voice, 'Wait for me here, Watson. I shall not keep you long.'

With that, to my surprise, he rose and walked briskly across the room to the entrance hall, where a middle-aged lady and gentleman, who had just entered the hotel through the swing doors, were about to mount the stairs. Giving them a slight bow as one might to acquaintances, he made some remark at which the lady smiled and the gentleman responded. Holmes then gestured to them to precede him and, as they began to mount the stairs, he fell in behind them.

For a few moments, I was deceived by this little charade, believing that Holmes had indeed met the couple before and that, for some reason known only to himself, he wished to accompany them upstairs. Certainly the hotel staff present in the foyer, the clerks behind the desk, the doorkeeper, the pages standing about waiting to be summoned, were taken in by the ruse and raised no objection to Holmes' intrusion into the private upper floors, normally barred to non-residents unless they had first made themselves known to the management. Once again, I found myself full of admiration at my old friend's boldness and ingenuity which to my knowledge no other person possesses to quite the same degree.

As he promised, he returned within minutes and, as he seated himself again on the sofa, I congratulated him on his quickness of mind at which he smiled, pleased with the compliment.

'One must always seize the moment, Watson, and, in my experience, if one waits long enough, the moment will always present itself.'

'And was the moment worth seizing?'

'Indeed it was, my dear fellow. I discovered two very important facts. Firstly, the Baron's suite, number twenty-four, is on the second floor and, being an even number, must face the back of the building. Secondly, the locks on the doors are of a standard pattern and, should it be necessary, could be picked without too much difficulty. And speaking of picklocks, it is time we paid a visit to an old friend of mine, Charlie Peak, a former screwsman,[12] or burglar to you, Watson, and an expert in the field.'

'Former?' I enquired.

'He is seventy-four, too old, as he himself admits, for breaking into other people's property. We will now pay the bill and take a cab to Sydenham where we shall sit at Charlie's feet,' Holmes replied, summoning the waiter.

[12] Underworld slang for a burglar who used keys or picklocks to carry out his robberies. Dr John F. Watson.

III

To my astonishment, the cab set us down outside a neat red-brick villa with lace curtains at the windows and a brightly-polished brass knocker on the door, more the abode of a respectable bank-clerk, I would have thought, than a retired burglar.

A trim little housemaid in a spotlessly white cap and apron showed us into a parlour, where Charlie Peak sat comfortably ensconced in a large armchair among the domestic comforts of potted geraniums, buttoned velvet and family photographs.

He was a white-haired, pink-cheeked, cheerful-looking little man, his slippered feet resting on a stool and a walking stick propped up beside him.

'Mr 'Olmes!' he cried out in delight as we entered, holding out both his hands in welcome. 'You'll forgive me, I'm sure, for not gettin' up to greet you but the old pins ain't what they used to be.'

Having shaken hands vigorously with both of us, he waved us towards two chairs which we drew up on either side of him, so that the three of us formed a triangle with Charlie Peak at its apex like a benevolent genius presiding at a feast.

After an exchange of tidings such as old friends indulge in after a long absence, Holmes came to the purpose of our visit.

'Now, Charlie,' said he. 'As well as to have the pleasure of seeing you again, I am here to seek your expert advice.'

'On locks, I suppose,' the old man replied with a twinkle.

'Of course.'

'What sort of locks? Door? Cupboard? Chest? Safe?'

'A metal container similar to a cash box in size, but very strong and fitted with, I believe, three separate locks, each requiring its own special key.'

Charlie Peak's face lit up.

'Ah, a Medici[13] casket!' he exclaimed.

'You have heard of it?' Holmes asked eagerly.

'I've done better than that, Mr 'Olmes. I've 'eld one

---

[13] The Medicis were a rich and powerful family of merchants and bankers who ruled over Florence, and later Tuscany, from 1434 to 1737. The most famous of them was Lorenzo de' Medici, known as 'The Magnificent', who was a patron of arts and letters. Dr John F. Watson.

'ere in these very 'ands. It was as beautiful an example of the locksmith's art as I've ever clapped eyes on. They're made by Signor Valori of Florence, a direct descendant, so 'e says, of Luigi Valori, the locksmith 'oo worked for the Medici family. 'E 'as a little shop in a side street be'ind that big church with the fancy black and white stonework . . .'

'The Cathedral of Santa Maria del Fiore?' Holmes suggested.

'Could be,' Charlie Peak replied, shrugging his shoulders. 'I didn't ask.'

'But you have met Signor Valori?'

'Indeed I 'ave. I'd heard of 'is special caskets and 'ow they're impossible to open unless you 'as the keys so, seein' as I made my livin' in those days by pickin' locks, I wanted to find out about 'em. So I went to 'is shop and talked to 'im about 'em.'

'How?' Holmes asked with genuine curiosity. 'Does Signor Valori speak English?'

Charlie Peak gave a wheezy laugh.

'No, Mr 'Olmes; no more'n I speak Eyetie. But when it comes to two men sittin' down to talk about a subject they're both in love with, if you follers me, they finds the means some'ow, whether its using the 'ands or drawin' little pictures or actin' it out. We managed it any'ow by one means or another. Signor Valori explained that he only makes them to order, usually for very rich people because they costs a great deal of money. In all 'is years, 'e's only ever made four. They're made of the strongest steel that no ordinary cracksman can cut through and, like you said, each is fitted with three locks, every one different and so crafted that even the most skilful screwsman can't get 'em open unless 'e knows the secret.'

'Secret?' Holmes demanded.

Charlie Peak winked and tapped the side of his nose. ''E wouldn't tell me, Mr 'Olmes, nor 'oo 'e's made 'em for, but as a very special favour to me, 'e showed me one 'e was workin' on. It was a beauty! Black-japanned, it was, with a brass bird let into the lid.'

Beside me, I felt Holmes' whole body become alert as if an electric charge had suddenly been passed through it. But his voice and manner remained matter-of-fact.

'What kind of bird?' he asked, as if only mildly interested.

'I wouldn't like to say, Mr 'Olmes. Apart from sparrers and pigeons, I can't tell one from t'other. All I can say is, it was a big bird with a bloomin' great beak and it was 'olding a leaf in its claws.'

'Oh, I see,' Holmes said, apparently losing interest. 'Pray continue, Charlie. You were describing the Medici casket Signor Valori showed you. Were you able to examine the locks?'

'I wasn't given the chance. I didn't 'ave it in my 'ands for more than a minute before Signor Valori took it off of me.'

'A pity!' my old friend murmured. It was quite obvious he was bitterly disappointed.

Charlie Peak watched him without speaking for a moment or two, his head on one side and his face alive with amusement. Then he said, 'But I can do better than tell you about them, Mr 'Olmes. I can show you! See that cabinet over there? Open the bottom drawer and you'll find a box. If you bring it to me, I'll let you see 'ow far I got in findin' out Signor Valori's little secret.'

Holmes did as he was requested and produced a plain deal box about ten inches square from the bottom drawer of the cabinet, which he carried over to Charlie Peak. It was apparently heavy and, rather than place it on the old man's knees, he set it down on a small table which stood by Charlie's side.

'Open it up!' Charlie ordered. He was clearly enjoying the situation hugely.

Inside was a jumble of locks of various shapes and sizes, each one identified by a luggage label. Several of these locks which lay on top, as if of more recent construction, were joined together in pairs or, in some case, in threes. On the very top lay a small bundle about six inches long wrapped in black felt.

'Take that one out!' Charlie Peak instructed Holmes, pointing a gnarled index finger at one particular lock of the triple variety.

As Holmes lifted it out, its label dangled free and it was possible to see the inscription on it, which read in capital letters: 'Medici Number Ten'.

'Number Ten?' Holmes murmured, raising an eyebrow.

'My tenth and last try at making a copy of the lock

to the Medici casket. That's what all them locks are, Mr 'Olmes – copies or originals of every lock in the land that I'd be likely to run up against in a day's, or rather a night's, work. It took a lifetime to build up that collection and years to break the Medici combination. Give it 'ere, sir.'

Holmes silently obliged but I could tell from the look of admiration on his face and the almost reverent manner in which he handled the lock that he was deeply impressed by the old man's skill.

'And them picklocks,' Charlie added, pointing to the little felt bundle.

It contained, as we discovered when Charlie unrolled it, about a dozen slender steel rods of various widths and lengths.

'A superb set of "bettys",'[14] Holmes remarked approvingly.

'I 'ad 'em specially made,' Charlie Peak replied, looking pleased at Holmes' compliment. 'Now, gentlemen, if you cares to gather close, I'll show you how to work the trick. And I'll tell you 'ow I found out about it.

'I didn't let on to Signor Valori that I was a screwsman. I let 'im think I was just an ordinary locksmith, sittin' like a little kid at the feet of an expert, oohin' and aahin' at 'is skill. 'E was flattered, just as I meant 'im to be. So, as a great 'onour, 'e gets out three little keys and opens up the casket for me. Now, I've got a good memory for

---

[14] Slang for picklocks. Dr John F. Watson.

the look of a key. It's part of my trade, like you with footprints,[15] Mr 'Olmes. So as soon as I left the shop, I drew pictures of the keys and 'ad 'em made up as picklocks when I got 'ome. If you look 'ere, you'll see each one's marked at the end with their own sign. This one's got a little cross on it. That's the one you use to open the centre lock first.'

As he spoke, he inserted the narrow metal rod into the central apperture before continuing with his explanation.

'Then you twists it about to and fro until you 'ears the wards give way. But I don't need to tell you that, do I, sir? By all accounts you're an expert screwsman yourself. Now what follers is the first part of the trick. You leaves that "betty" in place and puts in the second, the one with the two little cuts on it, into the keyhole on the left. But don't take that "betty" or the first one out, for it keeps them locks open. Then you moves on to the third keyhole. You get my meanin', Mr 'Olmes?'

'Indeed I do, Charlie,' Holmes said.

'Now watch this,' the old man continued, ''cos 'ere comes the best part of the trick. Once you've opened the third lock, the other two locks close. So you 'ave to go back to the first and second lock and open 'em again. Clever, ain't it?'

---

[15] Sherlock Holmes was adept at using footprints as a method of detection and claimed he could tell a man's height by the length of his stride. There are several references to his skill. *Vide*, among others: *The Sign of Four*. Dr John F. Watson.

'Yes; but not as clever as you in working out the trick. I take my hat off to you, Charlie. That is expertise at its very best.'

The old man, his cheeks flushed an even brighter pink, looked pleased as well as embarrassed by the compliment.

'All in a day's work, Mr 'Olmes,' he said gruffly and, to cover up his self-consciousness, began to busy himself with replacing the set of 'bettys' in the box, leaving aside the three he had used to open the Medici lock as well as the lock itself.

'If you like, you can borrer those,' he told Holmes.

'May I? Then I am eternally in your debt, Charlie. What can I do for you in return?'

'Nuffin' except to come and tell me if the trick worked for you, that's all.'

'I will certainly do that when I return the "bettys" and the lock,' Holmes assured him, putting these objects into his pocket before taking leave of his friend.

'A remarkable old fellow,' Holmes added when, having hailed a cab in Sydenham High Street, we drove back to our lodgings, a journey which he enlivened for me with accounts of the more colourful exploits of Charlie's career.

'I wish I had half his skill,' he concluded.

'But surely not his criminal record?' I asked dryly.

Holmes looked sideways at me and grinned broadly. '*Touché*, Watson!' he declared. 'But I do sincerely believe that had my interests leant towards committing crime rather than solving it, I could have been the most successful burglar in the business.'[16]

Our little excursion had evidently stimulated my old friend into renewed action, for hardly had we returned to Baker Street than he was off again, bustling out of the sitting-room and down the stairs, pausing only to call back at me, 'By the way, be a good fellow and make sure you have a pair of light boots with rubber soles and heels!'

'Why, Holmes?' I called back, much mystified.

But he had gone. All I heard in reply was the slam of the street door as he hurried out to whistle for a hansom.[17]

He was back about an hour after my own return from my bootmaker's with the prescribed footwear, bearing the fruits of a shopping spree of his own, which consisted of a small valise and a coil of strong cord which he placed inside the valise, together with a selection of implements from his burglar's kit.[18] He had

[16] Sherlock Holmes successfully carried out several burglaries himself, as for example in the case of Charles Augustus Milverton. *Vide* also: 'The Adventure of the Bruce Partington Plans' and 'The Adventure of the Illustrious Client'. In 'The Adventure of the Retired Colourman', Sherlock Holmes remarks that burglary was an alternative profession which he could have taken up. Dr John F. Watson.

[17] See footnote to p. 80. Dr John F. Watson.

[18] Sherlock Holmes bought a 'first-class, up-to-date burgling kit, with nickel-plated jemmy, diamond-tipped glass cutter, adaptable keys, and every modern improvement which the march of civilisation demands' in readiness for his planned burglary at Charles Augustus Milverton's house. Dr John F. Watson.

also bought, as I discovered later, the components of disguises for both of us.

'And you have the rubber-soled boots I recommended?' he asked me.

'Indeed, I have,' I assured him. 'But why should I need them?'

'You will find that out tomorrow night, my dear fellow, when Baron Kleist attends the opera and we shall scale the heights of the Hotel Imperial,' was his enigmatic reply.

Before I could question him further, he had disappeared inside his bedroom, taking Charlie Peak's picklocks and his copy of the Medici lock with him where, I assumed, he spent the next few hours practising opening the lock, a task which continued to occupy him for most of the following day as well.

IV

We had decided to set out for the hotel at seven o'clock and before we left we put on our disguises, simple ones on this occasion, although Holmes is an expert in changing his appearance and had, at various times, taken on the identity, among others, of an elderly Italian priest, a French workman and an old woman.[19]

For himself, he had chosen a dark waxed moustache which gave him the air of a stylish man-about-town. Mine was a brown wig *en brosse* and a pair of gold-rimmed spectacles. Thus disguised, we set off by cab for the Hotel Imperial, where we were to make use of the suite of rooms adjacent to Baron Kleist's where Nils and Oscar, the King of Scandinavia's agents, were already installed.

Oscar, who opened the door to us, seemed already

---

[19] *Vide*: 'The Final Problem', 'The Disappearance of Lady Frances Carfax' and 'The Adventure of the Mazarin Stone'. Dr John F. Watson.

acquainted with Holmes and I assumed that part of Holmes' expedition on the previous day was to inspect the lie of the land, as he expressed it, from the closer quarters of the interior of the hotel suite. Oscar was a tall, very blond young man, too conspicuous to be seen in public, whose role seemed to be to keep watch on the Baron's rooms. The small, dark agent, Nils, whom we had already seen the day before, sitting downstairs in the lounge, was not present. Presumably he was following the Baron as he spent the evening with the actress at the opera and dining at Claridge's.

Oscar showed us into the drawing room of the suite and from there into an adjoining bedchamber, the master bedroom, I assumed, judging by the opulence of its furnishings, including a huge mahogany wardrobe which occupied almost the whole of one wall. Holmes examined the lock on its doors in an almost negligent manner.

'That will be easy enough to pick,' he remarked with a shrug. 'Now I understand the servant's room where the Baron's bodyguard will be keeping watch is next door to the Baron's bedroom.'

'That is so, sir,' Oscar replied in almost perfect English. 'The one opens into the other. I can show you quite easily how the rooms are arranged, for this suite is like a mirror-image of the Baron's.'

Opening a door in the far wall, he led us into a much smaller and more simply-furnished bedroom containing a single bed where presumably an attendant valet or lady's maid would sleep.

Crossing to the window, Oscar raised the lower sash and then stood back to allow Holmes and me to inspect the route we would have to take in order to gain access to Baron Kleist's quarters.

It was the first time I had seen it and I confess my heart sank at the sight of it. It would be a dangerous approach indeed and I understood Holmes' remark about scaling the heights of the Hotel Imperial and also the need for rubber soled boots. No other footwear would have given one the necessary purchase on the route Holmes apparently intended we should take.

Unlike the front of the hotel, which was stuccoed, the rear façade was built of brick ornamented with stone cornices running horizontally across it, broadening out at regular intervals to form the sills of the windows which extended in tiers across the whole of the back of the building. Above each window was a triangular stone pediment which also jutted out a few inches from the brickwork, thus becoming part of a general geometric pattern of straight lines and angles.

The cornice was no more than three inches wide and the only visible hand-holds were those stone pediments above the windows. But, unlike the cornice, they were not continuous and between them there was a terrifyingly barren stretch of brickwork, offering no hand-holds whatsoever. Immediately below lay a sheer drop of two storeys, terminating in the glass and iron-work dome of the Winter Garden, for which the Hotel Imperial was famous. Lights shone up through the panes and

I thought I could faintly discern the moving shapes of waiters and hear the sound of voices and violins rising up from among the potted palm trees.

If we fell, I thought, with a sudden rush of mingled terror and hysteria, we would crash spectacularly down among the wine glasses and the starched napery to the sound of a Viennese waltz. I dared not think of the injuries we might cause both to ourselves and to others, nor of the headlines in the morning newspapers.

Holmes seemed unperturbed by such considerations. He was calmly unpacking the small valise he had brought with him and distributing the picklocks and other burgling devices about his person, including a small jemmy should he need to force open the window of the Baron's bedroom. The blue and gold leather case containing the copy of the Gustaffson Stone was placed in his inside pocket, which he then fastened with a large pin.

Catching my eye, he said with a smile, 'It would be a complete disaster if I dropped the whole object of our little excursion, would it not, my dear fellow?'

My mouth was so dry with fear at the thought of our 'little excursion' that I could only nod my head in agreement.

Lastly, Holmes took out the coil of strong rope and, passing one end round his waist and across his left shoulder, he handed the other to Oscar, who tied it securely to the foot rail of the bed. Then he softly slid the lower sash of the window upwards and climbed nimbly over the sill.

It was several seconds before I dared approach the window to look out. When I did so, I had to force myself not to look down but to glance to the right where Holmes was balanced on the narrow cornice, his body pressed against the rear wall of the hotel and his arms spread-eagled as with one hand he supported himself by clinging to the stone architrave above the window, while his other hand crept inch by inch across the brickwork, straining to reach the similar pediment above the adjoining window which I realised, from Oscar's account of the arrangement of the hotel rooms, was the bedchamber belonging to the Baron's bodyguard, Igor.

For a few seconds, Holmes stood there motionless, his heels projecting over the edge of the cornice, his arms stretched out wide like a victim subjected to some hideous medieval torture. I thought he would never move. Then with a massive contortion of his shoulder muscles, which I could actually see taking place beneath the taut fabric of his coat, the fingers of his right hand touched and then tightened over the projecting border of the architrave above the adjacent window and, little by little, he was able to loosen the grip of his left hand and to inch his feet along the cornice ledge, the rope crawling along behind him.

Its presence should have been a comfort, but watching as it slowly dragged its way from the bed, across the floor to the window and from there out into the night, it seemed far too flimsy to support Holmes' weight should he lose his balance.

After what seemed an eternity, Holmes reached the comparative safety of the adjacent windowsill, where he stood for several long moments flexing his fingers which must have been aching with the strain of clutching the pediment. His face was pressed close to the glass and I had the impression that he was using this pause not just as a respite but as a chance to peer inside the room. Seconds later, his head turned in my direction and I saw him raise two fingers of his left hand to his lips as a warning gesture for silence. Then his head turned away and he again began the same laborious effort of stretching out for the architrave above the neighbouring window which offered the next hand-hold.

To take my mind off his perilous journey, I counted off the seconds under my breath and reached the total of two hundred and sixteen before Holmes arrived at his goal and once more was able to step off the narrow cornice and stand upright on the broader ledge of the window to the Baron's room.

The window, thank God, was not fastened, a lucky chance which I fervently hoped could be taken as a good omen for the successful outcome of the whole enterprise. Within seconds, Holmes had slid the lower sash upwards and had disappeared over the sill into the room. Moments later, there came a slight tug on the rope indicating that he had untied it and, at the signal, Oscar and I drew the rope in hand over hand until the full length of it lay coiled up upon the floor.

I regarded it with the same horror as I might a poisonous snake, for the terrible truth had at last to be faced. It was now my turn to secure it over my shoulder and lower myself backwards out of the window.

I hung there for what seemed like an eternity, feeling with the toes of my rubber-soled boots for the cornice, which gave me some purchase on the stone, thank God. At the same time I was clutching desperately to the pediment above the window, as a drowning man might grasp at a life-belt. Knowing that if I looked down I would lose my nerve completely, I kept my gaze fixed upwards, straight into the face of Oscar, who was standing at the open window looking down at me, ready to pay out the rope as soon as I began to inch my way along the ledge.

I think it was his expression which persuaded me to move. It was rigid with horror at my predicament, as if it were a mirror reflecting what I imagined was the expression on my own face, and I realised I had two choices: either to scramble back ignominiously into the room or to follow after Holmes.

I chose the latter, more out of pride than courage. If Holmes could do it, then so could I. Indeed, I *had* to do it.

At that moment of decision, my right foot found

the edge of the cornice, although its narrowness struck me with terror. But I knew I was now committed and I took my first shuffling step sideways, my body pressed inwards towards the hotel's façade.

Bricks are familiar, commonplace objects. In London, or any town or city, one sees them everywhere and one assumes there is little more to find out about them other than their shape and colour. To see them less than an inch before one's nose was like a revelation. I saw in close-up their gritty surfaces with their coarse, open pores, and their colour, predominantly a reddish brown which was streaked in irregular patches with lighter and darker shades ranging from a dusky pink to a purplish black. I saw, too, the paler bands of mortar which bound them together, not smooth as they appear from a distance but pitted and scabbed. I also smelt them, a mingled odour of soot and damp cinders.

I was aware of nothing else about me, neither the rest of the hotel stretching up above me nor the lighted glass dome of the restaurant below.

As my feet crept painfully sideways, my right hand, as if attached to my feet, made the same slow, oblique progress across the wall, like a crab, feeling for the edge of the pediment above the next window, that of the room where Igor, Baron Kleist's bodyguard slept. My relief on reaching it and feeling my fingers grip the stonework is beyond description, except that I knew then the emotion a mountaineer must experience when he successfully gains the summit of some dangerous, rocky cliff.

Seconds later, my shuffling feet had, so to speak, caught up with my hand and I was able to lift them slowly, one after the other, on to the broad safety of the window sill.

Like Holmes, I rested there for several moments, aware for the first time of the pain in the stretched muscles in my arms and the backs of my legs. I also copied the action I had seen Holmes make, pressing my face close to the glass, and saw what he must have seen which had induced him to signal for silence.

Although the curtains were drawn across the window, a pencil-thin gap between their edges allowed me a glimpse into the room beyond. I could see little except for a strip of flower-patterned wallpaper and part of a cream-coloured bedspread together with the wooden foot-rail of a bed, similar to the one in the adjacent room to which Oscar had attached the rope. I could see no one, but something about the manner in which the cover was disarranged suggested that someone, Igor presumably, was either lying on it or had been recently. The sight of it made me strongly aware that, although absent, the Baron's malign influence was still potent, a thought which spurred me to move on, although I doubted if the occupant of the room could have heard anything above the sound of the orchestra below in the Winter Garden or the traffic passing by along Piccadilly.

The relief I had felt on reaching the first window was a mere tremor compared to the rush of emotion on my gaining the safety of the last.

Holmes had left the bottom sash open and was waiting inside the room to help me over the sill.

He said nothing, for he rarely expressed his feelings, but his face conveyed more clearly than words his own relief at my safe arrival. There was also both admiration and pride in his features as he took my hand in both of his and wrung it warmly, mouthing the words 'Well done, Watson!' as he did so. It was at moments like those that I felt closer to Holmes than to any other living person, my own dear wife excepted.

He had already scribbled down a note for my benefit which read: 'Igor is in the next room. Keep *cave* for me.'

He pointed to the far wall where a door connected the two rooms and I nodded in agreement to show I, too, was aware of Igor's presence, before crossing silently to the door and kneeling down in front of it. Like a little window, the keyhole afforded me a wider view than the narrow gap between the curtains. I could see more of the bed and the legs of a man stretched out upon it. I could also smell the pungent odour of a Russian cigarette and hear the crisp rustle as the pages of a newspaper were turned over.

While I was thus occupied, Holmes himself had been busy, for, by the time I glanced over my shoulder, the doors on the large wardrobe, the twin of the one in Oscar's bedroom, already stood open, although Holmes may have picked the lock before my arrival, and he was in the act of lifting out of it a leather valise, like a Gladstone bag only smaller, from which he extracted a black-japanned metal box with a strong steel band going round it, in the centre of which were three small keyholes.

With most of my attention centred on keeping watch on the Baron's bodyguard lying on the bed in the adjoining room, I was able to take only occasional quick glances at Holmes. By this means, I saw him carry the metal box to a dressing table with a mirror standing upon it, like the wardrobe an exact double of the one in Oscar's bedchamber, and, placing it carefully down on the surface, took from his pocket the three picklocks which Charlie Peak had given him.

The room was full of a heavy, dense silence which seemed palpable, as if an invisible fog had crept into the room, filling every corner and crevice. The only audible sounds were the tiny metallic clicks as Holmes manipulated the picklocks and, faraway, the distant sound of the Winter Garden orchestra, which was now playing extracts from Gilbert & Sullivan.[20]

It was evident that, despite the hours of practice

[20] W.S. Gilbert and Arthur Sullivan, the lyricist and composer of many highly popular operettas, began collaborating in 1871. In 1881, Richard D'Oyly Carte built the Savoy Theatre to house their productions, which included *H.M.S. Pinafore* and *The Mikado*. They were both knighted. Dr John F. Watson.

Holmes had spent at our lodgings, opening the Medici casket was not easy. Each time I glanced hurriedly over my shoulder at his thin frame stooped over the task, his long fingers were busy delicately probing, his head strained forward in the effort to hear the faint sound of the wards yielding to his skilful manipulations. He was totally engrossed, deaf and blind to anything else going on about him.

And then suddenly, he gave a long, soft exhalation of breath and with it, the tension in the room fell away as if a great pressure had been released. The locks had at last given way.

The whole of my attention was now centred on Holmes. As I watched, he opened back the lid to look into the casket and then, reaching inside it, lifted out a little case covered in blue and gold leather, the exact replica of the one Holmes had in his pocket.

As he did so, I was aware of a new and unexpected sound which came not from the room which we were occupying but from the adjoining chamber. It was an insignificant noise and had I not been kneeling with my head close to the door, it might have passed unnoticed, for it was nothing more than the faint creak of a bed frame.

Immediately, I clapped my eye to the keyhole only to find to my consternation that my view through the tiny aperture had changed dramatically.

I could no longer see the outstretched legs of Baron Kleist's henchman. Instead, I saw the lower part of his torso, his garments strained upwards, an odd perspective until I realised the man was standing upright and was stretching his arms above his head as if loosening his muscles. The next second, I lost even this limited view of him as he stepped forward towards the door.

It is astonishing how quickly one's mind can work in moments of danger. Although I had only a few seconds in which to act, I knew instinctively what I had to do.

I gave a low whistle to attract Holmes' attention and, as he turned his head, I got up from my knees and jerked my thumb urgently towards Igor's room. At the same time, I stepped to the right where, once the door was opened, it would shield me from view for at least a few seconds as Igor crossed the threshold.

The next instant, the door was flung back and a huge man with the build and muscles of a prize-fighter came into the room. His astonishment at the unexpected sight of a stranger standing by the dressing-table gave me a split second's grace. So, too, did the additional few moments it took him to absorb and realise the significance of what he was seeing – the wardrobe doors gaping wide, the leather bag discarded on the floor and the Medici casket lying on the table, its lid opened back.

It was only then that he prepared to attack.

As he stepped into the room, I also made my first move. Flinging myself forwards from my hiding-place behind the door, I seized him round the legs from behind in a rugby tackle[21] and, using my weight like a battering ram, slammed him face downwards on to the floor.

He collapsed with a grunt, dazed but not unconscious. As he struggled up on to his knees, Holmes, who had meanwhile strode towards us, delivered the *coup de grâce* with a powerful right upper cut[22] at which the man fell forwards again, this time unconscious.

Rubbing his knuckles, Holmes gave me a rueful grin.

'It was, of course, very unsporting to hit a man when he was down, but I am sure the Marquess of Queensberry[23] would have forgiven me. Your fellow members of the Blackheath Rugby Club would certainly have applauded your tackle. It was superb, my dear fellow.'

---

[21] When a medical student at St Bartholomew's hospital, Dr Watson played rugby for the Blackheath Rugby Club, in what position is unknown. After he was wounded at the battle of Maiwand, he had to give up the game. *Vide*: 'The Adventure of the Sussex Vampire' and *A Study in Scarlet*. Dr John F. Watson.

[22] Sherlock Holmes boxed while at university. Dr Watson decribed him as an 'expert' while McMurdo, a professional prize fighter with whom Sherlock Holmes once boxed for his benefit night, remarked that Sherlock Holmes himself could have turned professional. *Vide* among other references: 'The Adventure of the Five Orange Pips', *A Study in Scarlet* and *The Sign of Four*. Dr John F. Watson.

[23] The Marquess of Queensberry Rules were, in fact, drawn up by John Graham Chambers, a member of the Amateur Athletic Club (AAC) and were published in 1867 under the patronage of the eighth Marquess of Queensberry. The rules, which are still in use, governed the conduct and conditions for boxing matches, i.e. the size of the ring and the length of time each round lasted. Dr. John F. Watson.

However, while appreciating Holmes' compliment, I was aghast that my precipitate action might have not only ruined Holmes' plans but also those of the King of Scandinavia.

'What will you do now?' I asked anxiously. 'Once Igor regains consciousness, he will be sure to report to the Baron and the cat will really be out of the bag.'

To my surprised relief, Holmes treated the matter with an off-hand air.

'It is of little concern,' said he, with a shrug. 'I doubt very much if Igor will tell Kleist anything. To do so would certainly mean instant dismissal. But should the Baron be informed, his first concern will be to examine the Medici casket, which he will find securely locked and the Gustaffson stone safely inside it. It would not cross his mind that it is the fake he himself so cleverly passed off as the original. The King of Scandinavia, or rather to use his preferred title, Count von Lyngstrad, only recognised it himself because of the secret mark his so-called 'uncle' scratched on it without the Baron's knowledge. But if, by some unlikely chance, he does suspect something, what can he do about it? Inform the police? Hardly. It would mean admitting to fraud. Or would he try to hunt us down and force us or the King of Scandinavia to return the real jewel? Also unlikely for the same reason. As for identifying us, that too is out of the question. Because of our disguises any description of us by Igor or a member of the hotel staff would be quite useless.

'Consider also another aspect of the situation: Baron Kleist's arrangement to sell the Gustafsson Stone to Cornelius Bradbury, the American collector, who is due to arrive in this country in a few days' time. If Kleist admits the pendant is a fake then he will undoubtedly lose the sale.'

'No, my dear fellow. We have no cause to fear any of these contingencies. If the Baron finds out about the substitution, he will keep quiet about it. I know I would if I were in his shoes.'

'But Bradbury will be buying a fake!' I protested.

'Oh, Watson!' Holmes chided me, laughing heartily. 'The pendant is part of the Scandinavian crown jewels! The man must know it was obtained illegally. All I can say to that is *caveat emptor*, a very sensible piece of advice to anyone buying an article of dubious origin. You realise, of course,' he added, 'that because of this little *contretemps,* there will be no need for us to leave by the window. We can go out via the door like civilised human beings, a benefit for which I am profoundly grateful.'

'And so am I,' I agreed wholeheartedly.

'By the way,' Holmes added a few moments later as he placed the fake Gustafsson Stone in its leather box inside the Medici casket, 'have you noticed the emblem on the casket lid?'

In the general excitement of dealing with Igor, I had not given particular attention to the box, but now that Holmes had drawn it to my notice, I saw that the decoration was in the form of a eagle, inlaid in brass, its wings outspread and holding a single leaf in one of its claws.

The amused smile on Holmes' lips alerted me to its significance.

'But is it not the same design which Charlie Peak described as being on the lid of the casket that Signor Valori was working on in Florence?'

'Exactly so, Watson! Which means we have here the very same casket bearing Kleist's personal emblem, appropriated, I might add, from the Hapsburg insignia of the imperial eagle. The bay leaf, a symbol of victory, of course, is Kleist's own personal touch. The vanity of the man is overweening! It gives me enormous satisfaction to have beaten him at his own game!'

With an air of well-deserved self-congratulation, Holmes placed the casket, now containing the fake Gustafsson jewel, inside the leather grip which he locked. That done, he closed and secured the wardrobe doors with a flourish.

Between us, we carried Igor's recumbent form into his bedroom, where we laid it on his bed. After that, all that remained to be done was to tug on the rope to signal to Oscar to draw it in. Once it had slithered out of sight over the window sill, I closed the sash while Holmes made sure everything else in the room was as we had found it.

As I lowered the window, I stood for a few seconds looking down on the lighted dome of the Winter Garden and, remembering my earlier image of crashing down on to the diners below, I allowed myself a small smile at the extravagance of my imagination.

We left immediately afterwards, pausing for a few seconds to make sure the corridor outside was empty before Holmes locked the door behind us and we let ourselves into the adjoining suite of rooms where Oscar was waiting anxiously, fearing for our safety when the rope returned with neither of us at the end of it.

Holmes gave him a brief account of our adventures and then we left for Baker Street by cab, stopping briefly on the way so that my old friend could send a telegram to our client, Count von Lyngstrad, alias the King of Scandinavia, announcing the success of our mission.

It read simply but enigmatically to anyone ignorant of the facts: 'YOUR FRIEND GUSTAF IS ON HIS WAY HOME STOP SUGGEST YOU MEET HIM TOMORROW AT 11AM STOP'.

The following morning, precisely on the hour, our illustrious client, the King of Scandinavia, arrived at our lodgings and was shown upstairs to the sitting-room where, beaming delightedly, he offered both his hands to each of us in turn.

'Congratulations!' he exclaimed. 'It seemed an impossible task but between the two of you gentlemen, you have triumphed against all the odds! May I see the Gustafsson Stone?'

'Of course,' Holmes replied, indicating the table where the pendant was already laid out for inspection on a starched white napkin.

The king seized it eagerly, holding it up by the chain towards the light and letting it revolve slowly so that he could examine it from every angle, all the time murmuring, 'Excellent! Excellent!'

Then turning to Holmes, he added, 'Tell me, for I am longing to know, how you managed to recover it.'

After Holmes had given a brief account of our adventure, to which the king listened with great seriousness, exclaiming out loud at the description of the dangerous route we had taken to enter the Baron's room, my old friend concluded, 'I think we may assume that the matter is now concluded. If Baron Kleist learns of the substitution of the real jewel for the fake, he will keep silent for fear of losing the sale to the American millionaire.'

The king nodded in agreement and, returning the jewel to its leather case, he placed it into an inside pocket of his coat before again shaking hands with us and turning towards the door.

But the ceremony was not quite over. At the door, he turned back briefly to lay a large envelope on the white table napkin where the Gustafsson jewel had been displayed. Then, without a word, he bowed and left the room.

The envelope, which was fastened with an elaborate seal in red wax of the Scandinavian royal emblem of a crowned eagle, contained, as Holmes discovered when he opened it, a great number of English bank notes amounting to a fortune and a brief note which read:

'You will be committing *lèse-majesté* if you do not accept this fee as well as my eternal thanks, both of which have been honourably and courageously earned.'

It was signed Erik von Lyngstrad, the name by which he had first introduced himself.

'Well! Well!' exclaimed Holmes.

He seemed uncharacteristically taken aback by the lavishness of the gift. Seconds later, however, he had recovered his usual *sang-froid* and remarked, with a laugh, 'A truly king-sized fee, wouldn't you agree, my dear fellow, which could be the key to open our own Medici caskets.'

'I do not follow you, Holmes,' I replied, puzzled by the remark.

But he dismissed my question with an equally enigmatic reply.

'Money can buy many things, Watson; freedom, for example.'

I only understood his remark as it applied to himself some little while later when, not long before we set out together for a week on the Continent to escape from England while his arch-enemy, Professor Moriarty,[24]

---

[24] Professor James Moriarty, whom Sherlock Holmes referred to as 'the Napoleon of Crime', was a brilliant mathemetician who wrote a treatise on the binomial theorem and held the Chair of Mathematics at a provincial university. He later organised and ran a criminal syndicate. Sherlock Holmes vowed to destroy him and the two men finally met face to face at the Reichenbach Falls in Austria, an encounter which led to the Professor's death. *Vide*: *The Valley of Fear*, 'The Final Problem' and 'The Adventure of the Empty House'. Dr John F. Watson.

was arrested, Holmes spoke of his longings to live in a 'quiet fashion', as he expressed it, and concentrate his attention on his chemical researches, an ambition which the investigation on behalf of the Royal Family of Scandinavia, together with the inquiry he had made for the French Republic, had made financially possible.[25]

The relevance of the remark to my own affairs became clearer at a much later date, after Holmes had returned to England after an absence of three years following his apparent death at Moriarty's hand at the Reichenbach Falls.

In the meantime, my dear wife Mary had died[26] and, on Holmes' return, I sold my practice in Kensington and moved back to share my former quarters in Baker Street with my old friend. A young doctor called Verner had, to my great astonishment, paid the high price I had asked rather hesitantly for the practice. I was later to discover that Verner was a distant relative of Holmes' and that it was Holmes himself who had found the money, at least part of which, I am sure, came from the fee paid to him by the King of Scandinavia.[27]

And so, as he had suggested, the fee did indeed serve

---

[25] In 1891, Sherlock Holmes was engaged by the French government upon 'a matter of supreme importance.' *Vide*: 'The Adventure of the Final Problem'. Dr John F. Watson.

[26] See footnote to p. 50. Dr John F. Watson.

[27] The exact sum is unknown. Dr John F. Watson.

as a golden key to open more than one Medici casket, so to speak, for that money enabled me to live comfortably in Baker Street and to enjoy with the greatest of pleasure the renewed companionship of my old and very dear friend, Sherlock Holmes.

Read on for an extract from June Thomson's latest book,
The Secret Archives of Sherlock Holmes . . .

THE CASE OF THE CONK-SINGLETON FORGERY

It was about six years after my old friend Sherlock Holmes returned to London following his apparent death at the hands of Moriarty at the Reichenbach Falls[1] and my own return to our shared lodgings in Baker Street that I became associated with him in a curious case of forgery. It began prosaically enough with the arrival of a visiting card which the boy in buttons[2] brought upstairs

[1] The Reichenbach Falls is a series of waterfalls near Meiringen in Switzerland. It was where Sherlock Holmes met his arch-enemy, Professor Moriarty, for a final confrontation in May 1891. In the ensuing struggle, Holmes, who had learnt *baritsu*, a Japanese form of self-defence, succeeded in throwing Moriarty off balance and in consequence he plunged to his death in the ravine below. Dr John F. Watson.

[2] Billy was the young pageboy who attended Holmes at Baker Street in *The Valley of Fear*. A similarly named pageboy also appeared in several much later accounts, 'The Problem of Thor Bridge' and 'The Adventure of the Mazarin Stone', and it is generally assumed that this is a different pageboy and that 'Billy' was a generic name. Dr John F. Watson.

to our sitting-room and handed to Holmes who, having studied it with raised eyebrows, passed it to me.

It bore the name of Archibald Cassell followed by the words 'Art Dealer' and an address, the Argosy Gallery, Bond Street, London. Below this was a handwritten message which read: 'I apologise for arriving without an appointment, Mr Holmes, but I have a matter of some urgency about which I wish to consult you.'

'What do you think, Watson?' Holmes enquired. 'Should I agree to see this Archibald Cassell?'

'The decision is entirely yours, Holmes,' I replied, secretly pleased that he should consult me about the matter.

'Very well, then. As we are not overburdened with cases at the moment, I shall say "yes". Show Mr Cassell up, Billy,' Holmes instructed.

Moments later the client in question entered our sitting-room. He was a tall, silver-haired gentleman, distinguished-looking in impeccably cut morning clothes and wearing gold-rimmed eyeglasses. A small leather case under his arm suggested he was a businessman of some sort or another. There was, however, a harassed air about him which I judged to be out of character.

Having shaken hands with both of us and seated himself at Holmes' invitation, he remained silent for a long moment before bursting out, 'In all my years in business, I have never encountered a similar situation, Mr Holmes! I confess I am baffled by it! That is why I have come to seek your advice in the matter.'

'Then pray do so, sir,' Holmes replied coolly. 'I suggest you begin at the beginning.'

'Of course, Mr Holmes,' Mr Cassell replied, making a visible effort to pull himself together. 'As my calling card indicates, I am an art dealer and in my time many hundreds of paintings have passed through my hands, some of enormous value, but until this morning I have never been presented with such a dilemma. It is without precedence and, quite frankly, sir, I am at a loss to know how to deal with it.

'A lady arrived at my gallery yesterday morning who introduced herself as Mrs Elvira Greenstock, the widow of Horatio Greenstock, who died two months ago, leaving all his property to her. Among her late husband's effects were a number of oil paintings. It appeared Mr Greenstock was an art dealer in a small way; it must have been a very small way, for I have never heard of him, although I pride myself on knowing most of the dealers and collectors in the world of art. It was one of the paintings from this collection which Mrs Greenstock wished me to evaluate. It is not unusual for members of the public to request such a service, for which, incidentally, I charge a small fee. What they have to show me is generally not of any artistic merit and is worth nothing more than a few shillings. However, I tolerate such clients because there is always the rare possibility that what they have brought may be an unknown or lost work of one of the great masters. It has been known to happen.

'I should perhaps at this point describe Mrs Greenstock to you, because her appearance has as much to do with my decision to consult you as the painting she showed me.'

He paused as if gathering together his recollections of his client, a bemused expression on his face as if he were finding it difficult to recall the lady in any detail, a hesitation which was explained by his next remark.

'Forgive me, Mr Holmes, but there is very little I can tell you about her except to say that her appearance was most bizarre. She was tall, with an educated voice, but as she was dressed entirely in widow's weeds, including a long, thick black veil, I cannot give you any description of her features, not even the colour of her hair or eyes. She was carrying a small leather valise and from it took a painting which she laid before me on my desk and asked me to evaluate.'

As he was speaking, Mr Cassell opened his own portfolio which he had placed at his feet and took from it a canvas which he held up before us so that both of us could see it.

It was an oil painting not much more than eight inches by six depicting a rural scene of trees and hedgerows, richly foliated, as well as meadows and fields of corn stretching back to the horizon, where the spire of a church was just visible. Above was a sky full of sunlit clouds moving towards the right-hand side of the canvas as if propelled by a light breeze.

I confess I am not an art expert and, given the choice,

prefer portraits to landscape paintings. Nevertheless, I thought the picture captured most charmingly the beauty of the English countryside as it must have looked at the beginning of the century. I was therefore much taken aback when Mr Cassell remarked in a dismissive tone of voice, 'The lady said it was a Constable[3] but it is, of course, a forgery.'

'Of course,' Holmes murmured in agreement. 'The clouds alone suggest it is not authentic, although the artist is competent.'

'Oh, indeed!' Mr Cassell concurred. 'Whoever painted it is no amateur and might have convinced someone of less experience than myself that it is genuine. It lacks that fluid movement in the clouds that Constable was able to convey by a few brushstrokes, as well as the play of light across the leaves and grass.'

'Given those criticisms,' Holmes remarked, sitting back in his chair and bringing his fingertips together, 'I am at a loss to understand, Mr Cassell, what is the dilemma you referred to. As the painting is a forgery, all you need do is send for the lady and tell her the truth.'

'I agree with you entirely,' his client replied, 'and under normal circumstances I would have acted accordingly. Unfortunately, there are two drawbacks to

---

[3] John Constable (1776–1837). An English landscape painter, some of whose paintings, e.g. *The Haywain*, are world-famous. Born in Suffolk, he is considered, along with Turner, to be one of the greatest painters of the English countryside. Dr John F. Watson.

such a suggestion. In the first place, I cannot send for the lady as I have no address for her. She refused to give me one. She would only arrange to call at my gallery again in a week's time when I shall, of course, act exactly as you suggested.'

As he was speaking, Mr Cassell had laid the little painting face downwards on the table and Holmes glanced across at it as if idly.

I have known Holmes for many years and, although I do not claim to be acquainted with every aspect of his character, I pride myself on being sufficiently familiar with him to recognise signs of excitement on his part, however much he might try to disguise them. They are not glaringly obvious. Indeed, most people would not notice them at all. But on this occasion, a slight lifting of his right eyebrow and a general tightening of the muscles in his shoulders told me that something about the back of the picture had roused his interest.

Aware of this, I looked at it again more closely, trying to gauge what it was that had engaged his attention. But there was nothing that I could see, apart from a piece of quite ordinary brown paper which had been pasted across the edges of the frame, presumably to keep out the dust.

Holmes was saying, 'You spoke of two drawbacks, Mr Cassell. The first was the lack of any address for Mrs Greenstock. That, my dear sir, can be easily rectified, if you will allow me to make some simple enquiries. What was the second drawback?'

Mr Cassell looked a little abashed by the question. Giving a deprecatory wave of his hand, he replied, 'I am almost ashamed to admit it, for it is nothing more than sheer curiosity on my part. Who is this lady who calls herself Mrs Greenstock? As I have already explained to you, she is not to my knowledge the widow of any art collector that I have heard of. And why should she attire herself in a thick black veil, which she never raised once during my interview with her, unless she feared I might recognise her?'

'Excellent, sir!' my old friend exclaimed. 'An admirable piece of deduction on your part!'

His client seemed only partly mollified by this commendation.

'That may be so, Mr Holmes. However, that still fails to answer the question as to her identity. Are you prepared to look into the matter? To be frank, I am uneasy about the whole situation. I shall, of course, not buy the painting from her. But supposing she manages to persuade another dealer or a collector less experienced than myself to do so? I realise the old warning *caveat emptor* should apply to all business transactions, but there is the reputation of the art world to consider. I feel I cannot allow someone whom I know is a forger to pass off her work, or if not hers then someone else's, as a genuine old master. Apart from the aesthetic consideration, it would be condoning a criminal act.'

'I see your point,' Holmes replied suavely. 'To set your mind at rest, I will certainly look into the matter.

You said the lady will call again at your gallery in a fortnight's time?'

'That was the arrangement.'

'At what time?'

'At eleven o'clock.'

'Then, with your permission, Dr Watson and I will also present ourselves at your gallery on the same day but a little earlier, at a quarter to the hour. In the meantime, may I keep the painting?'

Mr Cassell seemed a little taken aback by this request but acquiesced with a bow and, having shaken hands with both of us, took his leave.

As soon as he had gone, Holmes gave a delighted chuckle.

'To work, Watson!' he cried.

'On what, Holmes?'

'On the painting, of course! But before I make a start on that, I shall look into the curious matter of the lady's identity. Be a good fellow and run downstairs and ask Billy to bring up a bowl of warm water, a towel, a small sponge and some clean white linen rag while I find the entry I need in my encyclopaedia of reference.'[4]

He was taking the volume in question from his

[4] Among his library books in the Baker Street lodgings, Sherlock Holmes had an encyclopaedia that he had compiled himself and that contained newspaper cuttings and other sources of material that he considered of particular interest. There are several references to this volume in the canon. Dr John F. Watson.

bookshelves in the chimney alcove as I left the room, surprised by his instructions. To what use was he proposing to put the articles he had listed?

I did not find the answer to this question immediately, for when I returned to the room, followed by Billy carrying the requested items, Holmes was standing by the fireplace, his encyclopaedia in his hands, ready to read out the particulars of the entry he had found as soon as the pageboy had left the room.

'Now, Watson,' said he, 'our client suggested the lady in question, Mrs Greenstock, failed to raise her veil in case he should recognise her features. But if, as he himself said, he knew no art collector of that name, it is highly unlikely he has ever met her. It therefore occurred to me that the lady wished to cover up some disfigurement which she preferred not to display in public.

'The thought recalled to mind a newspaper report of a tragic accident which happened four years ago in which a woman suffered dreadful injuries, and which I noted with particular attention because it occurred near Paddington station, where you had your first private practice as a doctor. The name of the lady was also very unusual; in fact, I had never come across it before. I therefore cut out the report from the *Daily News* and pasted it into my encyclopaedia. Here, Watson, you may read it for yourself,' he concluded, handing me the volume of reference open at the relevant page. It was a report under a headline 'TERRIBLE ACCIDENT

IN PADDINGTON' and read: 'A lady pedestrian, Mrs Lavinia Conk-Singleton, of Coombe Street, Bayswater, was knocked down and badly injured yesterday afternoon by a runaway hansom cab in Praed Street, Paddington.

'The lady, widow of Mr Horace Conk-Singleton, a retired banker and amateur art collector, suffered severe cuts and bruises to her face. She was taken to the nearby hospital, St Mary's, for treatment. The cab driver, Mr George Packer of Bethnal Green, who was rendered unconscious, was also treated at St Mary's.'

'So her husband *was* an art collector!' I exclaimed.

'Whom our client may have known had she given him her real name. He might even have recognised her, although I doubt that. She wore that thick veil, I believe, to hide her face, which is almost certainly still scarred from her injuries. We might be able to prove that supposition when we meet her in a week's time. Now Watson, we must proceed with the next step in our inquiry. If you would be so kind as to spread the towel over the table, I shall start my investigation of the painting.'

As requested, I spread out the towel and placed the bowl of warm water, the sponge and the clean linen beside it, to which Holmes added a scalpel from his workbench. I assumed his intention was to wipe over the surface of the painting to remove any dirt. To my surprise, however, he laid the picture face down, exposing the back of it and, dipping the sponge into the water, began to dab it along the edges of the brown paper which had been pasted over the frame.

'Holmes!' I expostulated. 'Should you be doing that? I know the picture is a forgery but, even so, it belongs to Mrs Conk-Singleton.'

'Indeed it does,' Holmes replied. 'But I shall not harm the painting itself. I merely want to remove the brown paper which someone, presumably Mrs Conk-Singleton, has recently stuck across the back of it.'

'Recently?'

'In the past few weeks, I believe, judging by its almost pristine condition. But why should she wish to cover up the back of the canvas?'

As he was speaking, he continued to dampen the paper until it was loose enough for him to run the scalpel under the edges and lift the whole sheet away, revealing what lay behind it.

It was another painting, also in oils, but so darkened by dirt and old varnish that it was difficult to make out its subject matter. It seemed to be an interior, for on the left-hand side I could vaguely discern a window through which discoloured sunlight was falling on two figures standing in the middle of the canvas. They were female, for I could just make out their dresses, one a muddy green, the other a dirty blue.

Holmes, who had gone over to his bench, returned with his magnifying glass and, taking the picture over to the window, began examining it more closely under the lens in the full daylight. When he had finished his scrutiny, he handed me the glass so that I could see the effect for myself. It was still difficult to see the painting clearly and, when I remarked on this, Holmes acted in what was to me at first a thoroughly irresponsible, not to say uncouth, manner. Picking up a piece of the white linen rag, he put it to his lips and, having wetted it with his saliva, wiped it across a section of the painting.

'Holmes!' I began, but before I could make any further protest, he had repeated this unseemly action before passing the picture to me.

'Now look, Watson!' he urged.

I looked and was amazed. The portion of the canvas he had treated in this displeasing manner had suddenly and unexpectedly cleared, much as a dirty window will become transparent when it is wiped over with a damp cloth, the discoloration vanishing to be replaced by a clear image of one of the figures which occupied the centre of the painting. It was that of a young woman with a fair complexion, her blonde hair braided on top of her head into an elaborate coronet. For a few seconds she smiled at me and then, as the saliva dried, the image faded and all I could see was a vague oval shape, obscured once again by the brown patina of dirt and old varnish.

Holmes burst out laughing.

'My dear Watson!' cried he. 'If only you could see your face! It is a picture itself of bewilderment and disbelief.'

'It is like a mirage, Holmes!' I replied. 'One second the picture is there; the next it has vanished. What causes it?'

'It is quite simple. When saliva, which is incidentally a mild solvent, is applied to old varnish which has become opaque because of the layers of dirt, it acts as a temporary lens through which one can see the underlying paint.

'However, once it has dried, the effect is lost and all that is left is a blurred smear. It is an old trick used by art dealers when confronted by a dirty canvas. Would you like to try it for yourself, Watson?' he added, handing me the piece of rag. 'The spittle can soon be wiped away with a little clean water.'

Much as I, as a doctor, disapproved of the unhygienic nature of Holmes' method, I was fascinated by its effects and, choosing the face of the second figure which stood slightly to the rear of the first, I applied the cloth to my mouth and, having liberally moistened it, I dabbed it on to that section of the canvas. Once again, the miracle happened. The dirt disappeared and I caught a glimpse of a fresh-faced young woman, rather solemn of expression, wearing a servant's white cap on top of her dark hair.

Such was my excitement that I might have gone on and treated the whole canvas had not Holmes, laughing at my enthusiasm, taken the cloth from my hand and, using the sponge with which he had removed the brown paper backing, wiped over the two areas where we had cleaned the paint.

'Enough is enough, my dear fellow!' he chided humorously. 'We must now finish our examination of the frame itself. I believe it will yield more clues.'

'What clues?' I asked. I could see nothing to suggest it held anything of interest. The frame was made of wood and, unlike the front of it which was gilded and heavily carved, it was undecorated apart from some traces of gold here and there along the edges where the gilding had spread on to the underside.

'Use this,' Holmes suggested, handing me the magnifying glass, but, even with its assistance, I could see nothing which by even the greatest stretch of the imagination could be called a clue, only the rough grain of the wood.

Holmes leant over my shoulder and, jabbing a long finger, exclaimed impatiently, 'Look here, my dear fellow! And here! And here!'

What he was pointing to were small nails driven into the inner edge of the frame at an angle to hold the canvas in position.

'You mean the nails, Holmes?' I asked.

'Partly, Watson. You are almost there. What else do you see beside them?'

'Ah!' I cried, noticing for the first time that the wood close to some of them was freshly bruised, exposing a cleaner inner surface. 'Someone has damaged the wood, either when the nails were removed or hammered back into place.'

'Suggesting?' he prompted me.

'That whoever forged the Constable first removed the nails and took out the original canvas so that the reverse side was uppermost and then tacked it back into position.'

'And?'

'Well, really, Holmes!' I protested, beginning to find the game a little irksome. 'What more is there to say?'

'Only that whoever replaced the nails was not a skilled picture framer. Mrs Conk-Singleton, for example?'

'Yes, of course,' I agreed, a little disappointed at so simple an explanation. 'Is that all?'

'Not quite,' he said, laughing. 'There is one more clue. If you look at the underside of the upper part of the frame, you will see a small blob of dried glue with a fragment of paper adhering to it.'

And indeed there was. For as soon as I reapplied the lens to the area he suggested, I immediately saw a tiny brown globule, hard and shiny like crystallised syrup, in which an even smaller speck of white material was embedded.

I confess I could not grasp its significance and refrained from asking Holmes, who was bustling into his coat.

'You are going out?' I asked. 'Where to?'

'To Mr Cassell's gallery, of course. Hurry up, Watson, and get ready.'

'Oh, Holmes!' I cried, deeply disappointed. 'I have promised Thurston that I would meet him at the club at noon for luncheon and a game of billiards.[5] It is far too late now to send him a telegram cancelling the arrangements.'

Holmes clapped me on the shoulder.

'Never mind, my dear fellow! The inquiry is by no means finished. You shall join it again, I promise you, at some later stage. And I shall, of course, inform you of any developments which take place this morning.'

Holmes was as good as his word and, when later I returned to our lodgings, I found him already there, his business with Mr Cassell having been concluded.

And what he had to tell me was very interesting. On hearing the name Conk-Singleton, Mr Cassell had become quite excited and had told Holmes all he knew about that gentleman, who had something of a reputation in the art-dealing world. He was a retired banker with private but limited means who, having had an early success in buying a valuable but unrecognised painting for a small sum, had persuaded himself that he was an expert and had haunted the auctions bidding for unlikely paintings in the hope that he could repeat his good fortune and sell them on for a huge profit. Some of the dealers, regarding it as a game, had deliberately bid against him, forcing up the value before withdrawing and leaving him to

---

[5] Doctor Watson played billiards with Thurston at their club. Nothing else is known about him, not even his Christian name. *Vide*: 'The Adventure of the Dancing Men'. Dr John F. Watson.

pay an inflated price for a worthless canvas which he could never hope to profit by. In the end, he died a bankrupt.

As for Mrs Conk-Singleton, Mr Cassell knew a little of her also. Much younger than her husband, she was a talented amateur artist who had had some professional training and, when money became short, had supplemented the family income by selling her work, usually landscapes, for small sums of money. After her accident, which had left her dreadfully disfigured, she had become a recluse, rarely setting foot outside her house in Bayswater.

'And what about the painting?' I asked eagerly.

'Ah, that!' Holmes replied with a twinkle. 'Mr Cassell will have it cleaned by a professional with Mrs Conk-Singleton's permission and will also enquire of her about a possible label which was once stuck on the back of the frame, leaving behind that tiny blob of dried glue. In the meantime, the whole affair is in the lap of the gods.'

'So it could be an old master?' I cried.

'Oh, Watson, Watson! One of your endearing qualities is your habitual optimism, a trait you share with the late Mr Conk-Singleton – and look what happened to him! The painting is probably by an amateur and therefore worth very little. We must wait upon events.'

It was not until a fortnight later that these events reached their climax when Holmes received a telegram from Mr Cassell which read: 'You are both invited to take tea tomorrow afternoon with Mrs Conk-Singleton at four o'clock in my gallery.'

The following day we presented ourselves on the hour and were admitted by Mr Cassell, the premises being closed as it was a Sunday, and were conducted through the gallery itself, hung with paintings, into our host's private office. Holmes was in high spirits and I, too, was full of eager curiosity to meet Mrs Conk-Singleton and to see the painting cleaned and restored.

The office seemed a suitable setting for the dénouement, for, like the gallery, its walls were lined with paintings, and furthermore it was furnished with rosewood cabinets on which stood exquisite *objets d'art* in marble and porcelain. It also contained for the occasion a small table laid with a lace cloth and a silver tea service, including a cake stand on which was set out a tempting display of little iced cakes. Four chairs had been drawn up to the table and Mrs Conk-Singleton sat on the one facing the doorway.

She was tall and thin and dressed entirely in black, as Mr Cassell had described her, including the thick black veil which covered her face.

Her sombre attire and her air of sadness cast a melancholy mood over the colour and glitter of the gilt-framed pictures and the beauty of the artefacts which surrounded her, but her voice, when Mr Cassell introduced Holmes and myself, had a gentle sweetness about it which dispelled much of that gloom.

The painting, the reason for our invitation to the

gallery that afternoon, was standing to the right of the table, displayed on an easel but covered with a black silk cloth so that, like Mrs Conk-Singleton's features, it was completely hidden from view. I saw Holmes glance towards it from time to time and I myself snatched several sideways glimpses of it, but it was not until tea was finished and Mr Cassell had rearranged the chairs in a semicircle in front of it that he allowed us to see it.

It was clear that our host was hugely enjoying the situation for, when the moment came, he bowed towards us and, showing an unexpected theatrical side to his nature, announced like a magician about to perform his most amazing and difficult trick, 'Madame! Messieurs! The painting!'

And with that, as if to a roll of drums, he whisked away the cloth and the painting was revealed.

What we saw was indeed like a magic transformation, for the picture we found ourselves gazing at was utterly changed from the original dirty brown canvas into an object of such beauty that I felt some sleight of hand must be responsible for it.

It was the interior of a lady's chamber, lit by a brilliant shaft of sunlight which poured in through a window on the left. In its radiance, the indistinct forms of the two women were transfigured, the first into a lady with corn-coloured hair, richly dressed in a gown of pale-green silk, decorated with lace and ruffles. Standing immediately behind her in the act of closing the clasp of a pearl necklace round the lady's throat stood her maid, more modestly attired in a white cap with an apron over a plain blue gown. She was young and pretty, not long up from the country, I imagined, for she wore an anxious, intent expression as she adjusted the clasp as if she were unused to carrying out such a delicate and intimate task.

Against the rear wall stood a table covered with a cloth patterned with blue and green diamonds, a design echoed in the tiled floor, only this time in black and white. A pair of embroidered gloves lay on the table together with a glass vase containing three pink roses. The light and colour were dazzling and so caught up was I in the vivid details of the room and its inhabitants that I heard Mr Cassell's voice as if in a dream.

'A genuine old master!' he was declaring. 'In fact, a Jan Vermeer, the seventeenth-century Dutch painter who specialised in such interiors.[6] Look at the light falling on the silk of the young lady's skirt! And the roses! They are superb! It is also an unusual subject matter. Vermeer generally included only one lady in his paintings, not two. An expert on his work, a Mr Claude van Heerden at the National Gallery, no less, has examined it and declared it authentic, a claim borne out by its provenance.'

'Provenance?' I enquired.

---

[6] Jan Vermeer (1632–75). A Dutch painter, born in Delft, he was famous for his paintings of household interiors containing a single female occupant, often occupied with some intimate or domestic task, e.g. *Young Woman Reading a Letter at an Open Window*. Dr John F. Watson.

'Its previous history – in this case the label which Mrs Conk-Singleton found on the back of the frame when she removed the canvas, the presence of which you, Mr Holmes, deduced from the small blob of glue still adhering to the frame. Fortunately, Mrs Conk-Singleton kept the label.'

Mr Cassell bowed to Holmes and the lady, acknowledging the part they had played.

'The label,' he continued, 'was dated 1798 and bore the name Bardwell and the number 275. With a little research, I was able to establish that in 1797 Lord Bardwell died at the great age of ninety-two, leaving a houseful of furniture, paintings and other works of art. His only heir was a great-nephew who, anxious to benefit by his death as quickly as possible, sold the house and auctioned off its contents. Apparently, nobody recognised the value of the little canvas which, according to the inventories I was also able to consult, had been in the family from at least the end of the seventeenth century. However, by the time Lord Bardwell died, it was probably already discoloured with dirt and therefore when it was catalogued as Lot 275, it was described merely as "An interior; Dutch School". Later it found its way into another auction, still unrecognised for what it was, and was bought by Mr Conk-Singleton.

'It was an extremely fortunate purchase,' Mr Cassell continued, bowing again towards the lady, 'for the painting is now worth a considerable sum of money.'

Mrs Conk-Singleton acknowledged the statement

and the bow with an inclination of her veiled head. Speaking in a low, sweet voice, trembling a little with emotion, she replied, 'I do not have the words to express my gratitude to all of you gentlemen for the work you have done in helping to discover the true identity of the painting. I leave the sale of the Vermeer in your hands, Mr Cassell, and offer my heartfelt thanks to all of you.'

She was clearly overcome with emotion and left soon afterwards, Mr Cassell escorting her to the door and summoning a four-wheeler to take her home.

He returned to the office smiling broadly and rubbing his hands together with delight.

'What a truly wonderful outcome!' he declared. 'Mrs Conk-Singleton is indeed a very fortunate lady. She will be financially secure for the rest of her life and there will be no further need for her to paint fake Constables on the back of old masters to save the cost of a new canvas!'

'So it was a happy ending after all, Holmes,' I could not help remarking later as we made our way back to Baker Street in a hansom.

Holmes threw back his head and laughed heartily.

'Your optimism is indeed vindicated, my dear fellow,' he replied, adding with a sly sideways glance at me, 'At least on this occasion.'